Ba'az of the Bengal Lancers

Ba'az of the Bengal Lancers

Uttiyo Bhattacharya

juggernaut

JUGGERNAUT BOOKS
KS House, 118 Shahpur Jat, New Delhi 110049, India

First published by Juggernaut Books 2019

10 9 8 7 6 5 4 3 2 1

P-ISBN: 9789353450267
E-ISBN: 9789353450281

Typeset in Adobe Caslon Pro by R. Ajith Kumar, Noida

Printed at Manipal Technologies Limited, Manipal

For
Bhaskar Bhattacharya, Lightbringer
Lady Sunanda, Wordsinger
Priyanka Pande, Starmaker
Broti, Ayesha and Indrani . . . Twats

Contents

Prologue

The Fall of the House of Timur

The English siege guns broke the gates of Delhi. The ragged redcoats retook the city. God was with them when they imprisoned the king. The country would be theirs again, perhaps this time for good. The rebellion quelled, they wreaked vengeance on the vanquished city, plundering and pillaging, reducing much of it to rubble.

As the mayhem played out and the corpses piled up, a one-eyed man listened to the whispers in the city, as he had always done. He carried them to his master, the captain. The captain commanded and the one-eyed spymaster acted. Sometimes he acted on his own. At other times, he used his ghosts.

~

The fierce old man sat in the mosque, drinking. It was not a mosque yet but it would become one soon – a house of god where the faithful would come to pray. Today, it was a place like any other. A place built with bare hands and bone. Brick with brick, lime with mortar, stone with plaster. A place which had taken seven years and seven days to build. Days of dust that needed washing down by the fiery liquor.

With his back to the wall and the earthen jar full of the fiery liquid by his side, he wondered what god would say. Drinking was a sin. But then, he thought, god might forgive him. If he did not, he would take it up with him when the Day of Judgement came. Soon, though, it would be time to join the others in the graveyard behind the mosque. He felt it in his bones.

He heard the clatter of hooves outside. He listened intently, eyes half-closed in concentration. One, two . . . three horses. Good. The boys all rode together. It bode well. There would be festivity and celebrations tonight. After all, it was not every day that you laid hands on the richest treasure of Hindostan. He took out three small earthen cups and poured liquor into them as he waited for the riders to join him.

~

Akbar dismounted first and tied his horse to a post outside the mosque. He went in. Iqbal and Abdullah followed. Even in the dim light, Akbar could see his father sitting in the corner. He saw the three cups waiting for them. He looked at his father and shook his head. With a sigh he sat down. The others squatted on either side of him. In unison, as if controlled by a single mind, they reached out for the cups and drained them in a single draught.

'It was not there,' Akbar began. He brought out a small ornate casket hidden inside the folds of his robes. Intricate silver work on hard wood. The heavy lid was opened to reveal nothing inside. 'And now, for attempting to take it, we cannot go back,' he said.

He began to narrate the events of the past week.

When he had finished, the old man spoke.

'So that means you are outlaws. You will be hunted. For the sake of nothing.'

Everyone was quiet. The silence continued unbroken, until they heard the sound of approaching horses. Four, maybe five. They rose, alert. The three young men loosened their swords. They formed a protective arc around the old man and faced the doorway.

The horses outside halted, and there was silence again. They heard footsteps. A tall, dark young man walked through the door.

The three relaxed. Akbar said with an edge in his voice, 'Oi, Bungalee! What brings you here so early?'

~

Bayaz-ud-din Waris Ali Khan, sometimes called Ba'az and at other times Bungalee, looked at the four men and then at the empty casket at their feet. Turning to Akbar, he raised an eyebrow questioningly. Akbar sat down and gestured to Ba'az to sit, too. The others joined them in a circle around the empty box.

'There was nothing inside,' said Akbar. He proceeded to repeat what he had told them a little while earlier. Ba'az listened quietly, nodding now and then, without comment.

'This should not be,' he said after a while. 'The information was accurate.'

There was silence again.

Then Ba'az said, 'It doesn't matter any more. In any case, I have news.'

He began, and spoke at length, in short, staccato sentences.

When he was done, the old man asked, 'Emperor Bahadur Shah Zafar?'

'Still in chains,' answered Ba'az.

'So the emperor remains captured, the exchange failed and the princes dead,' summed up the old man, heaving a deep sigh.

The inevitable question came from Iqbal.

'What happened to all the gold?'

Ba'az began to laugh. Without stopping, he looked at all of them. 'I was wondering who would be the first to ask. I brought it with me, of course. I thought it would make a good accompaniment to what you would bring. That treasure should have gone somewhere else, but fate has its ways. Instead, we have thirty thousand gold mohurs. Double mohurs, actually. The ransom for an emperor. It is outside, on the mules.'

The old man rose quickly. The others did, too. They went out of the mosque in a rush. They returned after a while, but at a slower pace. The old man stepped forward and embraced Ba'az. Akbar looked at him and gave a short, sharp nod as a salute. Abdullah returned his gesture with a salaam. Iqbal slapped his back and kept thumping it hard until Ba'az began to groan. All this while the old man continued to pour liquor into the earthen cups. They drank quietly, in relief and fear. Fear of what may befall them.

The old man then said, 'Rest for a while. Soon you must leave with the gold. There will be a price on your head. They are sure to be looking for you and the treasure.'

'What about the three of you?' asked Ba'az. 'You are wanted men, too.'

'We will stay here. No one will think of looking for us with you still at large. Besides, all we did was steal an empty box. But you must leave and hide the gold somewhere. Return when it is safe,' said Akbar.

Ba'az hesitated. The old man said, 'Do not worry.

We know you will come back. A lesser man would have kept the gold for himself rather than bring it here. Do you know what to do with it? It will be cumbersome to lead the laden mules.'

Ba'az thought for a while and then nodded his head in agreement. 'That makes sense. I know where to go. There is a man in Calcutta. Son of an Irish horse merchant who is like a father and a friend to me. He will help me.'

'Will you be safe on the road to Calcutta?' asked Akbar. 'The fighting still rages in Lucknow and beyond.'

'I will take the long road through the mountains. No one will think of looking for me there. Besides, I still have the dispatches of Hodson. I can always say I am delivering them. There are certain advantages of being a fighting scribe, you know. My letters will take care of some dangers. My sword and rifle will take care of the rest.'

The others nodded.

'May god be with you,' said the old man.

'May god be with us all,' said Ba'az, 'in these godless times.'

They all walked together to the door of the mosque. The old man and the three young men embraced Ba'az one by one and then watched him ride away into the darkness.

~

The one-eyed man stopped his mule in front of an archway. He saw the three corpses still hanging, as they had been the week before. Time had not been good to them. Carrion birds had stripped away their flesh. Scavengers of the human kind had stripped away their clothes and shoes. Their lifeless forms swayed in the warm evening breeze. Their blackened bodies contrasted against the red, sun-washed stones of the archway. The setting sun, low on the horizon, bathed them with fire. Shadows of their swinging silhouettes danced on the walls – an unruly, disorderly dance.

Till a week ago this was called the Red Gate. Whispers of a new name began after the captain shot the princes and left them to hang here. These were hushed voices in the alleys and bazaars, not meant to be heard by the victorious sahibs or their men. A misplaced word was reason enough to be blown up by cannon these days. But it was the business of the one-eyed man, Rajab Ali, to know exactly what was being whispered, when and by whom. He knew exactly what they were naming this arched gateway. *The Blood Gate. Khooni Darwaza.*

He waited till after the sun had set. He gave a low whistle, and a few shadowy forms emerged from inside the gateway. They cut down the bodies and loaded them on the waiting mules. Rajab Ali followed the train of mules on his mount. An hour later, skirting Feroze Shah's citadel, they stopped at a graveyard on the banks of the Yamuna. Three freshly dug graves awaited their occupants. The men dropped the bodies inside and quickly filled the graves. With just a word of acknowledgement from Rajab Ali, they disappeared into the darkness from where they had come.

Rajab Ali stayed there, looking at the unmarked graves that would soon merge with the earth and disappear. He whispered to his mule, 'So, Khwaja, this is it. The captain leaves his mark on this land. The House of Timur now lies here, and its glory fades away.'

Rajab Ali turned the mule around and set off at a leisurely trot back towards the fort. As they moved, he remembered a line from one of the captain's books. It was a play about princes and kings. In the language of the sahibs, he improvised a farewell speech to the two sons and the grandson of an emperor in chains.

'Goodnight, sweet princes. May flights of angels sing you to rest.'

Far behind him, a desperate, hungry crow pecked hopefully at one of the freshly filled graves.

~

When Rajab Ali reached the English lines, he made his way to the captain's office. Hodson sat at his desk, nose buried in a pile of papers. As Rajab Ali walked in, the captain looked up at him, and then stood up. He was a magnificently bald man. 'Report,' he said in a terse voice.

'It is done, sahib,' said Rajab Ali.

'Very well.'

'There is other news as well. About the other matters. The scribe, the Bungalee. As well as the three men who made off with the box in Agra.'

Hodson gave Rajab Ali a sharp look. He walked to the door and shut it. 'Speak,' he commanded.

'I sent my trackers after the Bungalee. They followed him to a village north of here, a place by the name of Haider Kalan. I have an informer there. Rafiquddin. This is the same village where his three friends come from. The three who made off with the box.'

Hodson sat down, his head bowed in thought, eyes closed. To Rajab Ali, it seemed as if he was praying. After a few long minutes, Hodson opened his eyes.

'The three are there then?' he asked.

Rajab Ali nodded.

'And the fourth as well – the Bungalee, that bastard scribe who should have been dead? Is he there, too?'

'No, sire. It seems that he left. I will send my three best men after him. They will find him.'

'The rains are coming. His tracks will get washed off,' said Hodson.

'My trackers can find a trail that is years old. They can track a decade-old caravan trail across the Rann.'

Hodson said, 'I am sending Captain Morstan and Major Sholto after the three to their village. Tell them where to go. A few troops and some of the new Irishmen will go with them. The swine needs to be made an example of. You know what to do about this, don't you?'

Rajab Ali nodded and then asked, 'The Great Moghul?'

'No one knows yet that the Great Moghul is gone. When found, he should be brought back only to me. The gold as well, when you find it,' said Hodson.

Rajab Ali nodded and turned to go. As he opened the door to leave, Hodson said, 'Ali, there is no room for a mistake here. The gold and the Great Moghul must be found. I have a lot to answer for already, for killing the three bastard princes. If they are not found, I am as good as finished.' He paused and then said, 'And so are you.'

Rajab Ali did not answer. He only looked at Hodson with his good eye. A cold, emotionless gaze that seemed to know everything.

Hodson flinched. 'Don't look at me like that, or I will put out that eye as well.'

'Worry not, sahib. My trackers are the best. They will hunt down everything.' Saying this, Rajab Ali left.

Part I

The Treasure of Haider Kalan

1

The Ancient Storyteller

The train jerked to a stop. I woke up with a start. I looked around, dazed, trying to figure out where I was. I could see Jami stuffing his belongings into his bag.

'Hurry up, man. It doesn't stop here for long.'

The haze in my head cleared a little. I remembered where I was.

I got up in a hurry, located my bag and lurched after Jami. Stumbling over legs, feet and other random appendages of humanity strewn all over, we moved towards the door. In a moment, we were out of the compartment and on the platform.

With a groan and a heave, the train began to move again.

After the train left, there was complete silence. A small shed stood in the middle of the platform, a dusty tree shading part of it. Underneath the tree was a water tap, which had run dry, over a tiled washbasin covered with dried leaves. My bladder gave a twitch. I needed to relieve myself soon.

'What now?' I asked Jami.

He did not say anything. Always a man of few words, our Jami. He only shifted his haversack from one shoulder to the other, looked at his watch and nodded.

I knew that meant we had to wait a little.

My bladder demanded attention. I saw a bush at the far end of the platform. It was as likely a candidate as any. After I was done, I looked around.

We were in the middle of nowhere, on the railway line between Ambala and Chandigarh. A tiny, nondescript station. The largest railway network in the world seemed to have forgotten its existence. A faded, yellowing signboard once had the station's name written on it. Now it was a patch of peeled and cracked paint.

We made our way out of the station. Jami raised a hand to shade his eyes from the blazing sun and peered at the dusty road. After a few minutes of waiting, doing nothing, he said, 'He should have been here.'

'Who?'

'There he is!' Jami pointed at a cloud of dust approaching from a distance.

With a clatter of hooves, a jangle of harness and a crack of whip, the cloud of dust came to a halt in front of us. As the dust settled, a four-wheeled carriage, drawn by a single mare, revealed itself. Perched on it was a giant of a man in a lungi and a knee-length kurta. His legs were splayed apart – one on the coachman's seat and the other on the yoke – as he crouched to balance himself. His tasselled red cap and a long, black leather whip matched the red leather of the seats and the grease-blackened wheels. With a flick of his whip and a flourish of his cap the man turned to Jami, exhibiting a set of gleaming, ivory-white teeth.

'Welcome home, Tiger!' he bellowed. 'You have grown taller since you were last here.' He burst into a deep, rumbling laugh that made his belly quiver.

I stared at him, despite myself. He appeared to have emerged from the pages of an ancient book. The man standing on the carriage was perhaps even larger than his usual self, towering over the both of us. The white mare, the carriage, the settling dust – all seemed far removed from the reality I was used to.

The man sensed my thoughts. He laughed louder and harder.

'Your friend – he should close his mouth, or else a fly will get in!' he told Jami.

He leapt out of the carriage. Landing like a cat, he enveloped Jami in a tight embrace.

After a few seconds, Jami managed to extricate himself. He slipped his bag off his shoulders and passed it on to the man. Then he introduced him to me.

'This is Mirza kaku. Our ride home. He . . . well, he likes to make an entry.'

And how! I thought.

Mirza kept the bag on the shelf at the back of the coach, before turning to me. 'You must be the Bungalee babu, our Jami's friend.'

He hopped on to the coachman's seat.

'Come on, let's go to Haider Kalan! An hour's ride lies ahead. Nusrat will take us there like the wind.'

Nusrat would be the mare, then, I thought.

As we clambered into the passenger seats, Jami muttered under his breath, 'He is a little cuckoo.'

The coach turned around and the mare broke into a brisk trot. Jami and Mirza launched into the easy conversational chatter of old companions on a long journey. Mirza spoke of adventures that Nusrat and he had had together, each tale wilder than the last. Jami rolled his eyes in mock disbelief. I listened with quiet disinterest. Jami spoke of life in Delhi and the architecture school.

As the countryside flew by, Delhi seemed far, far away. I thought of the grime and the noise of the city. The dread of failure. The plight of being broke and not knowing what to do about it. And then my mind wandered back to how we had reached here.

~

Baba exploded when the letter from the dean arrived. I had not expected it to be sent home, where I had just landed, with a plan for a lazy vacation. It was only my first day, and I was looking forward to some peace and quiet.

'What on earth is this?' he yelled. 'Why did you not tell me?'

The cat was out of the bag now. They now knew that I had been failing for the past two years. Instead of going into the third year, I would be repeating my first year. He screamed at me. He shouted some more. And then, he hit me.

I recoiled in surprise. Surprise turned to anger, and I stood up straight with hands clenched in fists of rage. But he carried on. 'History! History! You're no son of mine. I pay through my nose to put you through architecture school, and now you want to study . . . History!'

'Yes! History!' I barked. 'I will have to do what I have always wanted. I never could. It is you who wanted me to be an architect.'

Baba stopped short at my sudden outburst. I pressed on, floodgates unleashed, 'I am no architect! And like you say, I am no son of yours . . .' I took a step forward, drawing level with his face. 'YOU are no father of mine!'

He stood there stunned. I gasped at my temerity, sobbed, and ran out of the house that night.

When I came back the next afternoon, there was

no one at home. Only a message from ma stuck on the refrigerator door. Baba had been admitted for a severe ache in the back. I went to the hospital. He refused to speak to me. They wanted to keep him there for a few days. Observation.

Bastard died the next day. In his sleep. Everyone said it was sudden and unexpected. Ma knew nothing of what had happened between us. She went about her tasks like a zombie, while I went about mine like another. Mashi came from Delhi. My mother's sister, possibly our only living relative.

There are a million things that need to be done during a funeral. It took three days of continuous running around. Finally, everything was dealt with except the ritual feast after a month.

I left after that. I could not stay in that house even a day more than was absolutely necessary. Mashi would be there for a few more days to take care of ma.

I had returned to the hostel early. It was still the middle of the vacations. I could have gone to mashi's place, but I thought there would be no one in the hostel and the calm and quiet would be good for me. I could wallow in peace, without interference.

I couldn't have been more wrong. I found Jami in our room. Nira was there, too. She was standing, towering over Jami, as he cowered in a chair. I seemed to have walked into some sort of a lover's spat. 'Oh!' said Nira, cutting short whatever she was yelling at Jami. 'You're back?' The unasked question was whether I would be staying or just passing by.

'I could stay in Meghnad's room,' I replied. 'I have his keys.'

'No, it's all right. I was just about to leave,' said Nira, flushing a deep maroon. Jami looked the other way, saying nothing. Something was definitely wrong, and I had intruded at a bad time. But I didn't care. I opened the cupboard and tossed in my bag. The other package I was carrying I carefully kept among my clothes.

'Ciao,' said Nira. 'Nice hairdo, by the way. Looks good on you.' I ran a hand over the recent growth on my shaven scalp and shrugged. Once she left, I turned to look at our room.

It was cleaner than I had ever seen it before. Everything was in place – the beds, the bedclothes, the furniture, even my books were arranged in a neat little stack inside the smaller cupboard.

'What have you been up to?' I asked with a scowl. I hated anyone touching my books.

'Not me,' said Jami with a sheepish look. 'It was Nira. She wanted to clean up the place.'

'Everything all right?' I asked, knowing fully well it was not.

'Hmm,' said Jami, not confessing anything. Fuck these lovebirds and their romance. 'You are back early,' said Jami after a while, as I rearranged my books. 'Is everything fine back home?

'Yes,' I replied. I was lying but I knew there was no point confiding in Jami. It was an uncomfortable few hours of silence. I wanted my space. Jami wanted a place to get his rocks off – I didn't care. At long last he asked, 'Coming to the TV room? Finals tonight.'

I had completely forgotten about the finals in the mess and misery of the last few days. Football could heal any wound, they said. I might as well give it a shot.

That night Italia 90 finished with a whimper. West Germany extracted revenge on Argentina for the slaughter at Mexico four years ago. It ended with a single penalty shot. Diego Maradona walked off the field, a shadow of his former self. This would perhaps be his last World Cup. This would also be the last time West Germany would play as a country. Germania was on the path to reunification. The Berlin Wall had fallen a few months earlier. In four years, they would play the World Cup as a unified Germany.

If I had been a betting man, I would have put my money on Soviet Russia not playing again either. Not as itself, in any case. Holes had appeared in the Iron Curtain as well.

We walked back to our room, and I thought of the world as it was being rebuilt around me. Young men were hammering away at the walls of Checkpoint Charlie half a world away. People were making history and here I was, flunking year after year in architecture school, scraping through a deadbeat, broke existence.

My mind went back to baba. I thought about our last exchange and the derision in his voice.

'History! Now you want to study history?'

'Like it or not, baba, history it is from now on,' I muttered under my breath. My dearest wish to be remembered in history might also come true, in a warped sort of way. If word of how baba died ever got out, I would go down in history for patricide.

With nothing else to do, I picked up one of my many dog-eared, much-loved books and began to read.

Jami, meanwhile, was listless. He growled in frustration, echoing my thoughts. 'I have nothing to do,' he whined.

He sat there brooding while I read. Finally he looked at the book and asked, 'What is it?'

'Malleson's book on the mutiny,' I said.

'1857 stuff?'

So my companion knew a bit of our past. Life never fails to surprise you.

'Yes. Written by this chap not long after 1857. A collection of personal experiences and English accounts. Fascinating stuff.'

'The English bastards left India, but they left the likes of you behind,' said Jami. I kept reading. After a while he said with finality, 'It was not a mutiny. It was a revolution.'

It was an old dispute. 'Perhaps. The debate still rages,' I said, 'and it doesn't help that the only accounts of those times are written in English, by the British. All local accounts of the rebellion were destroyed by the English. Only the British versions remained. There have been oral narratives of history. Bards and storytellers reciting their tales, but only few of those remain. There is very little known or even heard from the other side. Only a few stories, long forgotten.'

Jami began to chant under his breath, '*Bundele harbole ke munh humne suni kahaani thi . . .*'

'Correct,' I said. 'That famous song. But not many like these remain. Everything else is lost. So mutiny it is, unless we can prove otherwise. And anyone who can do so would be an overnight star in academic circles.'

I thought about it for a couple of seconds and said wistfully, 'A find like that would be a treasure that would shed light on many buried truths.' I turned my attention back to my book. I was engrossed with the capture of Bahadur Shah Zafar, the last Mughal and the nominal leader of the mutiny, wondering what drove Hodson to kill Bahadur Shah's two sons and a grandson in broad daylight, when I thought I heard Jami say something.

'What was that?' I asked.

'All is not forgotten,' he said. 'Some stories are still told.'

'Say what?'

'You said every other account is lost. That might not be the case.'

'How?'

Jami fidgeted and said, 'See. . . My village. My ancestral village where I come from, that is. There is a story that my dada-jaan told us when I was young. He has been narrating it almost every day to anyone who cares to listen.'

I leaned forward, eyes narrowed. Jami continued, 'He heard it from his father, and it is a "thing" about our village.'

I did a mental calculation and interrupted him, 'So your dada-jaan's father – he would have been alive during the time of the rebellion, right?'

'I think so,' said Jami. 'So this story is about three men from our village who fought during the mutiny and how everyone in Haider Kalan was massacred by the English soon after.'

'Haider Kalan?'

'The name of our village. I don't remember the exact details of the story.'

'Where is it? The village?' I asked, intrigued. If an oral account of the mutiny had survived, it needed attention.

'Just a few hundred kilometres from here,' said Jami. 'A station before Ambala.'

'Tell me more of the story,' I said.

Jami shook his head in frustration. 'I just don't remember the details, man. It has been a while. There is something about redcoats killing everyone, some hidden treasure, and Zafar Bahadur or something.'

'Bahadur Shah Zafar!' I said, getting to my feet.

'Yes. Maybe,' said Jami. He saw my excitement and added, 'You should go there with me some day and hear the story yourself.'

Now was as good a time as any, I thought. I sat down again and began putting on my shoes. 'Let's go then,' I said.

'Now?'

'Why not?'

'We need to pack.'

'*You* need to pack. I have not even unpacked,' I said, rising to pick up my bag from inside the cupboard. I was ready. I saw him hesitate and sighed. 'Look, man. It is the middle of summer vacations. No one is in the hostel except for you and me. Nothing to do. And it is not as if you and Nira have babies to make or something.'

Jami, flushed, raised a finger at me and said, 'That you won't understand.'

'I know,' I said, pressing on, 'so let's go. Let's hear this story that has been told for so many years. This village of yours. Haider Kalan.'

My mind raced with the possibilities. If I could hear the story, maybe document it, it would be ripe material for a paper. Perhaps, Professor Venugopal could help. Perhaps, I could find lateral entry into a history programme. It could be a way out of where I was.

Jami, however, kept sitting. I exhaled and flung up my hands in despair. 'Look, man . . . I need to get the hell away from everything. All this . . . will keep my mind off things.'

'What things?'

'You know . . . things. College, hostel, home, things . . . All is not well at home, man. Everything is screwed in college. And if there is something more to this story, it might give me a way out of this shit I am in.'

Jami looked at me, thinking, and then shrugged. He rose to his feet and said, 'Cool. Let's go then. But it is a pretty lame place, you know, my village.'

He stuffed a few clothes in his bag and we caught a train a couple of hours later. We would spend a few days in Jami's village.

~

Jami nudged me awake. I opened my eyes. The sun was low on the horizon.

'We have arrived,' he said.

I felt stiff all over. The unsteady motion of the train had given me cramps. I looked around as I slowly moved my limbs.

The fields were now punctuated by an occasional single-storeyed structure, a rickety hut here, a burnt-brick shed there, or a solitary stack of hay.

A little ahead, silhouetted against the orange setting sun, was our destination. Haider Kalan. It was a tiny hamlet – a collection of single-storeyed houses. A few homes seemed to have an additional floor above, half built, seemingly abandoned.

As we drew closer, I took in the details. Most of the houses seemed to be low buildings, surrounding a courtyard. This was the pattern of village homes that was fast being replaced by an urban sprawl in most parts of the country. At the edge of the village, further away from the cluster of these houses, stood a structure that looked part mosque, part fort. It was a lime-plastered building, yellowed with neglect, the disrepair apparent even in the fading light of the evening. A solitary dome stood behind the slanting outer walls. The walls with bastions and weep holes made it look like the small outpost of a fort.

We stopped in front of one of the larger houses in the village.

Jami and I picked up our bags and got down. Mirza gave a crack of the whip and rolled away as we walked in through the door.

Jami said, 'We have come at a good time. Dada-jaan will be starting his rambles now.'

We made our way to the inner courtyard. I was greeted by the spitting image of a painting I had in our hostel room – a gift from mashi long ago. Inside on a cot was an aged man in white robes and a turban, with a few wide-eyed children sitting cross-legged on the floor. The end of the half-lit hookah occasionally disappeared into the flowing white beard that covered half his face. The children had gathered around to listen to the story he told them almost every day. The women hovered around the children, keeping an eye on them but also listening to the story that no one ever tired of.

Jami gestured me to sit down beside him, among the children. As the group became quiet, dada-jaan cleared his throat and began speaking with the measured ease of someone who had done this all his life, and enjoyed it.

2

The Treasure of Haider Kalan

'More than a hundred years ago, in this very village, there were three boys,' began dada-jaan. 'Like every boy who grew up in this village, they dreamt of a day when they would be soldiers. Soldiers in the army. Like their fathers. And their fathers' fathers before them. These three – Akbar, Abdullah and Iqbal – grew up together, played together, ate together and dreamed together. When the time came, they hoped to fight together.' He paused for a moment and then continued.

'Like every boy in this village, they were waiting for the drumbeat. The call to take up arms and march to battle. It came one day when the crops had been harvested and the fields had just been cleared. The rissaldar-major appeared with a troop of cavalry. A ritual played out. The same ritual that had been playing out every year, for years. The rissaldar-major spoke of life in the regiment, as was the norm. He held out a silver rupee for every new recruit, as was the norm. He read out the terms of service, as was the norm. Then, like every year, he called the boys of age to step forward. They all did, like others had done before them. They took their silver coins and gave them to my grandfather's grandfather, the venerable Rahat Ahmed Ali Khan. He also happened to be Akbar's father, so Akbar too is a forefather of mine. This was the tradition. The first rupee from the service was for the eldest family member. My grandfather's grandfather took their silver and sent the boys off. All the boys who put their mark on the rissaldar-major's register that day marched to duty, where they joined the others from Haider Kalan. Ninth Company of the Third Cavalry.'

Dada-jaan looked around, watching everyone listening intently. He noticed me and fixed me with a stare. I met his gaze and our eyes locked. He continued his story.

'The three boys of our story were different from their predecessors. They were brighter and sharper. Even before they completed a year of service, they were called up by the regimental major and sent to Delhi. There they were asked to leave the Third Cavalry and given other duties.'

Dada-jaan's gaze left mine and he continued, 'Their duties seemed strange and mysterious to everyone else.

They did not wear the red coat of the Company any more. They wore mufti and went around like common people. They did not have to ask any sahib for leave. They came and went freely. They were often found here, in the village, still on duty, still drawing pay, but not having anything to do. When they were asked, "What do you do?" they laughed and replied, "We are ghosts!" When they were asked, "Whom do you work for?" they laughed harder and said, "The Devil himself! We work for the One-Eyed Shaitan!"

'Years passed. Seasons changed. Eventually the times also changed. It was a time of defiance. A time of upheaval. A time of blood and gore. It was a time when the land was simmering with the rage of rebellion against the redcoat goras of the Company. It was a time when the land had become a powder keg, waiting for a spark. Soon enough a flame leapt up in far-off Barackpore. This flame spread far and wide and very quickly everything transformed.'

Dada-jaan took a deep puff from the hookah. He exhaled and the smoke travelled from his nostrils deep into his whiskers, emerging from his beard in wraith-like tendrils of fog. He paused for a moment and then continued.

'Everything changed. The Third Cavalry was part of the garrison at Meerut. It chose the side of the revolt. The three men of the Ninth Company, however, were built differently. They had to be loyal to the regiment, but the loyalty to our own ran deeper. They refused to be a part of the mutiny and also to fight the mutineers. They came back here instead, to stay out of it all. The rest of the Third Cavalry marched to Delhi and seized the Red Fort. Every now and then we received news of fighting. Of terrible liberties being taken in the name of freedom. Of the rebels being besieged by English soldiers. Of a battle on the ridge of Delhi. Of the changing tides of battle. Our village did not know what would happen next. We had no part in this war, but our fates seemed tied to the events in Delhi.

'One night, four horsemen rode into our village. Among them were the three boys of our tale, accompanied by a friend. They might have dressed in mufti when they last left, but that day they returned dressed in the red coats of the Company. They stopped for a while to rest and water their horses. They had a hushed meeting with my great-great-grandfather. No one knows what was said that day, but it was apparent something very strange was afoot. At the crack of dawn, the four left as quietly as they had come. This time they headed in different directions. The three boys rode east to Agra. Their friend took the road to Delhi.

'A few weeks passed. In spite of himself, my great-great-grandfather hinted at what was happening. He mentioned a mission of great importance on which the four were working. Something involving a treasure. And a ransom for the emperor. Speculation began. Speculation about who the boys were working for. Rumours flew about the happenings in Delhi. Rumours of victory. Rumours of defeat. With the rumours, there was also dissent. The younger men of the Ninth Company wanted to ride to the aid of the besieged in Delhi. The elders wanted them to remain out of the fighting. There were whispers about cowardice, rumblings about treachery and pleas of loyalty.

'Soon enough the debate became irrelevant. We received news that Delhi had fallen under the cannon fire of the English. The emperor had been captured. It was at this time that our three boys – the ghosts, as they called themselves – returned. They kept to themselves and spoke to no one. The elders put out word to keep their presence a secret from all outsiders. Of their friend, there was no news. There was a rumour that he rode in to meet them all one night and left as quietly as he had come. After the news of the fall of Delhi, more news reached us. The two sons and the grandson of Emperor Bahadur Shah Zafar had been murdered. Accounts of retribution also trickled in. Men of the Third Cavalry being tied to artillery and blown to pieces. There was uncertainty as well as an air of defiance all around. No one knew what would happen to the men of the Ninth Company.

'One night a company of soldiers surrounded our village. These soldiers seemed to be different from those we had seen before. White troops, led by two officers. Redcoats, but different from the redcoats of the Company. They were soldiers of the English Crown. All the men of the village were dragged out of their homes and lined up in front of the mosque. First, our three boys were singled out and questioned. They were beaten, whipped and questioned again. The English officers said they were keeping secrets that needed to be extracted from their bellies. Secrets about missing gold. They lined up the rest of the men and threatened them with death. The three boys only shook their heads in silence. My great-great-grandfather reasoned with the officers. No one here had any part in the rebellion or knew about the gold. But the officers showed no mercy. They shot him down like a dog. A riot broke out. There was mayhem. The English cavalry charged at the men. When the smoke had cleared, broken bodies lay everywhere. The soldiers looked at their papers and asked the names of everyone present – those who could still talk, that is. As they struck names off their lists – lists of men in the Third Cavalry – the two officers pronounced their sentence. Every adult male in the village, former soldier or not, was to be strung up from the nearest tree.

'Within a matter of hours it was all over. The trees sagged from their grisly burden. While leaving, for good measure, the English razed the mosque. It was all a warning of what happens when someone rears his head against the redcoats.'

Dada-jaan paused, eyes staring into nothingness. There was silence, the atmosphere grim and sombre. Then he began speaking again.

'One child, a boy, witnessed it all. He saw the brothers and fathers, uncles and elders of our village die that day. That boy was my grandfather. As he gathered the party of children and women to bury the dead, he swore a sacred oath upon the graves of the departed elders. He swore he would bring justice to the fallen, whose loyalty had been rewarded with death. At the same time, he wondered about the secrets that had died with the three boys of our tale, who danced at the end of a rope that fateful night.

'But the secrets were not dead. Just sleeping. Eleven years after that dark night, a man rode into the village. A tall, dark man on a tall, dark horse. His clothes were covered with the dust of many miles of travel. There was something about the man's bearing that my grandfather, who was only nineteen years old then, found magical. The curved sabre at his side, the musket on his back, the way he rode a horse like he was born to do so. That man was the fourth horseman who had ridden out that night with the three. He asked for them and for my great-great-grandfather. Then he met my grandfather. They walked together to the banyan tree where the three and my great-great-grandfather had been hanged together. They spoke in low voices, heads bowed, close to each other.

'This man went by the name of Bayaz-ud-din Bungalee. They called him Ba'az, the falcon. He was a man of many stories, but none of them mattered any more. The secret mission he had been on with his friends was of little consequence. The rebellion was broken. The emperor had been imprisoned and sent to far-off Rangoon. The country was under the rule of the English Crown.'

Dada-jaan paused for a moment and then continued.

'Ba'az made this village his home. He started rebuilding the mosque which had been razed to the ground. Working with my grandfather and the other men of the village, he put the mosque back together, brick by brick. Once the structure was complete, he began covering the insides with patterns and writings in Farsi. People would often ask him what they were and he would reply, "The word of god."

'One day, a year after his arrival, he mounted his horse and called out to my grandfather, saying, "Come with me. It is time." It was nearly dusk now. Ba'az rode ahead at a slow pace and grandfather followed on foot. Ba'az stopped at the foot of the tree in front of the rebuilt mosque – the same tree from which his three friends had been hanged. He sat in silence on the horse, head bowed, totally still, until grandfather began to think he was asleep. It was then, as evening turned to night, that grandfather heard faint hoofbeats in the distance.'

The children around dada-jaan sat open-mouthed in anticipation. They had heard this story many times before and it seemed to me they knew what would happen next. Dada-jaan spoke again, but this time in a voice that sent a chill up my spine. In spite of myself, I shivered a little.

'Grandfather saw three ghostly shapes come through the trees. They were three men on horseback, but their pale white images seemed to flicker – as if they were made of mist. Wide-eyed in fear, he saw that the hooves of the horses did not seem to touch the ground, yet made faint sounds for he could still hear the hoofbeats. Probably only in his head, he thought. As the three horsemen came forward, Ba'az whispered, "Do not fear. They are our own." Grandfather saw them clearly as they came closer. They were the forms of Akbar, Abdullah and Iqbal. The young men on horseback looked just like they did when they had died. They did not seem to notice grandfather and came up to Ba'az. In a hollow voice, Ba'az asked them, "Who comes to meet me?" The figures raised their hands in greeting and each spoke his name.

"Dost Akbar."

"Abdullah Khan."

"Iqbal Mohammed."

'Ba'az asked, "Where lies the treasure?"

'The horsemen replied, as if on cue, "Locked up."

"How do I find it?"

'The horsemen answered, "The key lies hidden."

"Where?" asked Ba'az.'

Dada-jaan stopped. He raised his right hand to his right ear and turned his head towards the children, gesturing them to provide the answer.

'Here. In Haider Kalan!' said the children in unison.

'Then grandfather heard Ba'az ask the horsemen, "How do I find the key?" They replied, "It is where it has always been. Look to the skies above the house of god. The stars will speak to you and tell you where to go." The horsemen stood in silence, as if waiting. Then one of them said, "Go seek it, brother, and let our souls rest. We will meet again here next year." Turning their ghostly horses around, they disappeared into the darkness.

'Grandfather was at a loss for words. He did not know whether he had imagined it all. Ba'az dismounted and said, "I am leaving. This time I may not come back. I have shown you all this for good reason." Grandfather listened, unnerved and confused. 'This village bears a terrible history. You have seen it with your own eyes. But this village also carries the secret to a great treasure which can make amends for what happened that day. The year my brothers died and Delhi was burnt by the redcoats, my three friends you just saw carried away thirty thousand gold mohurs from the loot of Delhi and hid them. No one knows where the treasure is hidden. The secret died with them. But every year, their restless ghosts come back here and tell me the same thing you heard today. Since I must leave, it is for you now to find the key to the treasure.' Saying this, he mounted his horse with a fluid, graceful motion. Grandfather stood there, looking up at his craggy face.

'Ba'az continued, "Look to the skies above the house of god. Let the stars speak to you. Knowledge lies in them. The truth behind the secret treasure of a badshah of India. A treasure worthy of an emperor's ransom," and then rode westward, soon receding from view.

'In the morning, grandfather called together all the men of the village who were boys when their fathers had been killed. He told them what had happened the previous day.

'A hunt for the treasure began in the village. There were muted whispers about the man named Bayaz-ud-din. Everyone dreamed of the hidden treasure. Buildings in the village were taken down and the ground was dug up to look for clues. Nothing was found. There was talk of digging around in the mosque that Ba'az had rebuilt, but the fear of god far outweighed the greed for wealth. They did look into the well inside the mosque, though, and tapped all over the walls, but did not find anything anywhere.'

Dada-jaan looked around at his audience in the dim twilight, the darkness increasing every minute.

'Many years have passed. Legend has it that every year, on a full moon night, as dusk turns to darkness, three horsemen come and wait under the tree outside the mosque. They have been coming every year since this story has been told. I have never seen them myself, but some say they have. They come and wait. And after a while, when no one comes to meet them, they turn around and leave.

'I have told you this story for many years, the same way I heard it when I was a child. From time to time, I have looked for clues about where the mysterious key lies – in the stars above the skies of the house of god. I have thought for long about this cryptic message that Ba'az left with my grandfather. But I have not been able to make any sense of it. My quest has come to nothing. The treasure has not been found. I tell you this story so that some of you may try to find it. This is the story of our village and the mystery in its history. Find this treasure if you can. If you cannot, tell this story to your children. Let our men who were hanged from the trees of Haider Kalan not have died in vain. Their souls shall not rest until the treasure they hid has been found.'

3

Questions in the Dusk

The children broke into protest.

'But dada-jaan, you promised!'

'The treasure has not been found today, either!'

'We want the treasure!'

The old man smiled and looked with benign amusement at his grandchildren and great-grandchildren. He said quietly, 'Who knows? We may find it tomorrow. Or maybe the day after?'

The children got up and started playing. Some variant of chasing one another. I continued to sit, deep in thought. My brain was in a whirl. A hundred questions flooded my mind.

Darkness had set in. Hurricane lanterns and an occasional electric bulb lit the courtyard. With my mind some place far away, I got up.

Jami took me to dada-jaan and introduced me.

'Dada-jaan, this is my classmate.'

Dada-jaan was puffing on his hookah, lost in thought. Hearing Jami, he squinted to look at me in the darkness. His eyes seemed to catch mine and he fixed me with a gaze like he had done while telling us the story.

'Very good. Very good. Bless you, my child. Where are you from?'

'I am studying in Delhi now, dada-jaan. But my parents are from Bengal,' I answered. Why do we all want to know where we are from, I asked myself. Is it not enough that I am here now?

Dada-jaan nodded. 'Our friend Ba'azuddin Bungalee was also from Bengal. Tell me, son, did you like the story? What did you make of it?'

I didn't know what to say. I hadn't made anything of it. Not yet, in any case. My thoughts were a jumbled mess and I hadn't even begun to sort them. I jabbered whatever came to my mind.

'Yes. Very much. In fact, this is the reason I came here with Jami. To hear an account of the events of 1857 from the people who lived them. There is so much to know. The Third Cavalry. Was that the same Third Cavalry that was stationed in Meerut? And you mentioned the Ninth Company was made up of people from here. Is it true that they stood down during the rebellion? If that is so, it is a piece of history that has never been told. And the reprisals by the English. The fact that they scoured the land so far away to hunt down the perpetrators. Or who they thought were the perpetrators of the rebellion. There must be some orders or dispatches in the English files that mention the purge that happened here. Who gave the orders? Why?' I stopped to catch my breath.

Jami began to laugh. I gave him a baleful glare. He did not stop sniggering. I ignored him and continued.

'And you said that the English were asking questions about a hidden treasure. And the man – Ba'azuddin Bungalee. Where was he from? Where does he fit in? The riddle that is talked about in the story – about a key. What did it say – something about stars and god?' I was quivering with excitement. The questions came tumbling one after another. A part of me wondered why as other thoughts raced in my head. Treasure! 1857! Rebellion! Mutiny!

Dada-jaan was looking at me with a strange expression. He said softly, 'The skies above the house of god. Where the stars speak.'

'Yes, that! What can it mean? Were these the exact words? Since when has this story been told? Who started telling it first? Can there really be a treasure? Thirty thousand gold mohurs? Or has the tale of the treasure changed with time? Has the amount of money changed with time – grown? This happens, you know. And if there is actually a talk of treasure in the original story, it may still be found,' I said.

Jami made a sound that was a cross between a snort, a snigger and a sigh.

Dada-jaan looked at him sharply and Jami became a baby-faced good boy again.

Dada-jaan said to me in a calm voice, 'These days young people have no faith in anything any more.' I saw Jami's jaw tighten. He did not say anything. The old man addressed me again. 'But not all young men are like that. You seem to be a bright, intelligent one. A boy with curiosity.'

'Not a boy any more. I have turned twenty,' I said. What did this guy think I was, a toddler?

Dada-jaan gave a hearty laugh, tossing his head back. 'And what is your twenty to my ninety-five?' he asked. Then he said, 'Come, sit with me. You have much to ask, it seems.' He gestured me to sit next to him on the cot. I joined him.

Mirza had come over and was listening to the conversation. He said to Jami, 'Come, help us with the tandoor, will you? Royal Bungalee wants to hear more about Ba'azuddin Bungalee! We, on the other hand, need to start the fire quickly, or we will not eat tonight.'

Illiterate imbeciles, I thought. Sitting on a gold mine of lost narratives and all they can think about is their bellies. I turned my attention to dada-jaan, a barrage of questions ready for him.

'Umm . . .' I began.

I wondered about where to start. Before I could say anything, dada-jaan said, 'The story was told by my grandfather first. I heard it from him ever since I was a child. The words "look to the skies above the house of god", "let the stars speak", "thirty thousand gold mohurs" have remained unchanged. I tell this story exactly as I heard it. No change. Nothing added. Nothing removed.'

'What can these words mean?' I asked.

'That, child, is the entire mystery, is it not?' he said with a deep sigh. 'I have wondered about them all my adult life. I have looked high and low for a meaning but found nothing. Now I am at the end of my days. I get more and more tired with every passing day. And the young ones here have no stomach for the stories of old men.' He seemed to have aged visibly in the light of the dusk.

'As for your curiosity about the men of the Ninth Company and the happenings at the time of the great rebellion, I do not have much to add beyond this story that I narrated. Whatever remains is buried with my grandfather and others, who were only children then. It was all much before my time, you see.'

I understood. Dada-jaan must have been born more than thirty-five years after the events.

'Let us talk tomorrow, shall we? I feel so weary these days. Tell me, son, you are studying buildings too, aren't you? Like little Jami?'

Little Jami. I made a mental note to use that the next time he boasted of his manly exploits. 'Yes, dada-jaan. I study architecture.'

'Very good. You know, the mosque in the story – the one Ba'az helped rebuild? It still stands. You must see it before you leave, and tell me what you think.'

'Tomorrow, perhaps?'

Dada-jaan nodded, gave me a piercing look and then turned away, deep in thought.

Jami was done with firing up the tandoor and came over. I got up to leave. The old man gave us his blessings, lost in his own world. Jami and I picked up our bags and made our way to a flight of stairs at the end of the courtyard.

As we climbed the stairs to the room where we would be staying, Jami said, 'What did you do?'

'When?' I asked.

'It is very strange . . .' he said.

'What is?'

'Dada-jaan's behaviour. He never talks for this long to people. No one.'

'Just being hospitable, I guess. I am a guest from far, far away, you know. And little Jami's friend!'

'Right!' I heard his unmistakable snort.

'Yes. You should treat me better. Here, carry my bag,' I said, tossing it to him as we cleared one flight and started another.

To my surprise, Jami took my bag and didn't toss it back at me. He said, 'And you know something, I have never seen him look so tired before.'

I shrugged. 'Age catches up, man. It will happen to all of us,' I said, as we reached the end of the stairs. I am sure he is just a little tired after entertaining my yapping. Right now, I need to clean up. Where do I go?'

Jami pointed to a bathroom at the end of the terrace. As I walked to it, I saw the courtyard below. Dada-jaan was still sitting there, head drooping, as if half asleep. Mirza was sitting beside him.

When I returned, the scene below was the same as before. But this time I noticed something more. Dada-jaan seemed to be mumbling something under his breath, eyes half closed. Mirza was listening, nodding slightly every now and then.

4

Questions in the Dark

It was late at night. Jami and I were wide awake. The rest of the household was asleep. Dinner was long over. But sleep was nowhere in sight. Old habits die hard, and bad old habits die hardest. Used to staying up nights making drawings and small talk, we did not know what to do with so much time on our hands. No television, no radio. We finally decided to kill time in the oldest way known to man. Drink.

A few discreet enquiries earlier in the evening had produced a bottle of local rum. Made from the same sugarcane that was the staple crop of Haider Kalan. Distilled at home, of course, without licence. Procured by none other than Mirza before he too turned in for the night. Two drinks down each, the heady brew started to take effect, liberating our minds and loosening our tongues.

More of Jami's tongue and mind, evidently, than mine. 'Buddy, I need you to do something for me,' he said.

'What?'

'Fix this mess between Nira and me.'

'What mess?' I asked. 'You guys are already an item, right?'

'I don't know any more, man. She has not been talking to me.'

'But you guys were talking yesterday when I showed up at the hostel?'

'Not really,' said Jami sheepishly. 'That was just a screwed-up attempt at making up. She has not been talking to me for weeks.'

'What happened?' I asked with some reluctance and impatience. Here was a huge treasure waiting for us and this idiot was mooning over imaginary problems.

He sat brooding for a while. Then he blurted out, 'Something happened a couple of weeks ago.'

I did not want to know. These lovers' tiffs are not my cup of tea. Best avoided. But there is no escaping Jami when he is fixated on something. 'What?' I forced myself to ask eventually.

More silence followed. I could almost hear the tick-tock of his empty little head. 'Come on, out with it!' I said.

'Well, it's like this. One afternoon things were beginning to get frisky,' he said. 'But before I realized, the damage was already done.'

'What damage?'

'Well,' said Jami, turning a deep shade of red, 'things were about to go all the way, when I did something stupid.'

Super idiot. What had he gone and done now?

'Listen, fucker . . .' I began, alert all of a sudden, 'you did not do something *bad*, did you?' This was dangerous territory and I wanted to steer clear.

He remained quiet for a second or so. 'More like I did *not* do something bad.'

The poor fellow had an expression that bordered on self-loathing and shame. 'I could not. *She* wanted to. I didn't.'

Oh fuck. What had I got myself into here?

'And that pissed her off no end,' he said.

Hell hath no fury . . . and this was Nira we were talking about here. I felt sorry for this poor idiot.

'But why . . .' I began to ask, but the look on his face shut me up. There were some boundaries, after all, that could not be crossed. I checked myself and asked instead, 'What is it that you want *me* to do?'

'Explain something to her. Tell her that I need time, or something,' he said, almost begging for help.

'How do I do that?' I asked. The chances of Nira

listening to anything I had to say were next to nothing. Unless it involved agreeing with her. 'Explain what?'

'I don't know. You have a way with words. You are a champ, man!'

No way. I was not getting embroiled in this one. Friend or no friend.

'This is your cross to bear, my friend,' I replied. 'You have to do it yourself.'

'But what? How? How do I even start? Where do I begin?'

'Say something nice to her,' I said lamely. 'Everyone loves to hear nice things.'

'Like what?' Jami exclaimed like a hungry, eager boy.

'I don't know. Anything. Tell her that her eyes are wonderful.' How on earth was I supposed to know what to say.

'Yes, they are,' said Jami with a dreamy, faraway look. 'What do I say about her eyes?' he asked. 'Give me the words. You are the one with the words.'

This was awkward. I was in a sticky place. 'Tell her that her eyes light up your skies like stars.' It sounded like something that would never work with Nira.

'Stars. Light. Skies. Yes. Yes. Yes!' Jami was clutching at straws.

I would like to be there when he says that to Nira and gets chewed up, I thought to myself.

'You really are a champ, man! Now quick, give me a few more lines,' said Jami, eager for more.

Enough. 'Forget it. She is too good for you,' I said with some malice.

What I said seemed to touch a raw nerve. It shut him up and I thought that was the end of it. I continued my fantasy, dreaming about what I would do when I swam in gold. Between the time I was driving a silver Porsche 911 to college and signing up Sharon Stone for my seventh film, I heard a deep sigh. Jami.

In a hollow voice he said, 'She is not too good for me. It is I who am not good enough.' He almost gave out a sob. Damn. This guy should be an actor on stage. He was completely wasted studying architecture.

'Why was I born here?' he asked and looked at me, face contorted in a grimace. This was getting serious. I wondered what to say. Before I could think of something, he continued, 'Why was I born in Haider Kalan? Why did I have to be a village boy who has nothing for a princess like Nira? Why could I not be born to someone in the city? A computer scientist like your father, perhaps.'

This was completely insane. 'Trust me, you would not want to be born to my father,' I said.

'At least someone who would be around, then? Abba had to go and get blown to bits in Kashmir. They could not even find his body. Fending for ourselves, amma and I, stuck in this hellhole, with no end in sight.'

This was something new. Something about Jami I had no idea of. I realized that despite being friends for over two years now we never really talked about our families or our past. Not our style, I suppose.

Jami gave a shudder and continued in a low voice, 'You are right. I am no good for Nira. I do not have a way with words or any money to give her a good life. And I cannot bear to be a wham-bam kind of fellow here. Not with her.'

You have a heart of gold, my friend, I thought. And true love can move mountains. I wanted to say that, fix up my friend for good and have him live happily ever after. Instead, the fox inside my brain said, 'There might be a way around that.'

'There is?' Jami asked. An expectant flash in his eyes. A ray of hope. He really liked the girl. I would have to do something about this whole matter sooner rather than later.

'Yes,' I said, 'all we need to do is figure out dada-jaan's story. The key he spoke of. Where the stars speak from the skies above the house of god, whatever. Find the treasure and you will have enough money for anything!'

'What?' asked Jami, a little bewildered. It appeared he was still trying to understand what I had said. He blinked twice. Squinted. Shook his head as if clearing it and said, 'Say that again.'

'Thirty thousand gold mohurs. They lie hidden somewhere. All we need to do is find them. Look, we find them and all our problems are solved. We are talking several crores here, give or take a few.'

'Crores?'

'Yes. If we solve the mystery, we will have more money than we can spend.' Somehow it hadn't sounded so silly when I had been thinking about it.

I fought my own misgivings. 'There is bound to be a large element of truth in the story. Dada-jaan said he narrates it exactly the way he had heard it. Now the ghosts and stuff are definitely lore, but there is a big cache of gold hidden some place. I am sure of it.' Jami did not say anything. He only poured himself a glass of water and drank it in one gulp. He seemed more sober than he was a minute ago. He poured himself a refill of the rum. I finished my drink as well and passed him the glass to fix me another. 'My heart says so,' I said in an almost desperate attempt to appear convincing.

'You, my Bungalee friend, have a heart of gold,' said Jami.

Wait. That was my line!

'You have been taken in by this fanciful story,' he continued, shaking his head. 'No, man. Forget it. Look, this is just a story. A fable. A fantasy. A myth that has grown with each repetition over the past generations. There is no treasure. Never was. When I was a child, I too imagined that there is some fabulous treasure hidden under our noses. Something that would make this village rich. But as I grew older, I realized that this story has been made up over the years. There were heavy reprisals by the English after 1857. What they called the mutiny.

What some people call rebellion. What some others call a war of independence. Whatever it was, it scarred this village in a terrible way. The story was invented by someone to give some meaning to what happened that night over a century ago. To a mindless act of sheer brutality. That night when every adult male of this village was killed, something was needed to give hope. This story gave hope. Nothing more. I can see that you are getting all excited and charged up, but there is no treasure in this place. Never was. If it had been there, it would have been found long, long ago. Every inch of this village has been explored. Most of the village has been dug up many times. Still, no treasure. At the end of the day, this place is a rathole where nothing ever happens, and nothing will. This is a nothing place.'

That was a long speech from the usually taciturn Jami. Probably the longest he had made in his life. I looked at him, thinking of what to say. I decided to be tactful. 'Maybe you are right,' I said.

We sat in silence for a while, looking into our glasses. Occasionally, we swirled the dark liquid and sipped. Both of us were lost in our thoughts. After a while, I broke the silence. 'But you are wrong about this village. It is not a nothing place.'

'Why?' asked Jami, gazing at the bottom of his glass.

'Perhaps you do not see it because you grew up here. You are too close. You know what? I studied through my childhood in Repton, England. In sodding old Blighty.

Same country that ruled us fuckers for years. And you know what they teach in school about colonial history? Nothing. Not a fuckin' thing. And here you have living accounts from 1857. This place is fascinating! It is as if it is stuck in a time warp. A place where history is still alive. There are questions and answers here. 1857 man, 1857! I have only read about it in books, but here it is still alive. In dada-jaan's story and in the minds of the people.'

Jami gave a wry smile and gulped down his drink. The liquor had turned his eyes bloodshot. He said, 'You are city-bred. So you find these things fascinating. Just your fanciful, romantic notions of village life . . . Another drink?'

I nodded as Jami reached for the fast depleting bottle. 'Don't get me wrong, Jami. Of course, I find this place fascinating. And it is not just because I love history and see bits of it alive here. There is more. You know, there are some things here that I find against the stereotype.'

'Stereotype?' asked Jami as he poured rum into the two glasses.

'Yes. You know, a Muslim village. In Haryana. Part of undivided Punjab before Partition. Still, the people here stayed on in India and did not move to Pakistan. And the way things are here is not like the image of Muslim communities presented in the media. No burkhas. No skullcaps. More Sufi than conservative. Mirza got us booze. Booze, man! I would have thought it would be impossible here. But no, here we are, with a bottle of rum distilled right in this village.'

Jami stiffened a little while listening.

I carried on, a little excited. 'We should do something about this place. You know, something we have the skills for. Like design and build a museum for this place. Bring it on the tourist map of India. Something that would bring visitors to this place. Let's make Haider Kalan a place to be proud of.'

I finished the drink in my glass, my mind racing with possibilities.

Jami continued sipping his drink slowly. He said nothing.

'So, what do you think of my idea?' I prodded.

His response surprised me. 'Frankly, I give a fuck about your ideas,' he said. I thought he would show more enthusiasm.

Uh-oh. Angry Jami.

I raised my hands. 'Look, I am sorry about the Muslim stereotype thing. I have nothing against Muslims. In fact, I know nothing about Islam, let alone its stereotypes. I was only making a point.'

Jami stood up, a little unsteady on his feet. 'I know. I, however, know enough about Islam and its stereotypes. And I don't care about them either.' He started pacing the room, unsteady on his feet.

'What I do care about is *me*. But first, let me satisfy some of your curiosity about this village. It has been like this forever. Generations of soldiers coming out of this village, and generations of illegal booze-brewing. In 1947, when one part of India was moving to Pakistan and one part of Pakistan was moving to India, there was blood and mayhem everywhere. But not here. This village, and the three Jat villages around, we had no part in that nonsense. All our men served in the same regiments of the British Indian Army, which became the Indian Army later. We have shed too much blood here and tilled the soil here for too many generations to just abruptly pack up and leave. Soon, all talk of Partition stopped when our regiments were sent off to Kashmir in 1948 to fight. The soldiers' bonds of brotherhood protected this village from the pillaging mobs. The bonds built over sessions of bootlegged liquor eliminated whatever residual threats that might have come our way. Besides, things were settled. Too comfortable to consider going to a new place with no future. The money from soldiers' salaries brought comfort. Sugarcane farming brought some more. This place is filled with stories of bravery and valour – in 1857. Before and after 1857, in the Afghan Wars. And the Great War, and then the Second. And then in every war of independent India. 1948. 1962. 1965. 1971.'

I listened, not knowing where all this was headed.

Jami paused and leaned against the wall, steadying himself.

'And that is my problem. This comfort. This satisfaction with the status quo. The lethargy it breeds.

I don't want any of this. I want out. None of this soldier stuff and farming and being Muslim. I wanted out for the entire village once upon a time. But now I just want out for myself. Don't you see? Nothing has happened here. No roads. No schools. No proper electricity. It is this time warp that you find so fascinating. I loathe it. It is this disdain that made me take that talent exam nine years ago and go off to the army boarding school. I wanted to get a real education and not end up like everyone else in this village.'

Jami hobbled back to where he had been sitting and crashed on the bed. He kept staring at the ceiling for a while. Then he spoke softly.

'I want to grow. To grow out of Haider Kalan. I want to be able to speak English as well as you and Nira. Why do you think I keep listening when the two of you are yapping? I want to be like those who have been to private schools in Delhi and London. I want to go to New York and be a hotshot architect there. Jami Ahmed Ali Khan will be like Peter Eisenman and Richard Meier. And for that I have to shake Haider Kalan off myself. And that is why, my friend, I give a fuck about your idea of making Haider Kalan a place to be proud of.'

I couldn't think of anything to say. There was silence for a while.

Jami turned on his side and curled up on the cot, pulling the pillow around his head in a cocoon. He was mumbling, drunk, half asleep.

'I will go to sleep now. Tomorrow morning, they will send me off to the sugarcane fields. I will be waving a stick around like an idiot, scaring off birds.'

He got up with a start and raised himself up on his elbow. He looked at the bottle of rum that the two of us had all but finished.

'Hide the bottle after you are done and wash the glasses, please,' he said. 'Amma should not know what we have been up to.'

With that he lay down and pulled the pillow around his head again. Soon he was snoring loudly.

I stayed up for a little while, thinking of all that Jami had told me. A part of me wanted to agree with his cynicism even as the other remained fearfully optimistic. My heart, made of gold or dirt, wanted me to believe that there was a treasure waiting to be discovered. It would solve so many problems in one stroke. More than anything else, the idea helped me escape my present reality. It gave me hope. Something to look forward to.

The sceptical part told me I was being foolish. Wishful thinking. There is no cure for optimism, it said.

But having hope is so much better, I thought. Better to be eager to wake up the next morning. Better than killing yourself over lost academic years.

Thoughts of baba brought the old misery back. The last words we had spoken to each other were filled with so much bitterness. I wished I could have a different memory of all that.

I took to the bottle again. They say liquor drowns out sorrow, lets you sleep a dreamless slumber where you can forget the shit-storm called life. I hoped it was true. I drained whatever was in the bottle in a steady guzzle, letting it run straight from mouth to stomach, missing the gullet.

I kept the empty bottle in the bag and rinsed the glasses with some water. Switching off the light, I stumbled to the other bed in the dark.

Drunken sleep overtook me quickly. My last thoughts were of ghostly horsemen riding into darkness and piles of gold and jewels. Unknown shadows danced in the dark, sabres flashing and rifles blazing.

5

Verses

I woke up feeling suffocated. The pillow was smothering me. Or perhaps I was smothering myself with the pillow. It was past noon. The heat was stifling. Mouth parched and head throbbing with a dull pain, I got up. A half-empty bottle of water lay on the bedside table. Remnants of last night's revelry. I drank the warm water, draining the bottle in one go. Bleary-eyed, I pulled a toothbrush out of my bag and stepped out of the room on to the open terrace.

The glare of the afternoon sun on the cement floor made me squint. I stumbled into the heat and crossed the terrace towards the bathroom at the other end. The courtyard below was deserted. Not a soul in sight. I wondered where Jami was. Had he been hauled off to the sugarcane fields? Perhaps. Along with everyone else in the house. I thought of how I would spend the rest of the day. I remembered what dada-jaan had told me. Yes. Going to see the mosque would be a good idea.

There was a washbasin and an ancient mirror outside the bathroom wall. After brushing my teeth, I splashed water on my face, head and neck. The water felt cool in that heat. I looked up and saw a large earthen tank on the roof that supplied water to the bathroom and the washbasin. I felt grateful for the natural cooling of the earthen walls of the tank and made my way into the darkened bathroom. The light did not seem to be working. I remembered Jami saying something about this place not having proper electricity. Shrugging the matter off, I aimed in the dark and took a long, much-needed piss.

Somewhat less hungover now, I made my way back to the room. I found a covered plate and a glass on the bedside table which I had missed earlier. Breakfast, or brunch. Parathas and lassi. Soggy parathas, lassi that had seen cooler days. But I was not one to complain. I wolfed it all down.

With food taken care of for the time being, I was craving a smoke. It had been a few days since I had had one. I remembered picking up a pouch of tobacco from Meghnad's room back in the hostel. Finding said pouch at the bottom of my bag, I stuffed it into one of the pockets in my pants. It had matches and paper – a self-contained unit to roll and smoke cigarettes, without having to pay an arm and a leg. I took my notebook and pencil as well, stuffing them into another pocket. Then I made my way down the stairs, crossed the empty courtyard and stepped into the street. I took the dirt path in the general direction of the mosque.

I walked for over twenty minutes before the path turned a corner around a rundown building and the mosque appeared in view.

I was thirsty again. After taking a long look at the mosque, I walked to a handpump that stood a few paces away from the building at the edge of the village. I pumped the handle and drank the water. My thirst quenched, I walked a little further, going closer to the mosque. There was a shady tree next to the mosque and I decided to sit under it for a while. With my back resting against the trunk of the tree, I pulled out my notebook and pencil and began to make short notes and some quick sketches.

It was a curious building, as far as I could tell. For one, it was small. Very small. Each side was barely ten metres. There was a courtyard with an enclosure at one end. The dome at the top was free of embellishments. Along with its small size, what struck me was the starkness of the structure. If I had not heard dada-jaan's story, I would have thought it was a modern building, not a late nineteenth-century mosque. I had expected a little more adornment than what I saw. The form had a severity that made the mosque seem more recent than it was.

I did a line drawing of the mosque. A perspective view, an elevation, the detail of a doorway. I turned the pages of the notebook and compared them with other sketches I had made of the historic buildings that dotted the landscape of Delhi. Tombs and mosques that were at every other street corner in some parts of the city. I noted the stonework in them, the inlay, the ornamentation. I saw the barren limestone plaster on the mosque in front of me. I thought of kings and courtiers building grand mosques and tombs, with marble domes and minarets. I looked at the aged, yellowed, cracked, pockmarked fascia of the building in front of me. This was how poor men and women prayed, then. The past was not very different from the present.

Philosophy and history dealt with for the time being, I turned my attention to more pressing things. I put the notebook back in my pocket and took out the pouch of tobacco. I pulled out the wad of rolling paper and peered inside the pouch. The tobacco was moist, like it usually was. A smoky, earthy smell emanated from the long leaves mixed with the smaller grains of tobacco. I took a bit of it and started to roll a smoke. I wished I was better at this. Like Clint Eastwood, who could casually roll a smoke, lick it and light it, while pumping off lead at bad guys on the roofs of a one-street town in the Wild West.

Having done the best I could, I lit the cigarette and inhaled. The smoke wafted down my lungs and

I coughed. It had been a while. I inhaled again and let the smoke ease into my lungs before exhaling. The smoke hit my nicotine-starved blood and my head spun. Half closing my eyes, I looked at the mosque again and resumed my idle thoughts on architecture, empire, civilizations and dust.

~

I stubbed the cigarette on the tree trunk and decided to get up. I tottered ever so slightly under the influence of the nicotine, heightened by hunger. I hazily made my way to the entrance of the mosque. A small wooden double door was ajar. I called out once, twice. No one answered. I took off my slippers, stepped inside and entered a small courtyard. The door closed behind me, on its own.

It was cooler inside. I shivered involuntarily and looked around. The place was different from what the outside suggested. It was a small courtyard with a fountain in the middle. Or rather, what used to be a fountain. Water for washing the sins of the faithful. I tried to work the pump. Nothing. Purity had dried out here, too. I noticed the inner walls of the courtyard and the small pavilion at the end. I guessed that it was facing west, the direction of prayers for the faithful. The pavilion was where a cleric would usually sit, calling out verses of prayer, while others would pray in the courtyard. The floor of the pavilion was level with the courtyard and covered with the same grainy, fine dust that was present everywhere. The mosque was not in use, I concluded. The faithful of Haider Kalan had found other ways to achieve communion with god.

I noticed the elaborate patterns that ran along the walls of the courtyard, along the columns of the pavilion and into the ceiling. I looked with curiosity at the patterns and tried to follow them. Relief work in limestone plaster, painted here and there in splotches of red, blue and black. The sparse reds became more prominent as the patterns wove towards the pavilion. I entered the pavilion and sat down, resting my back against a pillar. My mouth felt dry and everything seemed to be in slow motion, missing a frame every now and then. I should not have had such a strong smoke.

I got up and went to the handpump again. This time, instead of a few cranks, I pumped until my arms and shoulders hurt. Sure enough, a trickle of muddied water came out, splattering the floor of the courtyard. Encouraged, I pumped again. More furiously this time. Water started to rush out of the pump. Victorious, I pumped more. As the water ran over the flagstones of the courtyard, it washed away some of the dust. I stooped and drank the water. It tasted sweet. I stood up and took a few more turns with the vanquished pump before returning to sit in the shade of the pavilion.

I pulled out my notebook and started sketching

again. The roof was odd. There was a dome on top of the pavilion, but the underside of the roof was flat, covered with patterns and motifs. Not a true dome. A charlatan. Made to look like a domed structure, but in reality just a flat slab with a filled lump on top of it, passing off as a dome. Cosmetic, not structural. Professor Venugopal would be very interested in this. A semi-medieval structure, modernist on the outside and post-modern inside.

I finished sketching what I saw. I observed the patterns and motifs closely. There were no curvy, leafy, floral patterns here, which were usually found in the structures of that time. The smears of reds, blues and blacks followed a rigid geometric pattern. They ran over the walls and columns. Straight and jagged lines, forming squares and rectangles, crawling up the columns and then on to the roof, where they converged at the centre and abruptly broke their geometry.

I shook my head and blinked. My mouth had become dry. My head felt light and heavy at the same time. Relaxed and tense. Feeling thirsty again, I tried to get up. I felt the urge to have that tobacco again. Perhaps it was the empty-ish stomach, perhaps it was the water, or perhaps the smoke after days. Whatever it was, it felt . . . good. I skipped and floated to the pump and pushed the handle again. Cupping my hands under the streaming water, I drank till my stomach could take no more. As I made my way back to where I had been sitting, I saw that all the pumping had bathed the floor of the courtyard. A thin film of water covered the surface.

I saw that the patterns on the underside of the roof had converged to the centre. They formed an elaborate, spiralling floral motif. It also featured text that looked like Urdu or Farsi. Hymns and verses to god, most likely. The curvy, snaky squiggles made me dizzy as I tried to twist and turn my head to follow them.

I felt a wet patch on my bottom. With a start, I sprang up. The water had trickled into the pavilion. I looked at the floor. The dirt had been washed away and the water had formed a murky, mirrored surface. I kept staring at it. After a while it started making sense. I tried to follow the patterns on the ceiling and their reflection on the floor. I stood at the centre of the pavilion. I craned my neck up and down, right and left, following the story that was unfolding. I pulled out my notebook and began to draw feverishly. After a while, tired with all the effort, I lay down and fell asleep, overcome by exhaustion.

~

I was woken by a discreet cough and a nudge on the shoulders. It was Mirza. I took a moment to realize where I was. It was nearing dusk. The wetness on my back reminded me of the water on the floor. I immediately tried to locate my notebook, hoping it was not wet. It had a year's worth of sketches, as well as the sketches and notes I had made a little while ago. Not finding it in my pocket, I groped around where I was sitting.

I looked up to ask Mirza about it and saw that he had it in his hands. He was flipping through the pages with curiosity. He also had my tobacco pouch in the crook of his arm.

'My god, Bungalee Tiger! You are quite an artist!' Mirza chuckled. 'These drawings, they are not all of here, no?'

'No. Most of them are some mosques and tombs in Delhi. Humayun's Tomb, Jama Masjid, Safdarjung's Tomb and the Moti Masjid at the Red Fort. I have an interest in old buildings.'

'Hmm. And a very keen eye, too. Does Jami-baba also have this interest? I have never seen any drawing books like this with him,' said Mirza.

'Jami? He is more interested in other things,' I said, getting up and dusting myself. 'What time is it?'

Mirza reached the last few pages of the notebook and exclaimed, 'Ah! You have been making drawings of our mosque, too. Very nice!' he said, looking at me.

'Yes. It is an interesting mosque. Very different,' I replied.

Mirza closed the notebook and handed it back. I felt like I was getting a passport back after an examination by an immigration officer. Mirza also gave me my tobacco pouch. 'Yes. The tobacco you smoke is also very interesting. Very different.' There was a knowing smirk on his face.

I stuffed the pouch and the notebook into my pocket. 'I don't really smoke, you know. Only once in a while. And cigarettes are so expensive. Rolling is cheaper,' I said as we made our way towards the door of the mosque.

'Of course, of course. Don't worry, I will tell no one. Heh-heh,' Mirza said, slapping me hard on the back. 'Now let us hurry back home. Everyone has been looking for you.'

'They have?'

'Of course! Look, Bungalee-baba, this is not a big city. It is not good to stay out for too long, especially in the evening.'

I followed Mirza down the path back to the house, silently cursing myself for having slept for so long, and so suddenly. I also fingered the spine of the notebook in my pocket, thinking of what I had discovered in the mosque.

~

When we reached the house, Jami was waiting at the doorway.

'Where on earth were you, man?' he asked.

'I was at the mosque, making some sketches.'

'Sketches?'

'Yes, my history notebook, you know.'

'Yes, yes. But what took you so long? We have been looking for you for hours!'

'I . . . I slept off there.'

'Slept off! How could you sleep off?'

Mirza's barking laugh interrupted us. 'Jami-baba, your Royal Bungalee friend was having the leaves of heaven. Heh-heh!' Mirza said, before leaving us at the doorway and disappearing into the courtyard.

I pulled Jami close and whispered, 'I had a smoke. From a tobacco pouch I had taken from Meghnad's room before leaving. Thing is, it is not just tobacco that is in there.'

'Ah!' said Jami, understanding, rolling his eyes as if that explained everything. 'That pot-headed idiot. Are you all right?'

'Yes, I am. Just a little hungry,' I said. 'But I think I have found something. I need to talk to you about it. Soon.'

We stepped into the now familiar courtyard. Dada-jaan was there again, surrounded by children and a few other people, having just begun the story he told every day. Mirza was by dada-jaan's side, preparing his hookah. His eyes met mine and we exchanged a brief nod.

I took Jami's elbow and nudged him upstairs.

~

'I have found something in the mosque that you have all missed,' I said to Jami as we sat down.

'Pray tell,' said Jami sarcastically, 'something about the treasure again?'

No faith these days. Kids. Little Jami needed a lesson in belief. I began, 'I was sketching, sitting in the pavilion inside the mosque, when the stuff I smoked began to hit me. I don't know what it is that Meghnad mixes with his tobacco, but it is really potent shit. Before I knew it, I was thirsty as hell and scouring the mosque for some water. I tried the handpump in the courtyard a few times and some water began to come out of it finally. I drank that, and it seemed to take me on an even greater trip. I made some sketches after that. Serious shit . . . but architectural sketches. What I found later was more interesting.' I paused to pull out my notebook. Without opening it, I continued, 'In my enthusiasm, I pumped a bit extra. The water began to spread and covered the floor. I was sketching the calligraphy on the roof at that time. The Farsi text, or what seemed Farsi at first.'

'At first?' asked Jami, bewildered.

'Yes. When I felt the water soaking the insides of my undies, my tripped-out self got up to see what on earth was afoot. It was then that I saw the reflection of the ceiling on the floor and I realized it is not Farsi at all. It is Bangla.'

'Bengali?' Jami was incredulous.

'Yes, sir! Bengali. Alphabets broken up, morphed.

Made to look like Farsi. But written in mirrored Bengali on the ceiling so that no one would notice. And you know something? The script is Bangla, but the words are in Hindustani – Urdu, or Hindi. I understood bits of it. Something god knows how many generations of treasure seekers from Haider Kalan missed. That these treasure seekers could not read Farsi helped. If they could have they would have figured out it is not Farsi but gibberish. Here, see.' I opened the page that had both the ceiling patterns – one straight, one mirrored.

Jami looked at it for a while and asked, 'What does it say?'

'It speaks of the treasure,' I said. 'It is a verse. Here, let me translate.'

I took out my pencil, scribbled at the bottom of the page where I had drawn the patterns, and read aloud.

In the red earth of Udaipur
In the lap of mother's strength
By the water
With Jagat lies the key
Locked in the head
Is great treasure

'What does this mean? In the lap of mother's strength . . . by the water, at Jagat?' asked Jami.

'I do not know. But I think we need to start looking for the treasure in Udaipur,' I said.

'But where in Udaipur, man? There must be some place we are supposed to start.'

'I did not think of that. Frankly, I do not know,' I said, uncertain for the first time since I had begun speaking.

'Read out each line again. As it was written. We might have missed something in your translation.'

I recited the lines as they were written.

Rangi lal mitti Udaipur mein
Gode shakti mata ki
Jal ke kinaare
Jagat ke paas hai chaabi
Sire pe, taala bandh
Hai khazaana dhan

Jami became quiet. No words. No sound. That was belief sinking in.

'There is some treasure after all,' he said finally.

'Yes, my little Jami,' I said. 'Now let us head downstairs. Dada-jaan's story must be nearing its end. Let us give him the news.'

6

The Fakir

Dada-jaan was sitting on the cot smoking his hookah as Mirza fanned the flames. They looked up as we approached. Then they looked at each other.

Dada-jaan addressed me. 'Mirza says you have found something in the mosque.'

This was a surprise. News travels fast, I thought. I was also beginning to realize that Mirza was not the buffoon I thought he was. I did not say a word and opened my notebook instead. Finding the page where I had drawn the verses on the ceiling, I gave the notebook to dada-jaan.

He looked at it closely in the fading light. Then he looked at me and asked in a quiet voice, 'And?'

'Don't you see, dada-jaan?' asked Jami in an excited voice. 'He found this on the ceiling of the mosque, and he knows what it means!'

The old man did not respond to Jami. He was looking at me intently. Mirza was also watching me, as if waiting for me to say something.

I cleared my throat, uncertain where to begin.

'These verses say something, dada-jaan. And I think the lines in your story – the skies above the house of god, where the stars speak – are an allusion to these.' I proceeded to explain the Bangla script, the broken characters, the words they spelt out. 'I do not know yet what these lines mean, but it seems to say there is something in Udaipur.'

Dada-jaan nodded. 'And you can read this with ease?'

What sort of a question was that? I expected a little more enthusiasm.

'Well, yes. It was more of a stroke of luck. You see, I was looking at this as it was being reflected in the water. I managed to piece it together.'

The old man raised a hand to interrupt me. 'No, I meant if there is more like this, more words written like this, can you read them?'

More? Where? I looked at Jami thinking he would know something. He looked blank. 'Yes, I guess I can,' I said.

'But will you?' asked dada-jaan, eyes narrowed, his gaze fixed on me.

Why on earth wouldn't I? There was something here I did not know. I threw politeness to the winds and asked, 'Is there something you haven't told us, dada-jaan?'

Mirza gave me a sharp look, outraged at my temerity. Dada-jaan did not react. He rose to his feet and said, 'Come with me. All of you, inside.'

Dada-jaan slowly moved towards a door at the end of the courtyard which led to his room. Mirza picked up the smouldering hookah and went after him.

We followed them and entered the room. Mirza closed the door behind us, shutting out the twilight streaming in. He went to a dark corner of the room and lit a match, bringing a hurricane lantern to life.

Dada-jaan pointed to a bench and said, 'Sit. We have a lot of talking to do.'

We sat down as Mirza came forward and placed the hookah at dada-jaan's feet. Dada-jaan pulled the end of the long pipe to his mouth and took a long draw. He exhaled and the room began to fill with smoke, illuminated by the pale light of the lantern and making its way out of the sole window at the end of the room.

Dada-jaan turned towards Jami. 'It was nice of you to bring your friend to our village,' he said. 'Sometimes outsiders can see things that our familiar eyes miss. It took an outsider like him to see what was staring us in the face all this time. I think the two of you should know what I know.'

'Know what?' asked Jami.

'There is more to the story I tell every day. Listen carefully,' said dada-jaan.

We sat still, listening.

Dada-jaan took another deep puff of the hookah and began, 'Like I told you yesterday, the story was first narrated by my grandfather, Alauddin Ahmed Ali Khan. For years, till the day he died, he told the story, and for as long as I can remember, I heard it, till it had seeped into my being. Grandfather would say to me, "Remember this story. You must share it when I am gone."

'One day, when I was forty years old or so, grandfather lay dying. Age had caught up with him. His time had come. It was then that he called me and said, "The story that I have been telling you . . . it is not completely true. The fakir and I made up parts of it."'

'The fakir?' Jami asked.

'Yes,' said dada-jaan. 'I asked him the same question. He was a wanderer who lived here once. Grandfather said this to me as I say it to you now.

'The fakir and I agreed to tell the story as I tell it and not divulge the truth, because the truth was harsh. There was little to remember it for, other than the grieving over the dead. There are no ghosts that come every moonlit night. There was no Bayaz-ud-din Bungalee who rode into our village eleven years after the English came and killed everyone. In the story, we have the three boys of our village. How they arrived with a companion in the dead of the night, had a secret meeting with my grandfather and departed in different directions. How they came back and there were rumours that they had hidden a great treasure somewhere. How the English surrounded our village and summarily executed every adult male to set an example. All this is true. Except where our story spoke of the fourth companion – Bayaz-ud-din Bungalee – riding into the village eleven years after that day. A magnificent figure, the tall dark man on a tall dark horse. It could not be farther from the truth. Bayaz-ud-din Bungalee did come into the village that day, on a tall dark horse, but not riding it. He was wrapped in a cloth, his body laden on his horse. Dead.

'The man who had brought him was the fakir. When I was very young, one day the fakir walked in carrying Ba'azuddin's body. He told me how he had found him two days earlier in the ravines of Rohilkhand, east of Delhi. Ba'azuddin was lying under a tree, dying of his wounds and thirst. His horse stood grazing by him as he battled for life. The fakir tried to nurse him, but could not do much. Ba'azuddin spoke of how he was trying to reach Haider Kalan to ask about letters he had sent many years ago. On the road he was ambushed by an old enemy. His dying wish was to be brought to Haider Kalan, as his friends would know where to bury him. The fakir asked where he could lay Ba'azuddin to rest. Though most people liked to be buried in their native villages, it was not unusual for a soldier to want to be buried with his friends. The brotherly bonds forged over years of fighting together often became stronger than familial ties. So I pointed to the village graveyard. The fakir hauled Ba'azuddin's body there and buried him, among the graves of those murdered by the English. He was buried alongside his friends, to wait eternally until the day they would all rise again.'

Dada-jaan paused here and gestured to Mirza to light his hookah again, which had gone out. We waited expectantly. Drawing afresh from the hookah, dada-jaan continued.

'Grandfather told me about how the fakir made an elaborate platform over Ba'azuddin's grave. He dressed a piece of stone to act as a marker. He appeared to know how to work with tools. Grandfather asked him about it and the fakir replied that he used to work with stone and wood in a previous life, before he took to a life of wandering. Grandfather asked him to stay on in the village. Able-bodied men were at a premium. The younger boys who had survived the purge of the British were barely beginning to come of age. A man who could work with wood and stone would be a valuable addition to the village. The mosque also needed to be rebuilt. The fakir agreed.

'By then, my grandfather, who was quickly slipping away, told me to look among his belongings for a packet wrapped in oilskin. I found it quickly and saw that the packet contained letters written in a strange language. Grandfather told me these were the letters that the dying Ba'azuddin had mentioned to the fakir. They had come in many years ago. Three of them soon after the fateful day when everyone was killed. The last one many years after. Ba'az had told the fakir he was heading here because of these letters. They contained the detailed location of a great treasure.

'I had been unable to read those letters when they had come in. I could not read them when the fakir's words made me dig them out. I showed them to him, hoping that he – a holy man of letters and words – could.

'But alas. The fakir, too, was unable to read them – or so he said. He said that they need deciphering. As he spent his days helping rebuild the mosque, he attempted to work on the letters. He would scribble away on a book, saying that he was trying to make sense of them.

'It was on one of those days, when the mosque was nearly done, that he thought of coming up with a story to tell everyone. The same story that I have been telling you all these years.

'The fakir and I could not tell people about the letters, but we hoped that we could find someone who could read them. And that was why we made up the story about a secret treasure hidden in the village. The fakir copied those letters to create some patterns on the ceiling of the mosque. He made that part up about looking to the skies above the house of god so that someone would look at the ceiling in the mosque. Perhaps understand what was written. Whoever could would be able to decipher the contents of the letter.'

Dada-jaan had a distant look, as if he was remembering the day his grandfather lay dying, telling him one story that had led to the telling of another. Then, he spoke again, '"Keep these letters," my grandfather said to me, "until someone is able to read the writings in the mosque. Keep telling the story till that day." I promised him I would. I then asked him what became of the fakir. My grandfather replied, "The fakir was a strange one. There was more to him than what was obvious. It was evident to me he was no ordinary man, and that he had a past. But I never pursued the matter. It was better to let him have his secrets."

'Though the mad fakir lived in our village, doing all sorts of jobs for us, he never stayed here at a stretch for long. He would often go off for days and return as abruptly as he had left. He would regale children with stories of kingdoms and princes, treasure and adventure. He was a man of far greater depth and knowledge than he appeared at first glance.

'One day, after the mosque had been completed, and the telling of our story had become a habit for me, I thought of asking the fakir about the work he had been doing on deciphering the letters. The book he had been scribbling in all these years. It was something about his answers that made me suspect all was not well. One evening I decided to pay him a visit. The memory of that day is still so vivid in my mind that it seems like it was yesterday.

'It was a moonlit night. I was making my way to the fakir's hut. I decided to enter unannounced and saw him doing something that confirmed my gravest suspicions.

'He was scribbling away in his book, writing in the same manner as Ba'azuddin's letters. It was evident he had deciphered those letters long ago.

'I accosted him and demanded that he tell me the truth. I asked him where he had been travelling to all this time. He did not answer but merely tossed his book into a box where he kept his things. He was about to close the box, when I stopped him. Harsh words were spoken that day. We argued, and then we came to blows.

'As we fought, a lamp fell from its place and landed inside the box, setting it ablaze. The fakir tried to douse the flames even as we continued to grapple. He finally broke free and fled the scene. I followed but lost track of him soon. When I returned, his hut had been burnt to the ground. I never saw the fakir again.'

Dada-jaan stopped and looked out of the window. It had turned dark. 'Those were the last words my grandfather said to me,' he said, 'but there is a reason I am telling you all this.'

Dada-jaan turned to Mirza. 'Send for some food for all of us. This is going to take a while.'

Mirza left.

I felt that I had come out of a trance. I realized that my leg had gone numb. Jami, too, fidgeted. We had been sitting absolutely still, mesmerized by dada-jaan's account.

'I went through the packet with the letter and

pondered over what grandfather had told me before he died. I went to the mosque and looked at the writings, hoping that some day someone would decipher them and lead us to the treasure.'

The old man took a last drag from the hookah and set the pipe aside. He got to his feet from the low divan and slowly walked towards a wooden cupboard at the end of the room, saying, 'I asked you if you can read more of what was written on the ceiling of the mosque.'

From the cupboard dada-jaan took out a packet wrapped in oilskin. He handed it to me and said, 'This is the packet grandfather gave me. Perhaps you can read what is written in the letters and enlighten me about a mystery that has plagued me for most of my life.'

Part II

The Caesar Cipher

7

The Letters

I took the packet from dada-jaan's hands. Despite being small, about four by four inches long and two inches thick, it felt heavy. It was wrapped in oilskin and tied with a red string. Excited, I looked at Jami and exhaled consciously. I had held my breath for too long listening to dada-jaan. I untied the knot carefully, filled with reverence at handling something this old. Dada-jaan seemed to sense my hesitation.

'Go on. It won't crumble. I have wrapped and unwrapped it many times,' he said.

Mirza laughed. He had come in carrying a tray with a large plate of parathas and an assortment of bowls. He placed the tray on the side table and said, 'This packet may be old, Royal Bungalee, but Abba has taken good care of it. Go ahead, open it – it won't bite.'

'Or would you like to eat first?' dada-jaan asked me.

'You all please carry on. Let me see if I can understand what is written,' I said. 'I don't want oil on these papers.'

Dada-jaan gave a nod of approval. He gestured Jami and Mirza to start eating. I untied the string and unwrapped the oilskin. Inside were many sheets of yellowed parchment folded in a strange manner. A long fold along the margin and many lateral folds. As I looked at the folds with curiosity, dada-jaan explained, 'This was how dispatch horsemen folded confidential letters. Easier to swallow if captured.'

I felt a tingle of excitement when I saw the script. Jami leaned over my shoulder to get a glimpse. The snaky, beautiful script was spread across pages, the letters formed by black ink, possibly written with a quill. The same writing that was on the ceiling of the mosque!

'This looks like the characters in the mosque!' I declared.

I brought out my notebook and pencil. I began to make notes and worked on the letters. The others ate, leaving me undisturbed.

~

More than an hour later, I put down the letters and picked up my notebook.

'There are four letters here,' I said. 'Three of them seem to have been written and sent not too far apart from one another. It is these that I will read out first.'

I began to read and the others listened in silence.

The First Letter

19 February 1858
Denzong

Winter will soon pass and the road will open for the last leg of this journey. It has been close to a year since I left Haider Kalan with the gold. A lot has transpired in this time. I can only wonder what must have happened in the rest of the country.

When I left, the tide of fortune was already turning in the favour of the English. You know we had a hand to play in that, being instrumental in the fall of Delhi. But I am certain our names would not be recorded in history. It would be Hodson or Wilson who would find mention in the books.

In the lands I have travelled over the past few months, in the shadow of the mountains, news is scarce. The might of the English machinery never made many inroads into the areas of the fierce folks of the mountains. I wonder whether the fighting still rages, or whether the ill-fated rising has been quelled for good.

I shall find out soon enough. In a few months' time, I will be in Calcutta.

In these past weeks and months, I have faced snow and ice. A man of the plains is not used to the freezing cold of the Himalayas. My mules have been a hardy lot, faring far better than I seem to have. The six large chests loaded to the brim with gold have been borne well. I once thought of giving these mules names. I had Akbar, Iqbal and Abdullah in mind for them. I wanted to see your faces when I introduced them. Then I thought of naming them Nicholson, Wilson and Hodson, but better sense prevailed and I settled on calling them One, Two and Three.

I have passed largely unmolested and unquestioned through these lands. I would have thought three heavily laden mules would have aroused suspicion. Nothing of that nature happened, and for that I am thankful. This might also be because I avoided the plains and decided to go through the mountains instead.

I would think that my pursuers have lost my trail as well. My last sighting of those hounds was many months ago. I think they may be dead. The avalanche I set off with a small charge of powder is sure to have buried them. I wonder who they were, and who sent them. Could it be the captain, or was it someone else? Not many would know of the hoard of gold that I am carting around.

I might find answers when I reach Calcutta. I will have to tread carefully. I will have to find some way to stash away the gold before I enter the city. I wonder if young Harper still runs his trading establishment by the Esplanade. If not, I will have to find some other way to hide the gold.

I will always remember these mighty mountains. Every time I look at the curved dagger by my side, I will remember the valour of Man Bahadur Thapa. It will take thirteen slayings by this khukri of his to repay the debt of blood that I owe him.

I will write again soon, after I reach Calcutta.

Your Brother

I stopped reading and looked up.

'What else?' asked dada-jaan.

'Nothing. That is all there is in the first letter.'

'But there are three pages here,' said dada-jaan. 'How can it be so short?'

I showed him the letter and the notebook where I had translated everything. 'Every six or eight pieces form one alphabet. That is how the script has been broken up and mirrored to resemble Farsi.'

After pondering on this for a while, dada-jaan said, 'But this mentions something about hiding the gold . . .' and then fell silent.

'Let us read the rest of the letters and see what they have to say. The second letter is dated a few months later and was sent from Calcutta,' I said and began reading again.

The Second Letter

28 April 1858
Fort William

It has not even been two days since I returned to Calcutta and I must flee again. While a fast horse gets readied for a long march, I find some time to put down the happenings of the past few days. Whether I live or die, some day, when you read these letters, these truths will be known to you.

The insurrection against the Company and the Crown is all but over. Lucknow and Cawnpore are back in the hands of the English. This you must already know. The fall of Lucknow extracted a heavy toll. Captain Hodson fell during the action. No words can describe what a valiant man he was. It was my good fortune to have served under his command as his aide and scribe. In a better world and a different life, I hope I meet him again and not part on the strange terms we did.

I am an outlaw. There is a lookout in my name. A warrant for my arrest. An English officer has travelled all the way from Delhi to Calcutta to look for me. How he knew I was here, I have no idea. The three hounds who followed me out of Delhi, before I lost them in the mountains, could not have known I was coming here. How then did the English officer know exactly where to look for me? Unless he is part of a larger manhunt for me that has spread to every territory governed by the English. If that is so, things do not bode well for me. You, too, must take care.

All this was told to me by Sam Harper while we sat and worked on the terms of the exchange of the gold. Sam remains the fine young man he was when I last saw him. It is unfortunate that his father, the venerable Patrick Harper, passed away a few years ago. It was a fine period of service that I gave to him and the old general when I was but a boy of sixteen. Having reached adulthood with young Sam, and being his friend, is perhaps what saved me from arrest today.

Young Harper may only be a few years older than I am, but over the past two years, he has built an empire, financing both sides of the war. Now he manages his business by trading items of the loot in Delhi, and Lucknow, and Cawnpore, and god alone knows where else. He sits in his office at the Esplanade docks, donning an enormous turban. He has a Mamluke-like Habishi bodyguard. He looks like a turbaned white raja of modern times – far wealthier and more powerful than all the false kings of our land who rule only in name.

It was he who helped me bring the six chests of gold into the city. It was he, and his man in Lloyd's

Bank, who took the gold I carried off my hands. I feel much lighter now, after having carted it all over the mountains into Calcutta.

The fifty pieces of gold that remain with me will allow me to lie low for the next few years. A fast horse is ready to carry me.

I hear of the faraway kingdom of Udaipur, which has had no part in the rotten affairs of the past year. A peaceful region far away from the influence of the English. It would be a good place to hide and lie low. Sometime after all the heat has simmered down, I will head back to Punjab and meet you again. Till then, your names and mine on the paper I carry will serve as a sign of the four tigers who dared to heist the ransom of an emperor.

Your Brother

I looked up.

Dada-jaan had seemed a little let down by the first letter. This one seemed to deflate him completely.

'The gold . . .?' he said. 'It was . . . given away?'

I nodded and said, 'And it seems Ba'azuddin Bungalee is on the run. There is a warrant in his name.'

I saw an expression of utter misery on dada-jaan's face and said, 'But the letter speaks of fifty pieces of gold still being with him.'

Dada-jaan did not say anything.

I picked up the third letter and began reading it.

The Third Letter

15 May 1858
Udaipur

It has been a relentless race that has lasted two weeks, but I am finally a free man. Of the three who started hunting me from Delhi, two remained when I left Calcutta. By some act of divine misfortune, they found my trail the morning I was to leave. Which two of the three they were, I know not. They all looked alike. But they seemed to carry the fury and rage of a lost brother as they hounded me across the plains and mountains.

The third must have died in the avalanche I caused. That must have set their blood boiling. Hodson is dead! No one need chase me any more – I wanted to scream out to them. But whether they answered to the long arm of the law, or whether they acted for revenge alone, it mattered not. They were the hunters and I was the prey. There would be no peace until either they were dead, or I lay on the ground.

One after the other, I sent them to their maker. Being chased relentlessly is a tiring affair, particularly when you are riding across open ground. All that the pursuers need to do is keep you within sight. You run and run, as fast as possible, trying to lose sight of your hunters. They trot along on a leisurely pace and wait for you to tire out.

One day, though, I had had enough of the chase. So I just stopped and waited. As they charged at me, I loaded my rifle. I got the first one with a carefully placed shot between the shoulder blades. It caught him on the neck. I did not wait to see what happened next. I turned my horse around and fled.

The second one continued the pursuit until he, too, began to tire. Yesterday, within sight of the hills of Udaipur, I finished him off as well. Hodson sahib taught me good use of the sword. If it had not been for his teaching, it would have been me on the ground, but I lived to tell the tale.

Now, with the shadow of the hunters off my back and the weight of the gold off my shoulders, I can wait in peace and start a new life here, for a while.

This is a quiet place with peaceful folk. I am thinking of what to do with the time I would have at hand. The last seven years have all been spent in soldiery. I do not know, however, if they would have much use for a soldier here. Besides, it would not do well for me to draw attention upon myself. All the provinces of our land are still being scoured by the English for anyone who might have had a part in the rising. A solitary soldier with independent means would draw unnecessary attention.

While I ponder over what to do with my time,

I am sheltered at the temple here, under the guise of a fakir. They feed the poor twice a day and I stand among them, fed by a strange god.

I will write soon, after affairs have settled down a bit. Till then, may the gods look over you. Rest well with the knowledge that our treasure is safe.

Your Brother

I picked up the last one – the fourth letter. I looked at it and said, 'This one does not say when or where it was written. You say this came many years after the others?' I asked dada-jaan.

He nodded, looking very dejected. I cleared my throat and began to read the last letter.

Brothers,

I do not know if you have been receiving the letters I have been sending you all this while.

I had been hiding in Udaipur all these years, keeping our secret safe. I stayed out of sight all this time. But last year I had to flee the place. I was discovered. A matter of the heart, and of the loins. In my hurry I had to leave our treasure where I had hidden it. It is still there. I cannot go back to it. One of you must.

In the event that you do not know what has transpired all these years, you must know this – I have done very much like your father counselled.

Of the thirty thousand pieces of gold, I kept fifty with myself and gave the rest to the turbaned sahib of Calcutta. Those fifty pieces lie hidden with the letter in a sealed scroll, in the same manner we hid everything else. In the red earth of Udaipur, with the mother goddess, by the water. With Jagat lies the key. Locked in the head is great treasure.

This is for the four of us. All as one.

Your Brother

I folded the letters, wrapped them in the oilskin and carefully tied the string the way I had found it. I handed the package back to dada-jaan and reached for my plate. Three parathas had been left for me.

I began to eat. There was silence in the room. Dada-jaan seemed shattered.

'There is not much in the letters,' said Jami finally. 'Nothing that we can use.'

'Hmm,' I said between bites. 'Not really. We now know that there indeed was a treasure – thirty thousand pieces of gold. And fifty pieces remain hidden in Udaipur, like it says on the ceiling of the mosque.'

'Hidden where?' asked Jami.

I shrugged. 'I don't know. I think it is somewhere he could not return to but his friends could, which is why he wrote to them to find the treasure. He said, "Hidden in the same manner we hid everything else." It seems they would have known where to look in Udaipur.'

'Except that they were dead,' said Jami.

'So the treasure must still be hidden there,' said Mirza.

'What treasure?' croaked dada-jaan. 'Fifty pieces only? Does the letter not say that only fifty pieces remain? What good will that do?'

There was silence in the room.

Then Jami asked, 'So what do we do now?'

I continued eating while thinking about the situation.

'There must be something in Udaipur. I don't mind taking my chances for fifty pieces of gold,' I said finally. 'But before that we need to study everything we have so far, in more detail. Then we go to Udaipur.'

Dada-jaan spoke again. 'If only . . . I have wasted decades on this. Looking for signs to a fabulous treasure that would change everything. Thirty thousand mohurs. But this! Fifty pieces! What good will that do?' he asked querulously. 'I have now reached the end of my life. What a waste of time!' I thought he would start sobbing. Mirza came to his side and placed a hand on his shoulder to comfort him.

'There is mention of another letter as well,' I said, trying to be helpful. 'The fifty pieces lie hidden with the letter. Perhaps that letter says something?'

'Letters!' said dada-jaan. 'I have had it with letters! What this village needs is gold. Lots of it. What is a letter to that?'

Why does the village need lots of gold? I looked at

Mirza, who had an arm around dada-jaan now. Mirza shook his head and indicated we should leave.

Fine! Keep your secrets to yourselves. Was this sheer greed or had dada-jaan been so consumed with the idea of the treasure for so long that fifty pieces of gold meant nothing to him? Never mind. None of my business. I could definitely put fifty pieces to good use. Worth several lakh, at least!

Jami and I went out of the room quietly. As I left, I heard a sob.

8

The Plot Thickens

'There is something very strange about all this,' I said, putting my glass down. We were, as usual, drinking.

Jami seemed to be lost in thought. My words brought him out of his reverie. He put down his glass as well. 'I think so too,' he said. Then, after a while, he said, 'You go first.'

'This fakir business we heard of today,' I said.

'What of it?'

'Why?' I asked.

'Why what?'

'Today we learnt that the story was concocted by dada-jaan's grandfather and the fakir, and that Ba'azuddin never appeared in the village eleven years after the executions. The fakir brought him dead.'

'So?' asked Jami.

'Why go through all the trouble of bringing Ba'azuddin into the story, then? Why not stick to the truth that it was a fakir who brought him dead? Why spin a story like that? What is there to gain from hiding things like this?'

Jami gave a shrug. 'I don't know, man. You know I never believed the story. Then you found the stuff on the ceiling. Now, after hearing dada-jaan's version of the truth, I don't know what to believe any more.'

'The letters are real enough,' I said.

'Are they?' asked Jami.

'What makes you think otherwise?'

'Who wrote them?' asked Jami, looking at me.

'Ba'azuddin Bungalee, of course,' I said.

'And you know that because . . .?' asked Jami.

I did not say anything. I looked at him thoughtfully for a minute and then shook my head. 'I don't know. It did not mention any names. Addressed to Brothers. By another.'

'Correct. Now think of motives,' said Jami.

'What motives?' I asked.

'Everyone's motives. Let us go over what happened in story number one. The one you heard first – the same story supposedly being told for generations.'

'Supposedly?'

'Bear with me, please. It goes like this. Three boys in the village. Enlisted in the Company's army, but working in mysterious ways. One day in the dead of the night they show up here with a friend, this Ba'azuddin fellow. Then, they leave, but in different directions. Three to Agra, one to Delhi. Apparently, they have got wind of some treasure. Thirty thousand pieces of gold. Right?' said Jami.

'Yes.'

'How do we know that?' asked Jami.

'Er . . . because it's in the story,' I said.

'Yes, but how is it in the story? Who besides these four knew of the treasure? Do you remember?'

I thought for a while and then said, 'The great-grandfather!'

'Yes. Dada-jaan's great-grandfather. Rahat Ahmed Ali Khan. They told him. And he told a few others. That is the assumption, right?' asked Jami.

'I suppose so.'

'Now, these three return one day. The fourth guy does not. Then the English show up. Question everyone, kill everyone. According to the story, they are looking for the treasure. So far, both the story and the "truth", as dada jaan calls it, are the same,' said Jami.

'Hmm . . . so you too think dada-jaan is not telling us everything?' I asked.

'Hang on, man. I will get there. Let us now see where the differences arise. In story one, the fourth guy shows up eleven years later. According to the legend it's Ba'az. Rebuilds the mosque. Introduces dada-jaan's grandfather to the ghostly horsemen, buzzes off. At least that is what dada-jaan's grandfather said in the story.'

'Yes, that is correct,' I said with a chuckle. 'Buzzes off.'

'But in reality, according to dada-jaan, as told to him by his dying grandfather, this is not what happened. Letters appeared in Haider Kalan, written in code. Apparently from Ba'azuddin to the three. A fakir shows up with Ba'azuddin's body and buries him here, with dada-jaan's grandfather's help. Then they try to break the code in the letters, but are unable to do so. They leave a part of it on the ceiling of the mosque that the fakir – not Ba'azuddin – is rebuilding. Remember, Ba'azuddin is already dead and buried,' said Jami.

'Yes,' I said.

Jami continued. 'The fakir and dada-jaan's grandfather spin a story – the first version – in the hope that someone smart enough will look up at the ceiling of the mosque and figure out what is written there. The idea was that they would then bring this smart person to read the letters and find out where the treasure is hidden.'

'I suppose so.'

'Except that the smart person does not show up in time. Dada-jaan's grandfather is dying of old age, and the fakir, too, has fucked off. So he passes on the responsibility of finding the smart guy to his grandson, dada-jaan. And then one day, you show up. You get everything right. Decipher the letters. Everything should be cool now, correct?' asked Jami.

'Yes,' I said, 'except that everything is still not cool.

We don't really know what to do with what has been said in the letters. Everything is still not clear.'

Jami nodded. 'That is problem number one. Problem number two is bigger.'

'That we are not sure if the letters are from Ba'azuddin,' I said, following Jami's train of thought.

'And problem number three, or perhaps it should be promoted to number one, is that dada-jaan and his grandfather, in fact, the whole lot, right up to his great-grandfather, seem to know a few things they are not telling us,' said Jami.

'Like what?' I asked.

'First, how do they know there is a treasure hidden somewhere? Next, how did they know that the letters were from Ba'azuddin? Third, how did they know, or assume, or imagine, that the letters were about the location of the treasure? You see, they couldn't read the letters. There are too many loose ends here, man. Too many unexplained things,' said Jami, pouring himself another drink.

I handed him my empty glass and Jami poured one for me too. I said, 'I was also thinking of the fakir.'

'Yes. More questions there as well. More questions than answers. Who was he really? And where did he go? Why did he have an argument with dada-jaan's grandfather?' asked Jami.

I said, thinking aloud, 'A stranger comes from

nowhere, says he can't decipher the letters, creates a story to tell people, leaves a part of the letter on the ceiling. And a very critical part, at that.'

Jami sounded frustrated. 'It is like listening to a half-finished conversation that happened centuries ago and trying to understand it,' he said. 'Do we have *anything* here so far that should make us think any of this is true? That there is a treasure hidden somewhere?'

'We have the letters,' I said.

'Unsigned letters that talk of fifty pieces of gold, Udaipur and a rhyming riddle about something locked up in Jagat's head. I don't know, man. I think Jagat is the name of some guy and whatever we want to know is locked up in his head. He is dead. Everyone in the story is dead. And we have nothing to work with,' said Jami gloomily.

I was quiet. The euphoria of decoding the text in the mosque and the letters had evaporated. I morosely looked at the rum in my glass.

Jami said, 'You know what I think? I think dada-jaan is hiding something from us. Or maybe he is plain delusional. Either way, I don't like any of this. We should just forget about this. Put it all behind us and go back to being penniless students. All this talk of treasure is messing with my mind. It is making me think negatively of dada-jaan. He is my father's father, after all. I should be respecting dada-jaan, not doubting him.'

He stretched out on his bed and lay still, looking at

the ceiling. 'Until yesterday, I was convinced there was no treasure. Today, my mind is occupied by a treasure, multiple stories which don't tie up, a mysterious fakir and a whole lot of unanswered questions.'

I lay down too, lost in thought.

My mind was flooded with questions. Why did dada-jaan get so disheartened at the treasure being only fifty pieces of gold? Fifty pieces of antique gold coins would still be worth a huge amount. Who was the fakir? Could the fakir have discovered the location of the gold? Would the treasure still be there in Udaipur? Locked in the head of Jagat? What or who was Jagat? Was it a reference to the world? What did the riddle mean? And the letter mentioned the turbaned sahib of Calcutta. Why was he given all the gold, except for the fifty pieces?

Only questions, no answers.

Tomorrow we would head back to Delhi. Back to the grind. Away from this quiet Haider Kalan with its tale of treasure and mysteries locked in the minds of old men. Out of the rabbit hole and back into the dense wilderness of despair, monotony and mayhem.

As I waited for sleep, part of me wondered about truth and the telling of history. Dada-jaan had told us a story that was passed down to him by his grandfather. That story itself had distortions, and the lines between truth and fiction had been blurred to turn it into what it was. The reality of the fakir was an added layer that we learnt of later . . . I wondered how fiction sometimes adds to reality and makes for a greater story. How truth sometimes fades from memory, and the story itself becomes history. It made me think of the history that has been told to us. How much of it is true, and real, and how much of it fiction? How much of it changes over time, and with the telling? When does reality turn into fiction, and then to myth? I had no answers, and perhaps never would.

Just before falling asleep, I thought I heard the jingle of a metal chain outside our door. I opened it, but there was nothing there. Must be my overworked imagination, I thought. I went back to bed and was soon asleep.

9

A Tale of Two Meals

We were back in Delhi. It was a hot Sunday morning. Breakfast consisted of endless cups of tea. I thought of the treasure, the riddles on the ceiling, the cryptic letters and all the unanswered questions, while Jami whined about Nira.

After an hour or so of listening to him, I said, 'Fine!'

I went and made a few calls. It would not be a bad idea to secure a free meal or two and shut Jami up at the same time. I returned to him and said, 'Let's go.'

'Where?' he asked.

'We are having lunch at Nira's place. And then dinner at mashi's.'

'*You* are having lunch at Nira's place, you mean,' said Jami. He added something about a treacherous, back-stabbing swine.

'No, I told her you are coming as well.'

Jami scurried off to hunt for a clean set of clothes. Best of luck with your courting and rebuilding bridges, I thought to myself. I had no impressions to make. My jeans, unwashed since I don't remember when, would do. It was just that my underpants had begun to itch. I discarded them and decided to go commando for a few days.

~

When we got to Nira's house in Chanakyapuri, she was all by herself. Except for a retinue of servants, cooks and whatnot, of course. Her parents had gone to a ribbon cutting, or something of that sort.

How could a girl like her be born to such parents, I often wondered. Her father was the principal secretary at the Ministry of Culture and her mother the principal of a women's college. The most uptight people I had ever come across. Other than baba, of course.

Lunch was still an hour away. Jami was making small talk with Nira. Soon enough they were standing over a scaled model of what she had designed the past semester. Jami began to share his opinions. His critique.

Bad idea, I thought. Very bad idea. With any other girl you can show off your intelligence and charm yourself back into her pants. But not with Nira. I decided to make myself scarce. I decided to come back when the slaughter was over to pick up Jami's pieces off the floor.

I made myself busy in the dreamland that was Nira's library. I picked up a leather-bound volume of Conan Doyle's historical novels. Then I noticed another book. *Lonely Planet Rajasthan*. Thoughts of Udaipur came back to me and I forgot all about Brigadier Gerard and Sir Nigel. There might be something in the book which could be of use. Something that would help with the riddle. The book had to be borrowed. Without thinking, I headed back to Nira to ask her.

Jami was on the floor. Nira was straddling him, wrestling. They were . . . giggling! How on earth did Jami manage that? Romeo had some tricks up his sleeve that I needed to learn some day. I was about to clear my throat and interrupt them, when the bell rang downstairs. Still laughing, they let go of each other and got up. Nira headed downstairs, saying, 'That would be lunch. Come down, boys.'

Jami gave me a look. One of a small-time thief who had pulled off a great heist.

As we walked down the stairs, he whispered to me in a conspiratorial voice, 'You are definitely a champ, man. Those words of yours really worked.'

'They did?' I asked.

'Yes,' said Jami. 'When I told her that her eyes are like skylights, she just pounced on me giggling.'

What! I thought to myself. 'You told her that her eyes are like skylights?' I asked him incredulously.

Jami nodded proudly.

'Starlight . . . skies . . . stars,' I muttered to myself, shaking my head. 'Stars!'

I kept shaking my head from side to side as we went down the stairs. I needed to learn a lot about people, I realized. There was nothing I understood about anything, really. Skylights? And Nira found that even remotely *romantic*? Skylights!

Bloody architects.

~

Nira's parents were back in time for lunch and were waiting for us at the table. I made polite conversation with them about architecture school, the state of education and the nation at large. They attempted to talk to Jami. He, however, looked fixedly at his plate.

Nudging him slightly, I introduced Jami Ahmed Ali Khan from Haider Kalan to Nobonita and Debashish Basu of Chanakyapuri.

Somehow, after a while the discussion turned to Haider Kalan.

'So, what do your people do?' Nira's mum asked Jami, ever so casually.

'Uh . . . we are into farming,' Jami replied hesitantly. 'Sugarcane,' he added.

'Very interesting. Very interesting,' her father responded. 'That is very lucrative, is it not? There is a great future in sugar.'

Jami mumbled something about getting by.

As we were finishing dinner, Nira's mother rang a little bell and the plates magically disappeared. Dessert was next.

'How many acres did you say your family held?' she asked Jami. She had a shark-like look on her face. Nira seemed to be fuming, knowing well where the conversation was headed.

'Three,' said Jami, almost in a whisper.

'Marvellous! Marvellous!' exclaimed Nira's father. 'Three hundred acres! That is just splendid.'

Jami looked embarrassed. 'Not three hundred. Three,' he said awkwardly. He was looking down with great attentiveness at the small dessert spoon in front of him.

The parents exchanged glances. Nira's mother turned frosty, while her father donned calculated nonchalance. At one point, while passing the dessert, Nira's mother said to Jami, 'It is very much like the kheer your people make.'

Jami's grip on the spoon tightened. He shovelled a spoonful into his mouth and said, 'Yes, it is like the kheer we make.' Then he added, 'The sugar grown in smallholdings is sometimes sweeter, though.'

Nira slammed her spoon into the dessert bowl loudly.

'Meghnira Basu, you will please behave,' said Nira's mother sternly.

'As must we all,' replied Nira, eyes blazing.

Jami continued eating quietly.

The rest of the dessert was eaten in awkward silence.

Afterwards, Nira walked us to the bus stop. To fill the awkward silence, I blabbered about our plans for dinner. As we waited for the bus to the hostel, Nira asked, 'I would like to come for dinner, too. It has been a while since I got out of the house in the evenings.' Then, after a pause, 'That is all right, I hope?'

I said, 'Of course. E-29, C.R. Park, ground floor. We plan to be there at eight.'

Jami did not say anything.

~

We landed up at mashi's place at eight, as decided. She greeted me with her usual whining about mother calling her to enquire about me. She asked me when I would go back home. I said something about training and having to work in Professor Growler's studio during the summer. Jami gave me a sharp look. I realized that sometime soon I would have to explain matters to him, which is when Nira arrived. Jami and I were surprised. I had completely forgotten about her. I never thought she would show up so I hadn't even told mashi about an extra person for dinner.

Mashi, however, took matters in her stride. She went to the kitchen immediately and put on some more rice to boil. As she moved in and out of the kitchen, Nira joined us at the dining table, fidgeting and taking in her surroundings. Obviously, there were none of the luxuries around that she took for granted.

The food appeared. Glorious stuff. Course after course, force-fed lovingly by mashi. After a few valiant attempts at pride, Nira too succumbed. Soon enough, I saw that she was chattering away with mashi about the smell and texture of spices. Something about fish-jhaals and fish-jhols.

Jami and I were busy gorging on rice and fish, while Nira and mashi talked.

~

Sated, we sprawled on the sofas in the living room, and Nira went into the kitchen to help mashi. She was being such a sweet, obedient girl. Something was definitely afoot. I just did not know what. A little later, Nira came to the living room and looked down at us slumped in our food coma. Sensing a presence, Jami opened his eyes lazily and then looked away.

Nira raised a hand, gave a feeble wave and said, 'Right, guys. I need to be off. See you around.'

'But it's only nine,' I said. 'Stick around for a while.'

'Mum and dad will be pissed. I need to get home.'

'How are you going back?' I asked. Jami seemed to be gazing at his nails with intense concentration, cleaning them with our room key.

'The car is parked right around the corner,' said Nira. 'Mahinder is waiting.'

Of course. She drove. Or rather, her driver did.

'We will walk you there,' I said. Jami seemed not to hear and alternated between biting his nails and staring at them.

'Come along, man,' I said to Jami, as Nira and I made our way to the front door. Jami reluctantly got up and followed us into the street.

As we walked, I asked Nira, 'So what was that about fish-jhaals and fish-jhols?'

'What?' she asked.

'I have always wondered. Some Bengalis call the dish fish-jhaal. Some call it jhol. What is the difference?'

'Spices,' said Nira as we reached the car. Her driver saw us coming and stepped out of the car. He handed the keys to Nira and walked around to get into the passenger seat.

Nira continued, 'It is an East and West Bengal difference. You know, Ghotis and Bangaals.'

Jami had joined us by then. 'What is that?' he asked.

'A rivalry as old as time,' I explained. 'The Ghotis are from West Bengal. The Bangaals from East Bengal, what is now Bangladesh. I am from Bangaal. My family migrated here long ago.' Turning around, I said, 'So, Nira, you guys are Ghoti, right?'

Nira raised a fist in the air and said, 'Mohun Bagan!'

Jami gave a loud laugh. Louder than normal. He asked Nira sweetly, 'Do they make the same kind of kheer as well?'

Nira froze, her fist still in the air, and asked, 'What was *that* supposed to mean?'

'Oh, nothing. Nothing at all,' said Jami, raising his hands in mock apology. 'I just thought that being different and all, whether you Ghotis and Bangaals have the same taste in sugar. Like the sugar made from smallholdings.'

Nira quietly opened the door and got into the car. She said softly, 'Jami, this is so unfair.' I could not see her clearly in the dark, but I thought I could see her eyes smouldering. She slammed the door shut, started the engine and drove off, the tyres screeching and the poor driver praying fervently.

'What the fuck was that, man? What was that for?' I asked.

Jami shrugged and slapped me on the back. Wrapping an arm around my shoulders, he leaned on me for support as we walked back to the house.

~

When we returned, mashi was at the dining table. She was sitting in front of a pile of paan leaves, putting them neatly into a box. She heard us come in and said, 'There is some cake that I made yesterday. Why don't you take some of it to your hostel?'

Jami took a step forward, dropped down on one knee in front of mashi and said, 'If it is cake, madam, why some? We will take all of it.'

Mashi blushed red and gave a girlish giggle. 'Rascal!' she said. She shut the box and gave it to me to take to dida, my mother's mother.

'It is time for dida's paan. Take this box to her. She has not seen you for a while. And take Romeo away from my sight.'

I picked up the box. It was a little large for a paan box. And very heavy. It was made of dark wood with some kind of white metal on it. It looked very ornate. Both wood and metal had the stains of many years of use on them. It seemed out of place in a middle-class household.

'Careful with that box,' warned mashi. 'It used to belong to dida's mother. The only thing of value they brought back from Sylhet. She has been having paan from it all her life. If anything happens to it, I will not hear the end of it.'

I carried the box carefully. Jami followed.

~

Dida was sitting on her bed, fanning herself in the dimly lit room. Hearing us come in, she squinted her cataract-ridden eyes at us and asked feebly, 'Who?'

'I have brought you your paan,' I said.

'Oh, Shumon. It is you. Who is this with you?' she asked.

'My friend.' I put down the box in front of dida.

She ran her fingers over the lid, and with practised ease, opened it and began her paan ritual. While she pulled out the cutting tools from the drawers in the box and laid out the paan leaves with unseeing eyes, she asked me, 'You have been gone a while, Shumon. Where were you?'

I shuffled and hinted at Jami not to say anything, 'My friend and I had gone to his village. We had some work there.'

'You drink a lot of water, do you not?'

'Yes,' I said. I saw Jami's raised eyebrow.

Dida continued fanning herself. She began humming a song under her breath. A lullaby one might sing to a child. After a while, she seemed to notice us, as if for the first time, and asked, 'Who?'

'I have brought your paan,' I said again, my voice a little hoarse.

'Who, Shumon? You have been gone a long time. No, no. I just had paan. Can't you see, I am still having it.' Then she asked, 'You are both having a lot of water, are you not? It is good for Sumita. She is with child, you see.'

'Yes,' I said. 'We will go now.' I picked up the box. Dida had closed it after putting everything back where it had been with her seeing fingers. I gestured to Jami and we left the room quietly, closing the door behind us.

We returned to the dining room. Mashi was still sitting there, this time with a stack of papers in front of her. She must be correcting exam papers. I deposited the family heirloom on the table.

Mashi looked up at us over the rim of her reading glasses. 'How did you find dida this time?' she asked me.

'Same as before. This time, too, she thought I was baba,' I said. Mashi took off her spectacles and sighed.

I tried to think of sunnier subjects of conversation.

Suddenly, I remembered. 'Do you have a copy of the *Manorama Yearbook*?' I asked.

'We have the latest one, yes,' she said.

'Can I have it? I need it only for a few days.'

'Take it. But please bring it back,' she said with a look of reproach. 'I am still waiting for Toyne's book on English history.'

'Yes, yes,' I said quickly.

I found the book. I had completely forgotten to take the book on Rajasthan from Nira. This might have something of use, instead.

10

The Investor

Back in our room in the hostel, I sat cross-legged on the floor. I had surrounded myself with sheets of paper. They had my scribbles and notes. Half-opened books lay strewn around. In front of me was my notebook. Jami sat on a chair behind me, curiously studying what I was doing.

We had hurried back from mashi's place. First, I riffled through the copy of the *Manorama Yearbook*. The entry about Rajasthan, and particularly Udaipur, got me excited. I promptly pulled out a few books on Rajasthan from the collection in my cupboard. Quickly, I went over as many facts as I could. From time to time, I muttered to myself. Occasionally, I tried spelling out things for Jami's benefit, even though I did not have coherent explanations.

I stood up. I paced up and down our tiny room, collecting my fragmented thoughts. Finally, I said, 'It makes sense now. I know where in Udaipur we should look to find our treasure,' I announced. 'It is very obvious, really. Obvious to anyone who is not an arrogant, hasty idiot. I have been that, I am afraid.'

'Tell me!' said Jami.

'It started as a wrong translation. The original verses, on the ceiling, as well as the letter, go like this,' I said.

Rangi lal mitti Udaipur mein
Gode shakti mata ki
Jal ke kinaare
Jagat ke paas hai chaabi
Sire pe, taala bandh
Hai khazaana dhan

'I translated it into English the way I thought best. That is how I have been thinking about it all along.' I repeated my earlier translation.

In the red earth of Udaipur,
In the lap of mother's strength,
By the water,
With Jagat is the key.
Locked in the head is great treasure.

Jami had no idea what I was talking about.

'I translated "shakti mata" as "mother's strength". That is a literal translation,' I said. 'It should actually be Mother Shakti or Goddess Shakti. And then it begins to fall into place. There is a temple in Jagat, a short distance from Udaipur, dedicated to the Mother Goddess Shakti. It has been around since the tenth century. It is a likely place for Ba'azuddin, or whoever sent the letter, to hide the gold.'

'But what about the words "by the water"?' asked Jami.

'We will find out soon enough, my friend. Udaipur has many lakes. Let us work on this a little more. I think we are one step closer to the treasure, Jami. Treasure! Loot from the times of the last Mughal. Gold! Lots of gold! Fifty mohurs, if not more . . .'

'I don't know, man. It does not mean anything just because a name matches,' said Jami.

Bloody non-believer.

I looked over my notes and maps again, wondering how to change his opinion. I could not possibly go to Udaipur on my own. Besides, I had no money.

There was a soft knock on the door.

Alarmed, we looked at each other. No one was supposed to be around in the hostel, other than us. Not during the vacations, at this time of the night. We looked at the clock. It was one in the morning.

There was another knock. Slightly louder this time.

I pushed all the papers and books under the bed. Jami went to the door and opened it gingerly.

It was Nira. Seeing Jami, she flushed a little and asked, 'Can I come in?'

Finding Nira at the door, Jami stood speechless. He looked at me, turned to Nira, stood aside and nervously said, 'Sure.'

Nira walked into the cramped room. Dumping her tote bag on the drafting table with a thump, she announced, 'I brought you guys some rum.' Then, after a moment of silence, she softly said sorry to Jami without looking at him.'

'But,' Jami said with slight reserve, 'your parents . . . they . . .'

'I said I am sorry!' said Nira, flaring up. 'I am not responsible for them. They are not my fault!'

'No, no, not that,' stammered Jami, deflecting from what he was about to say. 'I meant, they would be quite mad. You in the boys' hostel and all. At this time of the night.'

'I don't care what they think. As if I have not done it before,' she said and parked herself on the chair that Jami had been sitting on. Seeing us looking at her, she asked, 'What?' She brushed aside a lock of hair from her forehead and said quietly, 'I had a bit of an argument with them.' She pulled out a bottle of white rum from her bag, placed it silently on the table and looked at Jami.

Jami stood there, confused. 'Don't just stand there, do something, idiot,' I said under my breath. I took out three cracked mugs from the cupboard and put them in

Jami's hands. Jami sniffed them and mumbled, 'I will go wash these.' Then he turned and asked Nira, 'You want some cola? I don't know whether we will get any at this time of the night. I can go and try.'

'Just get water from the cooler. This is good stuff from Dad's stock. Not the hooch you guys drink.'

Jami went to the bathroom to wash the mugs. I looked around the room, wishing the piles of dirty clothes would disappear. It was amazing how easily we changed the super-clean room to this mess. Nira stared at a poster of Clint Eastwood on the wall. She pointedly ignored the copy of *Debonair* magazine on the table.

Jami soon came back with the washed mugs and a bottle of cold water. Nira poured three large measures and added a little water.

Nira clinked her glass with Jami's and said, 'There is only one lord . . .'

'. . . and his name is Rum,' Jami finished her sentence, and they both gulped down their drinks.

I waved my mug in half toast but sipped my drink slowly. I felt happy that Nira was here. Now Jami would be in a better frame of mind.

Nira looked around, wrinkling her nose slightly. 'What is that smell?' she asked.

Jami looked at the bucket in the corner. He had soaked some clothes before we had left for Haider Kalan and had forgotten about them completely until now. He picked up the bucket and placed it outside the room. I figured I should also do something. I busied myself with collecting the clothes strewn all over. I gave a feeble excuse about books taking up all the place in my cupboard. I don't think she bought it. Nira took another look around the room before turning to face us.

'Now, tell me more about this treasure thing.'

Jami and I stopped what we were doing and looked at each other. How did Nira know?

'I was outside the door for a while, waiting to knock. You guys are loud. I heard some things.'

'What things?' Jami asked.

'Treasure. Udaipur. Some Bengali fellow. Gold,' said Nira with casual nonchalance. 'Is there something I can help with?'

Jami turned his head and looked at me. I nodded, ever so slightly. It might not be a bad idea to involve Nira in this. She was a good, resourceful person. And if I could convince her to look for the treasure, Jami was as good as in. In any case, Jami would tell her everything at some point.

Jami turned to Nira and said, 'Sit down. It is a long story.'

~

It took more than an hour for Jami to describe the events of the past week to Nira. She went through the books and the sheets of paper that I had pulled out from under the bed. She looked through the notebook with the sketches and the transcribed letters. 'Jagat sounds like a likely place. When do you plan to go?' she asked.

'Maybe later,' I replied. 'This is going to cost money. We are quite broke right now.'

'How much?' asked Nira, reaching for the purse inside her bag.

'Nira, it is going to be a lot. Getting there. Staying for a few days,' said Jami with considerable discomfort. 'At least three thousand bucks for the two of us. You can't be carrying that much.'

Nira gave a confused look. 'That is not a lot. Of course I am carrying more than that.'

That was what I spent in six months. And she carried it around like loose change.

Jami said, 'Even then, it is not as if we are going to achieve anything by visiting this place once. We might have to go a number of times.'

'You know we are going in blind. We have no idea what to expect,' I said.

Nira shrugged. 'Then take more whenever you guys want.'

How much money did she have?

'I have enough,' she said, as if hearing my thoughts.

'We couldn't possibly,' I said, embarrassed. 'What if we do not find anything? We can't repay you. Not till we pass out and get jobs. If we ever manage that.'

'You might not have to repay me,' said Nira, a canny

look in her eyes. Her mother had had a similar look – only more shark-like – when she was sizing up Jami in the afternoon.

'But how? Why?' I asked.

'Think of it as an investment,' Nira said.

'Investment? I asked. Jami and I exchanged a wary glance. Why did I feel I was selling my soul to the devil?

'I want a third,' said Nira.

'A third?' repeated Jami mechanically.

'You guys stupid or something? A third. Thirty-three point three three per cent of the treasure. Whatever it is. In exchange for financing the hunt for it.'

I thought for a second or two. Whatever she was, she was no shark. She could easily have demanded more. I was about to say yes when Jami said, 'But the treasure, fifty pieces or whatever, rightfully belongs to the village of Haider Kalan as well.'

Right. Screw over a deal going down sweetly. He did have a point, though. 'We couldn't have got this far without dada-jaan, his stories and the letters he gave us.'

Nira gave the matter a thought. 'Fine,' she said. 'We will have to give dada-jaan a share. Half?' she asked. 'Half for Haider Kalan, and the rest of it split three ways between us?'

Jami and I nodded. It sounded reasonable. There was a minor glitch, of course. That the villagers would find this unacceptable. But I put the thought aside for the moment.

'Let us close the matter then,' said Nira. She spat delicately on her palm and extended her hand to us. 'Isn't this how they do it in the movies?' she asked.

Jami and I looked at each other and then spat on our hands and extended them out to Nira.

'Eek! You guys are filthy!' cried Nira, drawing her hand back quickly. I wiped my hand on my pants and reached for the bottle.

11

Udaipur

From Delhi we caught a rickety overnight bus to Udaipur. We found a cheap lodge in the middle of the old part of town. After dumping our belongings in the room, we took the first shared jeep we saw to the temple of Jagat, two hours from town.

But when we reached there, we were at a loss for what to do next. We first walked around the tiny temple precincts. Then we went in. Initially Jami was a little reluctant about taking off his shoes and entering a place of worship that was not a mosque. We looked at the magnificent carvings with disinterest. It was all very fine to have come to bloody Udaipur but there seemed to be nothing in the lap of the mother goddess. We went to the shrine in the inner sanctum of the temple. Seeing the crowds I found it unlikely that anything inside could have remained undiscovered for over a hundred years. We hung around till dusk, with Jami trying to make conversation with the stall owners outside the temple. I pulled out my notebook again and made a few sketches. It was time for the temple to close. A little earlier I had dipped into my notorious tobacco pouch and rolled a smoke. My sketching seemed to improve dramatically as a result. This time, however, there were no earth-shattering insights. Nothing like what I had at the mosque in Haider Kalan.

Tired, we returned to our lodge. Over the next two days, we walked about the old town. Then we tried our luck at the Jagdish temple. And then we sought every temple that was dedicated to the mother goddess, in whatever form. But no result. I continued to dip into my fantastic pouch and look at the world with dreamy eyes, as Jami led our investigation with industry. Finally, sitting by the lake, Jami cursed in frustration, while I sketched the skyline against the setting sun. Jami raised an eyebrow when I paused to roll a joint. He tried to shake me out of my dreamlike stupor, but I just smiled at the beautiful universe. How would Jami understand? These smokes were opening new doors in my mind that I never knew existed. I was increasingly beginning to see things with new eyes. Many eyes. My own eyes, Jami's eyes, the eyes of the untrained stranger. Yes, this new herbal manna did take away a few faculties. Those of urgency and anxiety and anger. The sketches I was making of late were nothing like I had ever made before. A few quick strokes of the pencil had transformed the little island in the middle of the lake into a wondrous piece of cubism. A cross between a sketch, a watercolour, a perspective view and an elevation drawing. As if someone had flown around on the shoulders of a bird and unwrapped the island on my page. Capturing the palace, the shadows of the sun, the play of the light and the reflection of the water, all in a matter of minutes. Yes, imagination did get elevated, making me see between things. But over-see things too. Over-imagine. Why, the other afternoon I had been thinking of Mirza's wild tales about the adventures of Nusrat. I looked up to check the scenery again and I could have sworn that the man walking up the street ahead of us was Mirza. It was only when the man turned his head slightly that I saw that he was clean-shaven. None of Mirza's luxurious beard. When Jami heard of this, he pursed his lips in disapproval. Yes, it might be a good idea to smoke a little less of this stuff from now on. One never knew what I might end up seeing next.

Soon it was dark and both of us began to feel hungry. I closed my notebook and we went to get something to eat.

~

The next morning, emerging from the dark recesses of our room, Jami suddenly stopped in the middle of the street.

'Hey, we are idiots,' he said.

'We are? How?' I asked.

'Remember the verses on the ceiling? I think we have missed the obvious.'

'How?' I asked, looking around the deserted street of a town that was still waking up. I needed some matches. I was craving a smoke.

'Bring out the notebook,' he commanded.

'You have read and reread it a thousand times already, have you not?' I said.

'Not the words. The sketch you made yesterday. Of the palace in the middle of the lake.'

I searched my pockets. 'I think I left it back there among our things.' This was odd. More than the notebook, I was irritated that I had left my tobacco pouch behind. 'I will run back and get it,' I suggested.

'Never mind that,' said Jami, walking faster, nearly dragging me by the elbow. 'This is what our verses said:

Rangi lal mitti Udaipur mein
Gode shakti mata ki
Jal ke kinaare
Jagat ke paas hai chaabi
Sire pe, taala bandh
Hai khazaana dhan

'Yes. Sort of,' I said. 'But what about it?'

'*Jal ke kinaare, Jagat ke paas hai chaabi*,' said Jami. 'By the water, with Jagat lies the key. We have been to the Jagat temple. Even the Jagdish temple. We have scoured many temples of the mother goddess. But what about the most obvious thing, staring us in the face?'

'What?'

'That sketch you made. The Jag Mandir. Built on the lake, named after Jagat Singh, the local king during the time of the Mughals. The Jag Mandir and the Jag Niwas Palace, which can only be accessed from here,' said Jami, pointing to the gates of the City Palace, in front of which we now stood.

We sat on the bench at a tea shop next to the ticket window, taking in all the facts, waiting for the palace to open for the day. We talked about the possibilities as we sipped tea. But we did not make it inside the Jag Mandir. Getting there by boat required buying frightfully expensive tickets. The Jag Mandir, and the boats to it, were a private enterprise. Managed for the royal family, no less. We could have lived with paying an arm and a leg for the boat ride, if the liveried doorman had not turned us back at the entrance.

'Thar is a cover charge to vaisit,' the turbaned doorman with large whiskers said, his accent a residue from the Scottish couple he had just let through. 'Thar be a menu here, for yae purview,' he drawled. He did not bat an eyelid at Jami's chaste cussing about mothers and sisters in general.

The Jag Niwas Palace had been converted to a swanky restaurant. One look at the cover charge and the prices on the restaurant menu sent us back with our tails between our legs, but not before paying another fortune for the boat ride back.

~

That evening we sat at a tea stall and counted the little money we had left. From Nira's wad of three thousand, barely four hundred remained. Jami and I had dug deeply into the recesses of our wallets as well, pulling out even the emergency stash. Stuff we used only under the direst of circumstances.

'Just enough to pay the lodge, eat something and catch a bus back to Delhi tonight,' Jami said.

'When we find our treasure, I am going to buy this damned island,' I said darkly, finishing my tea and glaring at the Jag Mandir.

'If the treasure is still there. If there was a treasure to begin with,' said Jami gloomily, stuffing our combined wealth back into his pocket.

'Don't be pessimistic,' I replied. 'Everything points towards there being a treasure. Rumours in the village. Dada-jaan's story. The verses on the ceiling. His second story. The letters. I am convinced that whatever this treasure is, it lies on that island around the Jag Mandir.'

'What makes you sure it has not been discovered yet?'

'Just a feeling. We need to trust our gut on this one. My heart tells me it is still there.'

'Fine. I will go with your optimism,' Jami said, putting down his unfinished glass of tea.

'We still have a problem. The verses,' I said.

'What about them?' asked Jami.

'The words are the problem. Everything does not seem to fit,' I said. 'Let us start from the beginning. The red earth of Udaipur. There lies the first problem. I do not see how that fits into where we are. Udaipur this is, yes, but there is no red earth around. Water and Jagat seem to fit with the Jag Mandir, but the lap of the mother goddess – Shakti Mata – does not make sense. The Jag Mandir is a palace, not a temple. So we have two fits – Udaipur and Jagat, and two misses – red earth and mother goddess. Even if there is a shrine to the mother goddess somewhere in the Jag Mandir, where is this red earth?'

I added, 'Could be something about general violence in the land. The Rajputs were not exactly known for being peace-loving people. Come on, cheer up. I think we are on the right track. What we need to do is go back to Delhi, review and come back better prepared. It might be a good idea to do some more research before we return. Maybe pick Professor Venugopal's brains, if possible.'

Jami said, 'And arrange money. We need more money. Getting inside the Jag Mandir is going to be a problem for the likes of us. Let us see if Nira can get us there for long enough to look around in peace.' After a while, he added, 'I hate being poor.'

I shrugged. 'Yes, we will find more money. One way or another.'

We got up and began the walk back towards the lodge.

'The good thing is we have time. The treasure has been here for over a hundred years, and we are the only ones who know about it. It is not going anywhere in a hurry,' I said with satisfaction. 'Once we have found it, I will buy this damned island.'

12

The Last Leaf

After checking out from the lodge, we had a hasty meal and then walked towards the bus terminus. On the main street a sign outside a shop made me stop: 'STD/ISD/PCO/Photocopy/Fax'.

'Might as well tell Nira we are headed back to Delhi,' I said to Jami. 'Don't be too long. Keep it within ten bucks.'

'You crazy or something? You call her.'

'I thought the two of you were an item again.'

'Yes. No. Whatever. You make the call, man. Her mother or her lady dragon maid pick up the phone at her place.'

We went into the dingy shop that served as a phone booth as well as a photocopying and train ticketing outlet. A musty smell due to lack of ventilation assailed us from the dimly lit interior of the shop. Jami plonked himself down on the chair across the photocopy machine while I spoke to the shop owner. Jami leafed through an old magazine, looking at painted movie stars, as I went into the makeshift phone booth.

I dialled the number and carefully watched the red numeric display. A woman's voice answered. It was either the cook or the housekeeper. I asked for Nira. The voice at the other end was suspicious about who I was. No wonder little Jami quailed at the prospect of dialling the number. Security protocols fulfilled, the voice at the other end started hollering for a certain baby darling. That would be Nira, I guessed. I waited as the red numeric display kept flashing digits. I was seven rupees into the call when Nira appeared.

Three rupees left of the princely budget allocated for the call, I decided to condense the briefing.

'Bad news, Nira,' I said. 'Nothing here. We are headed back.'

I heard an exasperated sigh. Then she said, 'Tell me more.'

'Would, but can't,' I said in a hurry. The meter was ticking eight-fifty already. 'I will tell you the whole story when we get back.'

'Fine,' said Nira in a terrifyingly cold voice. 'Put Jami on the line, please.'

'Err . . . Nira, we are really short on cash right now,' I said. Nine-fifty.

She was about to say something when I slammed down the phone. The display read exactly ten. I would face Nina's wrath later for disconnecting the call.

When I turned around, I found Jami towering over the shop owner seated at the counter who was waving a sheet of paper in his face.

On seeing me, Jami thrust the paper at me without a word. He had a questioning look on his face. He also pointed to a few more sheets of paper pinned behind the shop owner's chair. What I saw made me forget everything else. They were all enlarged photocopies of a sketch of the island on which the Jag Mandir stood. As if the artist had flown around the place and unwrapped the building in a wondrous piece of cubism that was a cross between a sketch, a watercolour, a perspective view and an elevation drawing. It was the same drawing that I had made the afternoon before.

'Where is your notebook?' Jami asked me in a steely voice.

I unslung the haversack from my shoulders and opened it. The notebook should be in the bag. It was the second thing I had looked for after returning to the lodge from the Jag Mandir jaunt. The first being the tobacco pouch, of course. I had stuffed everything into the haversack in our hurry to pack up and leave.

The notebook was indeed there, nestled between a sock and a pair of used underpants. I pulled it out and flipped the pages. Everything seemed to be in place. Including the page with the sketch.

Jami quietly went to the entrance of the shop, shut the door and turned the 'Open' sign to 'Closed'. He also switched off all the lights outside the shop. Then, with a cold smile, he pulled a plastic chair and sat in front of the shop owner, resting his elbows on the table.

'So, as I was saying, this is a very nice drawing. Where did you get it from?'

The shop owner was quite flustered. 'I just told you. A man came here this afternoon with a notebook full of sketches. Made a copy of the whole thing and left.'

'This notebook?' I asked.

The man's eyes lit up. 'Yes, yes. This one. What beautiful sketches. Some of Udaipur as well. I asked that man if I could keep a few copies. But he seemed to be in a hurry. After making the copies, he left as quickly as he had come. Did not even bother to collect his balance money.' He licked his lips nervously and extended his hand tentatively. 'Can I have a look at them again, please?' he asked.

Jami and I looked at each other. Jami gave a slight nod. I handed over the notebook to him.

The shop owner put on a pair of spectacles with thick lenses and lovingly opened the notebook, leafing through the pages carefully. 'These can be turned into such beautiful paintings, embroideries, prints. People will be willing to pay good money for them. I kept telling that man to let me take another copy, but he was so curt and brusque,' he said. 'Who made these?'

Jami did not answer. Instead, he pointed to the sheets of paper that had drawn his attention in the first place. 'How, then, did you make so many copies of this sketch?'

The shop owner took off his glasses and said, 'Oh, this new photocopy machine. It has memory. The last page that the man photocopied was stored in the memory of the machine. I made a few copies after he left.'

Jami was deep in thought. He looked at me and then towards the man again. 'Tell us more about this man who came to make the copies. What time was it? Afternoon, you said?'

'Yes, a little after one,' replied the shop owner.

I said to Jami, 'We were at the Jag Mandir then. The notebook was in the lodge.'

Jami's brow furrowed in worry. 'Describe the man, will you?' he said.

'Tall, big fellow. Clean-shaven. Almost looked baby-faced. Would be about forty.' Then he shifted slightly in his seat and said, 'Look, I don't want any trouble. Why are you asking me all this? Has anything been stolen?'

'No. Nothing seems to have been stolen. Technically,' said Jami. 'Thank you.' He got up and extended a hand towards the shop owner to take the notebook back.

He seemed reluctant to part with the notebook. Suddenly, Jami asked him, 'How much?'

'What?' asked the man.

'How much will you pay us for a copy of all the sketches here?' asked Jami.

'Fifty for the lot,' said the man quickly.

Before I could respond, Jami said, 'There are about fifty sketches here. We will let you copy any ten for six hundred rupees. That is about sixty rupees a sketch.'

After a few minutes of haggling, they settled on five hundred rupees for the ten. As he made copies, the shop owner grumbled about his starving children. Jami commended him on his ample girth and asked him when those children were due.

Our pockets a little heavier than before, we stood outside the shop in silence, trying to understand what had happened.

After a while Jami said, 'You were right. I was wrong.'

'About what?' I asked.

'It was indeed Mirza you had seen the other day on the street. You were not hallucinating. It could be no one else. And it was he who went to the lodge, took your notebook and put it back before we returned. This is the only explanation that makes sense.'

'But why would he do that?

'I don't know. But Mirza would not have acted without dada-jaan telling him to do so. I think it is time to pay them a visit again.'

~

Before we left, I made another call. Again to Nira.

'I thought you guys were short of money,' she said after I got past her chaperones.

'Some things happened,' I said. I proceeded to tell her what had happened over the past few minutes. 'Makes sense for us to pay another visit to Haider Kalan,' I said.

Nira agreed. I figured it was time to help make peace. And give Jami a treat. I said, 'Here, talk to Jami for a bit. I need to step out for a minute.'

There was silence for a second, and then she giggled.

'Stay within fifteen bucks,' I told Jami. 'I have already spent fifteen and we need money to go to Haider Kalan.'

Jami spent fifty rupees, saying goodness knows what.

It was very late at night when we caught the last bus to Ambala.

~

This time we arrived at Haider Kalan in a jeep, a rickety Second World War model. It ran an irregular service connecting the railway station to the surrounding villages. By the time we reached Jami's house, it was almost noon.

Jami went in first. I followed. We heard sounds of wailing from the house. Jami looked at me, worried.

'Wait here,' he said. He kept his bag down and went inside. I waited.

He was gone for a while. When he returned, he wore a grim face.

'Dada-jaan. He died last night. In his sleep. His heart gave way.'

13

The Grave

I let Jami's words sink in. Then I asked, 'Mirza?'

Jami pursed his lips. 'He reached a few hours before us. They said he had gone somewhere. He left the day after we did.'

He handed me his bag. 'Take this upstairs. I must go.' Then he added, 'Mirza's beard is gone.'

~

I sat in Jami's room in the sweltering afternoon heat. I had discarded my shirt long ago. The rivulets of sweat on my body welcomed the slightest trace of breeze that blew. When it did. When it did not, I sat drenched.

The funeral had been a quiet affair. Other than Mirza weeping loudly. A discreet funeral, but elaborate. People had come from miles away to pay their respects to the patriarch of Haider Kalan. Dada-jaan had been washed and dressed. Then he had been taken to the mosque, where the muezzin prayed for his soul, following which he was taken to the graveyard and laid in the grave. Everyone dropped three fistfuls of earth into the grave. Mirza was still sobbing loudly. It was only when the last piece of earth had been deposited that he stopped and sat on his haunches in stony silence, praying.

Jami and a few others left shortly afterwards. A prayer ceremony was to take place a few miles away in the mosque of Shahbad, the nearest mosque still in use. Mirza remained by dada-jaan's grave. I stayed by his side for a while. Then I, too, returned to the house, leaving Mirza alone, sitting still beside the freshly filled grave.

I went up to our room and sat there, thinking of the conversations I could have had with dada-jaan. I did not know the old man well enough, but I still felt some sadness.

There was a soft knock on the door. I rose to open it. It was Mirza. Standing like a deflated giant.

'Come with me,' he said hoarsely.

~

I walked with Mirza in silence. We were at the graveyard again. Mirza stopped at dada-jaan's grave. I stood with him, wondering what he was up to. After a few moments of silence, Mirza said, 'Bungalee Babu, I will miss him.' I stood there awkwardly, not knowing what to say, wondering if I was expected to say anything at all. Something welled up inside me and formed a lump in my throat. Something I thought I had buried weeks ago.

'That evening when we last met. Abba was heartbroken. What would only fifty mohurs do for us, he had asked,' said Mirza.

I was about to ask why fifty mohurs meant nothing to him, when Mirza continued, as if to explain, 'I did not know until that day that this village owes a huge amount of money to the sugar mill. They built the canal for us forty years ago. Abba agreed to their terms then. We were to get fresh water for the sugarcane crop. With that, over time, we would pay back the cost of building the canal.' Mirza shook his head. 'The payback never happened. Each year we could barely pay the interest with whatever we could grow. The debt mounted. It troubled Abba. The villagers do not know but the mill owns everything we have now. He was counting on finding the treasure.

'I had harsh words for him. Those were the last words I said to him. The next day I went to Udaipur, desperate to find something, thinking that even if it was a few mohurs it would do something towards paying our debt. I wandered for a few days until I saw the two of you there. I knew that you were on to something.' He rubbed his now smooth chin.

I did not ask him why he had taken the notebook from our room and copied it. It did not seem important any more. I also did not want to hear about harsh last words. Anything to take my mind off them would be welcome. I turned my attention to the rest of what Mirza had to say.

'And now, here we stand,' he said. 'Abba's responsibilities are mine. There is crop to be harvested. Money to be paid to the mill.' Mirza went silent for a while, staring at his father's grave. Then, he said, 'I will do what I can, but there is something you and Jami-baba need to do. If there is anyone who can find the treasure – if there is a treasure – it is you. You must give me your word.' He looked into my eyes. It was a look of deep despair. I understood what he wanted. I also remembered the conversation Nira, Jami and I had had the other day.

I cut to the chase. 'Half,' I said.

He seemed to think for a while, as if calculating something. Then he nodded and said, 'Half.'

He put a hand inside his shirt and pulled out a package wrapped in newspaper. 'Here is something that might help you,' he said. Before handing it to me, he said, 'Remember what Abba told us the other day? What his grandfather told him before dying? About the brawl with the fakir, and the hut that burnt down?'

I nodded, looking at the wrapped packet.

'Everything did not burn,' said Mirza, and put the packet in my hand. 'See if you can put any of this to use.'

He began to turn away, his business apparently finished, but stopped midway and said, 'About the debt that the village owes to the mill. No need to tell Jami-baba anything about it. Okay? He needs to keep his mind on other, bigger things.'

I nodded. Jami would continue his dream of being a hotshot architect in New York. Mirza walked back towards the village, taking long strides.

As I saw his disappearing form, I sat down and unwrapped the packet. Inside was a burnt notebook. A diary. Bound in leather. It seemed very old. Only a few pages remained. From the binding it seemed to have been a thick volume. I turned the pages very carefully. The writing was very familiar. Written in code. Bengali characters, broken up and mirrored. I felt my breathing become heavier. My heart thudded with anticipation.

Not everything in the diary was written in code. There were some journal entries. Each of them had a date that was in English. 1868. About eleven years after the rebellion. The first page had a scrawl on it. A snaky, beautiful hand. Letters formed in black ink, possibly written with a quill. In plain English, not in code.

The Diarie of Bayaz-ud-din Waris Ali Khan
9th Bengal Lancers

I slammed the diary shut, unable to contain myself.

I sat still. Then I wrapped the notebook in the newspaper. I got up. The sun would set soon. I needed to clear my head.

I began to walk. Not towards the village, but away from it. I wandered in the graveyard, my mind racing. I was thinking of the numerous possibilities. I thought of what I knew of the treasure so far. I wondered what the diary would reveal. There was a lot of work that needed to be done. Many pages that needed deciphering. I hoped they would give answers, and not raise more questions.

As I kept walking, I realized I had reached the far end of the graveyard. There, away from all the other graves, stood a solitary grave. Dressed in stone. A platform. I noticed the elaborate stonework. A large headstone atop. I remembered what dada-jaan had said a few days ago. About the fakir bringing in Ba'azuddin Bungalee, dead. Burying him here. This must be his grave, then. The notebook I carried was written by the man buried here, in front of me.

The light of the setting sun fell directly on the headstone. I looked at the grave closely. The stone had a very interesting texture. Smooth. Without blemish. I went around the grave and stood behind the headstone to examine it closer.

This was strange, I thought. Such a thick slab of stone. But the grains on the front did not match those at the back. I noticed the rough-hewn surface of the back of the headstone. No, this stone was definitely different from the stone in the front. The headstone was like a sandwich. I squatted and ran my fingers over the surface. I could feel a neat rectangular crack. My heartbeat quickened. I prised open the joint. It was loose. I tapped the flat outline of the crack. A flagstone had been built on the face of the headstone. I gave another tap and the rectangle inset into the stone slab toppled towards me. I caught it before it hit the ground. I held my breath. A cavity appeared where the stone had been. A hollow, about a foot square, eight inches deep.

It was dry. Untouched by damp or dirt. I put my hand inside the cavity and groped blindly. There was nothing. I somehow felt there had been something there.

I put the slab back in the headstone and stood up. Darkness seemed to be falling faster than usual. As I crossed the edge of the graveyard, I turned around to look at the stone-clad grave of Ba'azuddin Bungalee. Did the fakir find the diary among Ba'azuddin's effects? Was this the book he was scribbling in, trying to decipher the letters? Did he hide them in the false headstone? Was this why he had an argument with dada-jaan's grandfather? I had no answers yet.

I was about to turn away, when I thought I saw something. I looked again in the distance. There was nothing there.

I quickened my pace as I walked back towards the

house. I was tingling all over. I shook my head. No. It could not be.

But I knew in my heart what I had seen for a brief instant.

Shadowy forms behind the grave. Shadowy forms on horseback, as if looking straight at me. Four of them.

14

Coconut

Back in the house, Mirza was nowhere to be seen. I went up to our room and unwrapped the package again. My hands were shaking. I willed my hands to be still.

'Calm down, idiot,' I said aloud to myself.

I pulled out my own notebook from my bag. I opened the diary. The evening was young and there was a lot of decoding to be done.

~

Two hours had passed. I was looking at the words in front of me. I had finished transcribing the letters in the first journal entry.

Nothing made sense.

It was a string of incomprehensible gibberish. The letters that dada-jaan showed me had joined to form whole words. Here, nothing made sense, neither in Hindi nor in Hindustani. It did not make sense in Bengali either. Maybe it was in a language I did not know. For all practical purposes, I seemed to have hit a blank wall.

Night had fallen. My stomach growled. I realized it had been a while since I had eaten anything. Where could Jami be? It had been ages since he had left. I wanted to tell him about the last few hours. Mirza. The diary. Everything.

I lay down and drifted off to sleep. The scrawl of letters in the diary swam about in my head. I was half asleep, on the border between wakefulness and dream, when I heard Jami call out to me. There was mention of food. I mumbled something to him in my dream-addled state.

'What?' he asked, leaning in closer.

I drowsily said in a slur, 'The food of love, my friend, doth nothing to the truth. It behoves music as 'tis fair broth.'

'Wake up, you coconut,' I heard Jami say in my sleep.

'A nut by any other name, roses . . . roses,' I mumbled on.

'Bloody angrez!' he hissed. 'The damned English left us long ago, but left you behind. Idiot even dreams in English.'

I dozed on for a few more moments, before waking up with a start. 'Jami! Jami!' I cried.

'What is it? Is everything all right?'

Of course everything was all right. It was now. I was fully awake. 'What did you just call me?' I asked Jami.

'A coconut. Brown outside, white inside. You were talking in your sleep. In English! Who does that?'

'That is it! I have it now!'

'What?'

'It is in English!'

I looked around. I must have been asleep for an hour or so. I began to tell Jami about my conversation with Mirza. The diary he gave me. I left out the part about the debt the village owed. I had, after all, given my word.

'Yes. I had a word with him as well,' said Jami. He was looking at me strangely, as if wanting to tell me something. I put that thought aside and continued telling him about the diary, the first fragment I had transcribed and the dead end.

'I have it now!' I said to him. 'It is a simple substitution cipher.' I brought out my own notebook where I had transcribed the scrawl.

'See, it is like this,' I began. 'The vowels in Bangla convert to the equivalent vowel in English. The same with the consonants. Don't you see? The diary is written in English!'

Jami did not say anything. He only continued to look

at me with concern. There was something gnawing at him, but I did not have time for that right now.

'The diary. It can tell us something about this treasure of ours,' I said.

Jami seemed to be consumed by whatever train of thought he was preoccupied with. 'Yes. Of course,' he said, without any enthusiasm.

What was wrong with this guy?

Then I understood. Dada-jaan's death must have cut deep. And he must have gone and confronted Mirza about the Udaipur affair. I let that be. I did not care about anything else at that moment. Nothing but this diary. The treasure.

I silently ate the food he had brought. He had eaten already. While I ate, he said, 'I will go to sleep now.'

I finished eating and picked up the first page of the diary and began transcribing the Bangla characters into English.

As I wrote, I read.

15

On Writing

The Diarie of Bayaz-ud-din Waris Ali Khan
9th Bengal Lancers

Haider Kalan
9 January 1868

It is such a joy to have my personal belongings with me again. To look upon the books that gave me strength during my times of silence. To unwrap a fresh, empty journal and put ink to paper and words to thoughts. It has been so long since I found pleasure in scribbling my thoughts on blank sheets of paper. It has been so long since I possessed a good nib and good ink that the words are flowing faster than they ever have.

The things I had left behind in Haider Kalan survived my absence of eleven years or so without being disturbed. It was a web of lies and counter truths that I had to spin to get my hands on them. After all, it is not easy to lay claim to a large number of books when their owner is supposed to be resting in a grave not a stone's throw away.

My effects were something that did not receive much regard from the people here. Neither did my name or my memory. I could sense disdain and loathing in the way my books had been strewn around. I quietly gathered them and slunk away to look over them lovingly. I was disguised as a harmless fakir, living with people who hated me, having faked my own demise to get to the bottom of why my name lay sullied.

In the dim lamplight, I read the books after the village has gone to sleep. It would not do me good for them to know that I can read the language. It is after a few weeks of being here that I picked up the courage to start writing in this journal. If they ever find a beggar writing and reading in the language of the Englishmen, there will be too many questions, which I cannot afford to answer. Yes, it is courageous of me to write in secret. Or perhaps it has been cowardly of me not to write more and tell some of the stories I know.

When the old general taught me the letters, little did I know what I read would swim around in my head and slowly change me. As I read the odes of Coleridge and Keats again and again, their words pierce me with an intensity that even flying lead could not. As I read about the iron-clad knights of Walter Scott, I imagine myself as them, brave and shining. When the general's son, Major Lassan, threw the first journal at me and asked me to start writing down my thoughts, I had begun haltingly and hesitantly. The thoughts were in my mind, and I struggled to put them down on paper. Lassan had looked at my journal entries and smiled, saying that I needed to write more and more, until the hand and the quill became an extension of my thoughts even before they were formed. It has taken a while for that to happen.

I can sense that my crafting of sentences has become better with time. My thinking has increasingly become like that of the white man. It was a few years of writing my first journal, a few years of reading and rereading books and many years of living under the English that shaped and formed my thoughts. With many years of not writing and not reading, I thought that my writing skills were lost. After all, there was very little to think of or write about in Udaipur. It is only now, when I have my books again, that it has all come back with a rush, and I realize that I cannot but write.

Not writing is perhaps like sleep and rest – you keep doing it in the recesses of your mind, without quill or ink, until it breaks loose like a waterfall and fills up pages and pages. Of late, I have begun to think in English, dream in English. I sometimes fear that under my skinny brown exterior has grown the soul of an Englishman. It fills me with revulsion, as well as pleasure.

Major Lassan once told me that whatever I write must reflect the times I live in. This is what makes it different from others' writings. I tried to write like that in my first journal. As I am writing now, I would be very curious to see what my thoughts would seem like to a reader. How it must have changed over the years.

I think I will try to do this for a while to see how it goes. It will be difficult picking up the threads of what I wrote of in the past. But there are other pieces of the past that I have not written about before, that I can put in here instead. Of how I came to be here again, eleven years after I left. Of how there is a grave nearby with my name on it and why I am a fakir here. Let me find the time to write about the day I stumbled into this village again a few months ago.

It is a story that starts from the middle, and over time a beginning and an end may appear. Let me start from a few days ago, trying to make sense of what has been happening to this mercenary Bengali boy who is in equal parts a soldier, a beggar, a thief, a lover, a spy and a frightened knight.

~

I finished reading the entry and closed my notebook. There were a million questions racing in my mind. I switched off the light and sat still in the dark. Jami snored soundly by my side.

16

Shelves Sixteen and Twenty-four

Jami, Nira and I were on the terrace of the hostel. The sun was beginning to set and the banks of the Yamuna were bathed in twilight. I looked over the ruins of the old arched bridge of Khizrabad. There, long ago, the armies of Timur and Khizr battled the Lodhis for domination over Delhi. Today, it stood witness to the particularly hairy quandary I was in.

Nira had questions. I did not have all the answers. Silence, however, was not an option. Not when you were dealing with Meghnira Basu. And not when she was armed with a list of things she wanted to investigate.

'So tell me this, guys,' she said, 'where do we stand on Udaipur?'

She was met with silence.

'I mean, I thought you guys would have a picnic there and return with a hoard of gold or something. And what do we have instead? A burnt diary, dada-jaan gone for good and all sorts of unanswered questions.'

I should have expected it. Nira or anyone else, investor anxiety runs deep in any operation. And what she said was true. We had been hasty in rushing off to Udaipur. The diary was a good find, though. I was sure it would bring us one step closer to realizing our dream of finding the treasure. I said as much.

'True, it was stupid of us to rush off to Udaipur. But not for nothing. The letters have already told us a lot. For one, we are now certain that there is definitely a fair amount of wealth involved. The burnt diary clearly talks of six chests full of gold.'

'But the letter also says that this Ba'azuddin gave it all to this Harper fellow in Calcutta,' said Nira.

'To be deposited in Lloyd's Bank. We need to look up where that is. And after that, he reached Udaipur, with fifty pieces of gold. This is corroborated in the letter dada-jaan showed us when we met him last. I am quite sure the letter was from Ba'azuddin. And he mentions in it that the treasure lies hidden in Udaipur. So to answer your question, we stand well on Udaipur. Everything still points to Udaipur. We need to look more closely at the meaning of the verses we found in the letter and on the ceiling.'

Nira made a clacking sound with her tongue, as if frustrated with the whole matter. What did she think? That finding the treasure would be easy? Of course, I didn't say that. You can't annoy your investor. Instead, I said, 'The fragments of the burnt diary might be able to help us.'

Jami spoke for the first time in the last hour or so that we had been wondering about what to do next. 'We seem to be at a dead end,' he said gloomily.

'I wish I could tell,' I said. 'I have read only the first entry so far. It adds something to what we know. Something very interesting.'

'What?' barked Nira.

Oh, impatient one, I thought to myself. I began to speak.

'It is possible that the fakir was Ba'azuddin himself.'

Jami's eyes narrowed into slits. 'Meaning?' he asked.

'I mean, from the first entry I decoded we know that the fakir was Ba'azuddin. Ba'azuddin was the fakir. The fakir that dada-jaan spoke of – the fellow who rebuilt the mosque.'

It was Ba'azuddin all along, hiding in the village in broad daylight.

I continued, 'This throws up some embarrassing possibilities, and interesting questions.'

'Yes, it does,' said Jami.

'Why did he live for all those years in Haider Kalan as a fakir, and not Ba'azuddin himself? Why live in hiding?'

'Why indeed,' said Jami.

'The rest of the entries might tell us more,' I said.

'So read them!' said Nira.

'That is the trouble,' I said. 'I can't.'

'What do you mean you can't read the rest?' asked Nira. 'You have already read the first entry. What is the problem with the rest?'

'See, it is like this,' I replied. 'The entry I have transcribed was unlike what I found in the letters. The letters were Bangla characters for text written in Hindustani – or what we call Hindi. The diary entry is, instead, in English. The first entry was easy to read. It was a simple substitution code. The letters of the Bangla alphabet, substituted with the corresponding letters of the English alphabet. The rest of the entries follow a different code. I am trying to figure out what that is. So far I have not succeeded.'

There was an awkward silence. All three of us looked over the terrace parapet at nothing in particular. I tried to raise their spirits. 'Look, I know there are more questions than answers. But a few things have also become clearer. One, it is highly likely that fifty pieces of gold lie hidden somewhere in Udaipur. Two, these diary fragments are of far greater value than they may seem. It is not every day that you acquire an account written over a hundred years ago and touch and feel words written by a person long dead.'

Nira sniffed. Or was that a snigger? She clearly did

not share my enthusiasm for history. All that these morons appreciated was the treasure. No respect for scholarship at all.

'Come on, Nira. We will find something,' said Jami as he tried to support me. 'And even if we do not, we will find a way of giving your money back to you,' he said with valiant confidence.

Nira seemed to turn a deep maroon. 'It is not about the money, Jami, you fool!' she burst out.

It was not? Oh!

For a moment, I was glad it was Jami under fire. I was also about to bring up the matter of returning Nira's cash but, thankfully, Jami took the bullet that would have surely come my way.

'But,' said Jami, continuing with his foot in his mouth, and Nira's boot up his behind, 'you told me . . .'

'Screw what I told you! Yes, it is about money, but not for me! It's for New York!'

At that moment, the two of them seemed to realize that I was also there. They abruptly clammed up about whatever they were talking of. There was clearly something interesting afoot there. I thought of asking Jami about it later. For the time being, I decided to stop being the convenient third wheel, and steered the conversation towards something else.

'So what will you guys do with the money anyway?' I asked. 'If and when we find something.'

Jami gave a snort. 'I really have not thought about it,' he said.

'It depends on how much we find,' said Nira.

'It does?' asked Jami.

'Yes, Jami,' she said, turning on him with venom. 'It does. I have plans and so do you!'

'Uh . . .' said Jami, mumbling something, caught between a rock and a hard place. The poor fellow just kept getting it from Nira. He asked me, 'What will you do?'

I thought for a fleeting second about the number of books I would buy and the things I would do. First head back home to get Ma. I shoved those thoughts aside and said instead, 'I haven't really thought about it either. And I suppose it depends on how much there is.'

'Fat good all this is!' said Nira. 'All this is daydreaming if we cannot figure out what is written in those diaries.'

I thought for a moment. 'I think I know someone who could help us with the diaries,' I said.

That caught their attention.

'What time is it?' I asked.

'Six-thirty,' said Nira.

'Can your driver take us?' I asked her.

'Where?'

'It is time we paid Professor Venugopal a visit.'

They both recoiled in mock fear.

'Bungalee Babu!' they said together.

That running joke would be the ruin of me. Once,

just once, he had called me by that name in class, and it just had to stick with him and me forever.

'Would it be okay for us to show up at his home just like that?' asked Jami.

Nira added, 'And you know where he lives?'

'Of course,' I answered both questions together. 'You take us, I will tell you where to go,' I told Nira.

'You are such a professor's pet,' said Nira as we made our way down to the parking lot. Her driver saw us coming and dutifully stepped out. He handed Nira the keys. Jami sat with her in the front and I made myself comfortable in the back. The driver made himself even more comfortable next to me and promptly fell asleep.

~

'But this is college,' said Nira, when I told her to stop outside the Architecture Block.

I did not say anything. Instead, I took my bag and stepped out of the car. I gestured them to follow. The driver slept soundly in the back seat.

As I entered the building and walked up the stairs, I explained. 'I found out last year, when the professor wrote to my parents. It was about a paper I missed turning in. Huge embarrassment for me at home. Anyway, it was then that I noticed the address at the bottom of his personal letterhead.'

'He has a personal letterhead?' asked Nira.

'Yes. I mean, it is the university letterhead that all senior professors get. The residence address was a strange one,' I said as we reached the second floor where the department library was. 'It said Stack 16-24, Architecture Library. He lives here, apparently.'

I let that sink in for a moment. Then I continued, 'I eventually asked the office. They confirmed that he does, indeed, live in the library. Official accommodation. Something to do with being close to his research material. All lies, of course. The department has been kind to him. His stature in academic circles, you see. He needed a place to stay. About seven years ago, his wife kicked him out of the house for reasons best known to her.'

'This guy has a wife?' asked Jami with a snort.

'Evidently so. Anyway, I have visited him here over the last few months. We are working on a very interesting paper together. It is called "Exposition in Architecture of Religion – Literacy and Liturgy",' I declared with great pride.

'What does that even mean?' asked Jami.

'You are getting to collaborate with him?' gushed Nira.

Better. At least she had a bit of a brain. I nodded.

'But yes, what does that mean?'

No, she did not.

I let the imbecility of lesser mortals pass. 'Never mind that,' I said. 'But he has a very sharp and canny mind, if you can penetrate the fog. He might take an interest in our story, and our notebooks,' I said, patting my bag. I knocked softly on the glass door of the library. There should be no one around during the vacations. But having been here dozens of evenings after hours, I knew better.

The old library watchman appeared behind the glass pane. He saw me and opened the door a crack.

'The professor,' I said. I had never ever gotten around to asking the watchman what his name was. 'I need a consultation.'

The watchman did not say anything, but only looked at me and the others balefully. I pulled out the quarter bottle of rum from inside my bag and showed it to him.

That let us in.

The inside of the library was dark. Only the reading room was dimly lit. The watchman would enjoy his reward there in the light, while we went into the darkness of the stacks. Poetic as hell. I hoped there would be some illumination at the end of it all.

In the dark, the library stack room is a fearsome place. I reached the end of the stack room where a plyboard wall ran from the shelf numbered sixteen to the one numbered twenty-four. I knocked on the makeshift door in the middle of it, a pale crack of light illuminating it. Behind me I thought I heard Jami and Nira hold their breath as I knocked. Once, twice, thrice.

'Come in,' said a voice from far inside.

I opened the door and stepped in.

The sight was familiar to me, but it would have been new for Jami and Nira. Piles and piles of books surrounded Professor Venugopal, who was bent over a book at his desk. In the dim light of the single bulb that hung from the ceiling, he squinted at whatever he was reading through a cloudy lens. There was a cot somewhere in a dark corner. It would be occupied by books and papers as well.

We waited by the door as the professor continued reading. He was also taking notes in a tome of a notebook. I shook my head at Jami and Nira, asking them to remain put. Finally, he finished whatever he was doing, and looked up at us.

'What is it, young man?' he asked, addressing me.

I shuffled to him and brought out my notebook. I put it on the table in front of him.

'There is something I needed your help with, professor,' I said. Jami and Nira had also walked in closer tentatively.

'It all began with a story I heard a few weeks ago,' I started. I told the professor about the story dadajaan had told me in Haider Kalan. From time to time, Jami interjected with a few details. I told the professor about the mosque and opened my notebook to show him the sketches and drawings. Professor Venugopal kept listening with a bored expression and without interrupting. From time to time he turned the pages of my notebook to look at the sketches of the verses. When I reached the part about Udaipur, he flipped to my sketches of the temple at Jagat and then the Jag Mandir. I told him about the letters dada-jaan had showed us in Haider Kalan. I showed him the transcribed letters as well as the original letters. For the first time, I saw interest in his eyes. He fingered the original folded letters that I had carried back from Haider Kalan. When he heard about the diary Mirza had given me, he gave me a sharp look. Then, with almost religious reverence, he opened the diary. I told him how I had figured out the substitution cipher. I showed him the transcription of the rest of the diary – the part I was unable to decode. I finished my account of the past few days. 'You see, professor, I think it is vital that I decipher the remaining entries. I am sure the later entries will have some answers.'

Professor Venugopal kept running his fingers lovingly over the diary. Then he opened my notebook and glanced at my translation of the strange entries. He went through the diary. Then he looked up at me and said, 'And what if I tell you how to read all this?' There was a look of yearning on his face that I understood at once.

I felt Nira tense up. She must have been thinking that the professor wanted a share in the treasure as well.

'Why, professor, you can keep the diary when we are done with it. Whether you can help us or not,' I said at once.

He broke into a million-watt smile and said, 'Spoken like a true man of letters.' Somehow, hearing that from him made me feel better than I had in months.

He took another look at the scrawled words in my notebook and said, 'Caesar Cipher. Look for *e* in *the*. You will have your key.' Saying this, he got up and went to one of the shelves that lined the wall. He began to pull out one book after another, dusting them and stacking them on his arm.

Jami and Nira looked at me. I was looking at my notebooks, realization dawning on me. I turned to them and nodded. I had the solution!

Professor Venugopal returned and placed the books on his desk. 'Now be off, gentlemen and my dear lady. I have work that needs to be done.'

Jami and Nira made a hurried exit. I was about to follow them when the professor stopped me. 'Please tell Abdullah on your way out that he can take off for the day.'

For a moment I was confused. Then I realized he was not talking about the Abdullah of Haider Kalan, but the library watchman. So his name was Abdullah, too.

I nodded and was about to leave, when another thought crossed my mind. A germ of an idea. 'Professor,' I said.

'Yes?' he said.

'Would you like to have lunch at my aunt's place tomorrow?' I asked with some hesitation. There were certain lines too dangerous to cross.

He did not say anything.

'We are going there tomorrow in any case and I thought it would be a nice change.' I gave an uncertain feeble wave at our surroundings.

A few seconds passed, during which he stared into my eyes and I shat a million shits in my pants, before looking down uncomfortably.

Then he said softly, 'It will be my pleasure.'

'E-29, C.R. Park, ground floor,' I squawked, and fled.

~

I walked past the dark stacks and reached the reading room. It was still bathed in light. Abdullah was nowhere to be seen. Neither were Nira and Jami. I was wondering where they had gone off, when I heard them coming into the reading room from behind me. Behind me. What on earth were they doing there, I wondered. They were startled when they saw me waiting. Seeing their flushed faces and embarrassed grins, I knew. I thought of facilitating their romance for a little longer.

I put my notebook and the diary on a table.

'Nira, can you guys do me a favour? Please hang around here awhile. I need to sit here and transcribe the code.'

'What did Professor Venugopal tell you? Caesar Cipher?' asked Nira.

'It is quite obvious, now that I think of it. The Caesar

Cipher is another substitution, but with characters shifted a certain interval in the alphabet.' I saw their blank expressions and thought it best to demonstrate.

'Here. See. He asked me to look for the letter *e* and the word *the*. The letter *e* is the most commonly recurring letter in English, and *the* is the most common word.

'Now see this page,' I said, pointing to the one in front of me. I scanned it briefly. 'The most common three-letter word here is *wkh*, written as *va-ka-ha* in Bangla. This occurs seven times on this page. Now suppose *wkh* is *the*. This would mean . . .' I calculated using my fingers, '*e-f-g-h* – four. There is a shift of four. Use this shift of four on *the* and you have . . .' I started counting again.

Nira said immediately, '*w*, *k* and *h*! And the professor saw that in a matter of seconds?'

I was glad to observe the reverence in her tone.

'And how do you know all this?' she asked me. 'Caesar Cipher and all?'

I shrugged. I did not know how I knew. I just did. Probably came from being a lonely kid. 'No TV at home when I was growing up,' I said. 'I used to read instead.'

'Ah.'

It is embarrassing sometimes when your friends hold you in awe. Time to reward these kids. 'I need some time to write all this down,' I said. 'Can you guys give me an hour?'

'Sure,' they said together. A little too quickly.

I sat down and began to transcribe the letters. When I looked up a while later, they were gone. Good.

I kept writing till my fingers ached. I resisted reading as I wrote. I would read peacefully when I was done. That would be a while. I could, however, not resist taking a peek at the first few words. *Haider Kalan, 11 January 1868*. Barely two days after the first entry.

Part III

The Fakir Who Came in from the Cold

17

A Small Incident

Haider Kalan
11 January 1868

A series of misplaced accidents of youth bind me to this place and have brought me back. Misplaced accidents that began with Haider Kalan and still linger on in the winds of darkness here. Some day, it will all end here as well. That is what a nagging ache in my thigh from an old wound tells me. But truth be told, nagging aches in thighs cannot speak, and it could be a soldier running into middle age imagining things. Imagining that an old adventure which began eleven years ago would end here. That the gold I carried away from under Hodson's nose would be ours. A hope that the key to unlock at least a part of this treasure, a key that lies hidden in Udaipur, will be recovered.

But then I come back to reality and see the fakir's life that I live. I remember how useless I have become. How penniless I am. I remind myself that of the four who started out with the gold, only I remain. Akbar and Abdullah died here only days after I left Haider Kalan the first time. How all this came to be, I will write of shortly. Iqbal has not been found yet. I will have to go looking for him soon. I cannot go to Udaipur on my own to claim what I left there – the key that would lead to our gold. It would have to be Iqbal. I will have to seek Iqbal and find him. I must. I must.

Otherwise, what good would gold worth a hundred thousand pounds be?

My first day in Haider Kalan was the most remarkable. That evening eleven years ago, when the four of us rode in, flush with exuberance. Of my having brought unimaginable wealth for ourselves, dreaming of a rich life ahead. I remember writing about that evening in my first journal. I remember describing our revelry, when I had my first taste of the arrack distilled here. I remember penning down how Akbar's father, the venerable Rahat Ahmed Ali Khan, gave sage advice about hiding the gold. I remember writing about how I rode out the next morning at dawn, promising to return. That first journal of mine has it all and I would very much like to see again how I had written about that day.

But that little red leather-bound journal Major Lassan gifted me is lost to me forever. I have no means of going back and getting it.

It is now time for me to put down on paper what has happened over the past few months and how I came to be here.

~

I will digress a little, for just a while, before I come back to writing about what happened. Many years ago, when I began writing the first journal, Major Lassan gave me books to read. As I took the bound volumes of Dickens and Scott and the poetry of Coleridge and Keats, the major carelessly tossed towards me an old copy of a magazine printed on cheap newsprint. I asked him what it was.

'A penny magazine,' he said. 'I use it to wipe my arse. Wipe your mind with it, if you please, Bayaz-ud-din.' He shook soundlessly with mirth, at a joke I did not understand then. The major explained.

'These books I am bequeathing you, they are very valuable. The finest writing in Her Majesty's language. Reading them will help you write better. But to know what is good, you also ought to know what is bad. And that is why I give you this magazine with these dreadful stories. Read them sometime if you can. You will see how bad writing can get and that my father's countrymen, too, can write what is nothing but rubbish.' He paused, and with a gentle fatherly caress in his voice, continued, 'And you will also know that even if I rant at your badly written strings of words, they are better than most of the filth in here.'

I saluted and went away. Later, I read the magazine and I loved the stories far more than the hollow, sad darkness of Dickens. The stories in cheap newsprint did much to race the blood in my veins. Dick Turpin and Sweeny Todd. Highwaymen and heaving bosoms. Ah, those were real stories.

I am tired of writing strait-laced accounts of my life. I now present to a future reader of my journal (if anyone will ever read this, that is) an account of my adventures in Haider Kalan and beyond. Adventures that transpired over the last two months or so. In five parts, dreadfully written, valued at only a pice each.

Part One
A Small Incident

It was a winter afternoon. I was half a day away from Haider Kalan. Udaipur was far behind. A year had passed since I had fled the place. I had laid low there for close to nine years, hiding, waiting for some word from my brothers, but when my guise was revealed, I took the chance to head back here, where the story had first begun. I assumed that the English would have stopped looking for me. The warrant was, after all, very old and I was not the twenty-year-old young man I used to be. I was right. I passed unchecked even on the Grand Trunk Road to Delhi.

Still, I was careful to give Delhi a wide berth and circled eastwards, on to the forest road to Patiala. Taking the old, familiar shortcut at the Kos Minar before Shahbad, I stopped at the stream to get some water for myself and my horse. I would reach Haider Kalan before nightfall the next day and my mind was occupied with what I would do once I got there.

Questions were gnawing at me. Why had my brothers not acted upon the letter I had sent them? I had told them about the warrant and that they would need to come to Udaipur. Why had they not come? Had they been captured? If so, would there be anyone in Haider Kalan I would know? Who would I ask for? What would I say? These thoughts were on my mind as I drank from the running water and wet my neckcloth, wiping away days of dust off my face. I was about to rise, when I heard the familiar click of a pistol lock behind me.

I raised my hands slowly and turned around to find someone I thought was long dead. It was Small. My nemesis, and once my worst nightmare. It was he who had put the scars on my back at a flogging post many years ago. It was he who had later made my days in Hodson's company a living hell. It was he who I had left for dead, bleeding with a smashed skull, just before

I fled with Hodson's gold. It was he who was now standing over me, astride a large stallion, pistol pointed unwaveringly at the spot between my eyes.

The years had not been kind to him. His skin looked like yellowed parchment, as if disease had consumed him. His clothes were dishevelled, a far cry from how immaculately he would present himself on the parade grounds. There was a slight tremble in his left hand that held the reins of his horse.

'Fancy finding you here! Just when I had given up on ever seeing hide or hair of you lot. They told me at the village that you have not been seen hereabouts since the day you left, and hey, coolie, I run into you.'

'Pleasure meeting you, too,' I said through clenched teeth.

He made me turn around, and everything went black. When I came to my senses, I found myself sitting up with my back against the trunk of a tree, my hands and feet bound. Small was hobbling about, riffling through my pack and trying to get a fire going at the same time. A stump of wood was what served as the remainder of his right leg below his knee. His horse was tied close to where I was bound. Of my horse, there was no sign. When I asked him where he was, Small gave me a malevolent glare with his good eye and told me that I would not be needing it where I was going.

Things were not looking good. Dusk was approaching and the shadows had grown long. I realized that if I had to stay alive, I needed to keep him talking. When I tried, he snapped and asked me to shut up.

'I will be asking the questions, Bungalee,' he said.

~

'Where is Hodson's gold hidden?' he asked me as the sun set.

I stayed quiet. He slapped me across the face.

'I have ways to make you talk, my coolie. I have dreamt of this day. I did not spend the last ten years locked up in that hellhole at Port Blair to suffer your silence. I will ask you one last time before I start using other means. Where did you coolies hide away the loot?'

I maintained my silence, although my mind was racing. Small drew a foot-long dagger and hobbled over to the fire. He sat cross-legged across me and began to heat the blade over the glowing embers. The firelight and his yellow pallor turned his face a sickly orange. His yellow eyes glinted with manic glee as he looked at the flames, whispering to himself.

'They did not let me question the others properly the last time. Sholto and Morstan are gentlemen, you see. When we tracked the four of you to Haider Kalan, and found only two, they did not let me have my way with them.'

I kept quiet and let him talk, as he turned the blade over the fire. Him talking was a better proposition than whatever else he was planning to do with me. At the same time, I wondered what he meant. My curiosity got the better of me.

'Two?' I asked.

'You had left earlier with the gold. And that kaffir Iqbal bloodied two of our men before he fled. That left the bastards Akbar and Abdullah. I told the majors Morstan and Sholto that I would make them squeal. Spill the beans about you lot. But no. They were officers and gentlemen, you see. They wanted to ask questions. Speak and banter with you thieving lot.'

Small spat and continued his story.

'I always wondered. You must have moved very fast and very skilfully. We sent our best trackers after you but found no trace of you or the gold. Tell me, Bungalee. How did you move three mules of load so quickly, and where did you hide it?'

The old story would need to be stuck to. I stared at him for a while.

'Move three mules?' I asked.

Small looked at me thoughtfully across the fire and then spoke, as if to himself. 'Or perhaps you never moved the gold from Delhi. Perhaps you hid it there. But no, that cannot be. We scoured all of Delhi for that gold. You must have moved it.'

I shook my head and told him what the four of us had decided upon many years ago.

'I took the gold with me to Calcutta. But *three mules*?

I took only a sackful of Hodson's gold.'

Small seemed to go berserk and started to speak, froth forming at the corners of his lips. He spittled and sputtered and shrieked.

'They said the same thing! You coolies. You bastards. You made the story up. Made me look bad in front of the majors. How was I to know that it would all come down on me? I wanted to skin them alive. I could make them talk, I said. But no, the majors said. The two must hang as deserters. I pleaded with them. I said that they would know where you took the gold. But they said the same thing. Just a sackful. Just a sackful!'

He stopped and then spoke in a calmer voice.

'But I can make you talk now. You see, there are no gentlemen around. I will make you pay for taking ten years of my life.'

He hobbled up and squatted in front of me, his face inches away from mine. The dagger in his hand glowed a dull orange. I had to think fast about how to stop him.

'Why would we want to do that?' I asked.

'What?' he asked.

'I really don't understand what you are talking about. I know nothing about the three mules of load. I took only fifty mohurs after hitting you on the head. I thought I had killed you.'

'Kill me, did you?' Small asked with a vicious hiss and sank the dagger into my thigh.

I screamed. The pain was like nothing I had ever

felt before. The flogging at the barracks that this man had administered years earlier seemed nothing in comparison. I closed my eyes. Everything turned red. And then it was dark.

When I regained consciousness, it was darker. I was trussed up against the tree, but facing it this time. Night had fallen and Small was leering over me, pouring rivulets of cold water down the stab wound on my thigh. Spasms of burning cold pain wracked through me as Small droned on in his low voice.

'There is a thing or two I learnt in the stockade in the Andamans. A thing or two they did to me that taught me about pain. This burning, it feels delicious, does it not? Now will you tell me what you did with the gold?'

I started blabbering.

'I swear to you! I just wanted to run. While leaving, I took only fifty mohurs.'

'You lie!' he roared, and I felt a slash of leather on my back. I started giggling. My laughter sent Small into an even bigger rage, like it had at the flogging post at Meerut years ago. I felt another slash of leather on my back and my giggles turned to maniacal laughter. As I laughed louder, he whipped me harder. As he whipped me harder, I recited poetry in my mind, like I had done earlier.

Torture seeks to inflict pain, to make a man talk. To silence thought and make pain the only thing on the mind, until the man will say anything to stop the pain. The trick is to keep thinking while the pain rages. There was nothing I wanted to say, no secrets I wanted to spill, but I needed to keep Small at my back, whipping me. His eyes had to be away from my hands tied around the tree. I recited all the poetry in my mind and laughed away, as Small worked on my back. By the time I had finished reciting Kubla Khan, the strands around my hands were loose enough. By the time Shelley met the traveller from an ancient land, I had dislocated my left thumb, timing it with a spasm of pain from the whiplash. The bonds loosened. As I freed my hands between two strokes of the whip, in a delirium of pain, I spun around on my uninjured leg and roared at Small.

'My name is Ozymandias, King of Kings!'

With all the strength I could muster, I caught his throat and squeezed it hard as we fell to the ground. He grappled with me, totally surprised. I scratched and bit in madness and pain. With anger born out of desperation, I found purchase and sank a finger into his good eye. As I released him, he screamed and thrashed around blindly. I stood over him panting, totally out of breath.

'LOOK upon my works, ye Mighty, and despair!'

And brought the rock that appeared in my hand down on his skull.

~

I rested for a while. I snapped my thumb back in place, tied it up and then fed the fire. Dawn was not far. I bathed in the river and dressed my wounds. Then I roused the now blind man and began to interrogate him in my own delicate manner.

He did not have much to say. He was dying, but I pieced together some facts about what had happened after I rode away from Haider Kalan with the gold.

I heard of the torture, the murder and the destruction and realized that Ba'azuddin Bungalee might not be welcome at Haider Kalan. I asked Small about what had transpired in Delhi after I knocked him over the head and made away with the gold. He was fading away by that time. All I could get from him was that when he had regained consciousness after our last meeting, I was gone. The troops had been sent after me to Haider Kalan with the two majors and Small. They did not find me, but they found the others. Iqbal fled, but Akbar and Abdullah were not so fortunate. After the night of questioning and hangings, a warrant was issued against Iqbal and me. It explained the heat I faced after leaving Haider Kalan. Sholto and Morstan concluded that Small had a part to play in the disappearance of the gold. He was incarcerated in the new prison camp in the Andamans, where the remaining rebels were lodged.

I wanted to ask Small more, but by then he was dead.

When dawn broke, I understood that I would have to go to Haider Kalan to find out more. But I could not go there as Ba'azuddin Bungalee because I feared the villagers believed I had brought upon them the ruin of that fateful night. Small would have to become me, then. I wrapped him up and heaved him on to his horse.

[End of Part One]

~

I will write tomorrow about what happened next.

One day, I rode into this village to meet my three brothers. The next morning, I rode out with the gold. Weeks after, the company of soldiers with Small, Sholto and Morstan arrived, killed every adult male and razed the mosque to the ground. On that day of anguish, the village howled out my name as the one who had caused their pain. Eleven years later, I hobbled in, carrying the corpse of the man who was one of the executors that fateful day, burying him in a grave that still bears my name.

That tale, of the day I walked into Haider Kalan again a few months ago, is the second part of my story.

18

The Fakir Who Came in from the Cold

Haider Kalan
12 January 1868

Part Two
The Fakir Who Came in from the Cold

The hot breath of the horse kept my neck warm as I led it through the foggy path. The sun was rising somewhere behind me. The path ahead was enveloped in darkness, but behind me, when I looked over my shoulder, I could see the light of dawn through the mist. The flies, too, were beginning to wake up. The wound on my thigh drew a few of them, as did the healing welts on my back. But these did not draw as many of them as did the load the horse carried. The wrapped body of Small, trussed on the back of the horse, was the reason I chose to walk and lead the horse, and not ride it. The seeping blood that had made its way through his clothes drew a swarm of flies, which buzzed and formed a cloud that kept pace with us.

I was carrying Small's body for a reason. I thought that carrying a body into Haider Kalan could be a plausible explanation for my being there. I was making up different stories in my head but could not come up with anything that sounded logical. So I decided to become the fakir, as I had done all these years in Udaipur, and see what happened. It was not as if the body was recognizable as human any more. I had tried for half a day to ride on the horse and drag the body. It had turned into unrecognizable mash and pulp. The smell of blood had become strong and fearing predators, both human and animal, I wrapped it in a shroud, hoisted it over the horse and walked instead.

As we approached the village, a few dogs began to bark. A lantern or two appeared in the distance. An old, mangy dog came up to us. It sniffed around, whimpered and came and nuzzled at my leg. I stopped. The horse shied a little because of the dog, but I patted him to calm him.

I bent down and patted the dog on its head. It seemed to be familiar with this gesture and rubbed itself against my hand. I would not have been surprised if it had detected a familiar smell as well. Its fur, now in tatters, would have been black and white once. I remembered a black-and-white pup during my last visit here. We had taken a fancy to each other and played through the night while the others drank. I searched my memory for the name I had given the dog, but nothing came to mind. I gave him a final pat on the back and straightened up. I began to walk again, leading the horse towards the village.

I saw two lanterns coming towards me through the grey mist. Two dark shadows wrapped in blankets, warily scanning in front of them for what had woken up the dog. Then they noticed this mysterious shadow of a man and a horse. I stopped and waited for them to walk up to me. What happened over the next few moments would be crucial.

The two came closer. They were merely boys. Tall for boys, but very young, nevertheless. One was taller than the other but seemed younger than him. The older one was broader at the chest and shoulders. I raised an open hand in greeting.

'Salaam. Is this Haider Kalan?'

'It is,' said the younger boy.

'I am here to see a man named Rahat Ahmed Ali Khan,' I said.

The two looked at each other, and then the same boy replied.

'He passed away long ago.'

'I was told that it might be so. His son, then, Akbar Ahmed Ali Khan?'

The two looked at each other again. Then the same boy gave a sad shake of his head.

'If he too is not here, then I was told to ask for Abdullah and Iqbal. I do not know their family names.'

This time the older boy answered.

'What are they to you? Who are you and what business do you have here?'

'I am nobody. I am but a passing fakir, here to act on the wishes of a dying man. The same man who lies dead on this horse. He said his name is Ba'azuddin.'

The younger boy scowled. The older boy spat and said, 'Come with us. We will take you to Alauddin.'

They turned towards the village and I followed. A few minutes later, we reached the edge of the village. The older boy pointed to a post.

'Leave the horse here. Alauddin will decide what to do with him.'

I did not argue. I merely hitched the horse to the post. They walked on and I followed, hobbling.

In the early morning light, I began to take in some details, tallying them with the last time I had been here. There was a forlorn, desolate air about the place. I wondered who this Alauddin might be and what I should tell him. It was then that two things struck me.

First, there were none of the usual sounds of a village of this sort waking up at dawn. No sounds of morning fires and cooking pots. No sounds of children wailing or playing. The other matter was of the mosque. Or where the mosque should have been. I looked to the far left of the path we walked down. The mosque where we had met that night should have been there. In its place stood a pile of brick and rubble. A large tree cast its shadow on the ruins. Over time undergrowth had claimed the ruins. Vines grew thick under the tree and on the stones around it. An occasional crow cawed from the sombre wreck.

The two boys approached a house. It was slightly larger than the rest. I remembered it. It used to be the house of the venerable Rahat Ahmed Ali Khan.

The younger boy told me to wait and went inside. The older one kept me company. Or probably stood guard. I was shivering in the chilly air.

The dog appeared again. It must have followed us. It quietly sat between me and the house, with its back to me. Erect. Tail whisking away an occasional fly. Ears sharp, looking at the closed doorway.

After a while, the door creaked open. The younger boy reappeared. He gestured to me.

'Come inside. Alauddin will see you now.'

I followed him through the doorway. It opened into a courtyard, just like I remembered it.

There was a young man seated on a cot in the middle of the courtyard. There seemed to be no one else around. He stood up as I came in. He was very young. Barely twenty or so. But there was an air of authority about him. A quiet, all-seeing aura of a man used to commanding. His eyes were gentle as they took in my appearance. He gave a slight nod and motioned me to sit on the cot with him. He sat down, too. The two who accompanied me remained standing.

After a few moments of silence, and without preamble, he said, 'Speak.'

I began my story as I had planned, making things up along the way. I had decided it would be wise to stay as close to the truth as possible.

'My name is Lalan. I wander where I can. Some call me a fakir. Some call me a pir. Others come to tell me their worries and woes. I see myself as a man who tries to comfort those around me,' I began.

'Three nights ago, I was walking down a forest path. It was nearing dusk and I wanted to find shelter for the night. It was then that I heard a blood-curdling scream. I cautiously and quietly made my way to where I thought the sound came from. I was not afraid of thugs, for I had nothing which belonged to me or could be taken away from me. So I went ahead fearlessly. I arrived at a clearing and what I saw was far different from anything I could have imagined. A white man, an angrez, was standing over a man tied to a tree. A fire was burning and the white man wielded a glowering, red-hot knife. The tied-up man was groaning and screaming. The white man was saying something to him in a low voice. I crept closer to try to hear him.'

The seated young man raised a finger to stop me. 'The white man. Describe him.'

I gave a description of Small. A tall, sickly-looking white man with a wooden leg. The young man looked over my shoulder to where the two boys were standing and gave an imperceptible nod. He gestured that I continue.

'As I came closer, I realized that the white man was speaking in English. I could not make out much of what was being said. The other man was in great pain and did not seem to be giving answers to what the white man was asking. The prisoner cried out in a cringing, beseeching voice. The white man kept repeating the same question. The only word I could understand from it was "loot". The prisoner kept shaking his head, denying and pleading. The continuous denial seemed to make the white man go berserk. He sank his dagger again and again into the legs, arms and thighs of his prisoner. Screams rent the air, and then died out abruptly. I realized that the man had become unconscious. I heard the white man howl in frustration. It was as if a demon had possessed him. He began to kick at the unconscious man's face, screaming some words I know not the meaning of. They were nothing pleasant, that is all I could understand. The unconscious man's face turned to a bloodied pulp, but the white man did not stop. He kicked until he himself began to pant. He lifted his weapon and was about to stab the man in his face, when something came over him, and he threw his dagger away in anger. It fell at a spot not very far from where I was watching, hidden. The white man gave another fearful howl and clawed at and ripped the man's face with his bare hands, saying the same sentence again and again. I heard the word "loot" repeated many times. I did not know if the prisoner was still alive to hear anything.'

The young man spoke. 'The white man was asking the prisoner about loot?'

'I think so. I did not gather much, but it was evident that the prisoner did not have the answer. No man could stand the torture and remain silent.'

The young man sat in silence for a while, deep in thought. 'Continue,' he said.

'As I watched them, the white man untied his prisoner, who immediately fell on the ground. The white man turned the man over and kicked him again. I thought him dead. The man lay there unmoving, bloodied, face unrecognizable as that of a human. Then . . .'

I faltered, uncertain about the next part of the story.

'And then what?' asked the young man.

I stayed silent. A distant memory stirred in me, of me at the flogging post at the barracks many ages ago, and Small coming to me after the call to quarters in the evening. I flushed a deep red, took a deep breath and tried to bring a quiver in my voice.

'And then he tried to do to him what no man should do with another, man or animal, living or dead,' I began, and stopped.

There was a moment of embarrassed silence in the courtyard. Bravo Ba'azuddin, I thought to myself. That was close. The morbid fear of a good buggering helps in most perilous situations. You should try your luck at the West End some day. Bravo. I continued the performance.

I averted my eyes, staring into nothingness.

'I am a man of god. Peace-loving. But that day brought out the devil in me. I was already seething at this white man beating one of our own. When he began his vile work, I saw red. Before I realized what was happening, I was upon him. We fought and thrashed about the clearing. I felt a hot sting on my thigh. I had been stabbed. I bit and clawed like an animal and before I knew what was happening, I had a dagger in my hand and it was plunging into his back, again and again. The white man fell groaning, and was quiet. I dropped the dagger with a clatter. I was out of breath and trembling. I have never attacked any living being before. I spent some time trying to compose myself. Then, I tended to the prisoner. He was alive, but barely so. I examined him to see if I could do anything for him, but he seemed too far gone. Night had fallen. I waited there, in the company of a dead white man I had killed, and another man who was dying, thinking about what to do next. After many hours – I think I had dozed off – I heard a weak groan. It was the prisoner. With his face smashed to a pulp, he was looking at me with whatever eyes he had left. His bloodied lips were moving and a hoarse sound came from his mouth. He was asking for water.'

I stopped and looked at the young man sitting next to me. I had his complete attention. I also felt the other two behind me listening intently. 'Do you have any water?' I asked abruptly.

The young man impatiently waved a hand and I sensed one of the boys behind me, possibly the younger, lighter-footed one, go away. He reappeared shortly with the water and I drank deeply. I looked up at the young man across me, who was fidgeting, waiting to hear the rest of what I had to say. I decided to toy with him a little more, as I brewed the rest of the story in my head.

'You must be Alauddin then,' I said.

'How do you know that?' he asked.

I pointed at the two boys behind me and said, 'They said so.' I drank some more water. The young man glared at the others. Very good again, Ba'azuddin. Sow the slightest seed of discord among your listeners and they will believe your word as the truth.

Now came the trickiest part of my story. It was important that they believe the rest of what I had to say. I finished the water and continued with the story.

'I gave the dying man a drink of water. He rested for a while, drawing one rasping breath after another. There were bubbles of blood on his lips. Something inside must have been punctured in the beating. It was clear he would not last the night.

'A while before dawn, he called out to me again and asked me who I was. Just a passing fakir who decided to help, I told him. He asked me to bring him here, to this village of Haider Kalan. As gently as I could, I told him there was only one place he was going to from there and that would not be of this world. He lay silent for a while and then asked me a favour – from a holy man to a dying one. He asked that he be taken to Haider Kalan and buried in the shadow of the mosque that Rahat Ahmed Ali Khan had built. He also asked that I ask Rahat Ahmed Ali Khan a question if he is alive, or his son Akbar Ali Khan, if he is not. If I find neither, I was to ask that question of Abdullah and Iqbal. Then that man, who gave his name to be Ba'azuddin, died.' I paused, looked up at the young man and said, 'So where are Rahat Ahmed Ali Khan, Akbar Ahmed Ali Khan, Iqbal, or Abdullah? I have a sacred promise that I made to a dying man and I intend to keep it, if I can.'

The man sitting across me, Alauddin, looked me in the eye for a few moments. Then he glanced at the two men behind me. I heard them turn away and leave. Alauddin addressed me.

'What is the question Ba'azuddin charged you with asking them?'

I shrugged.

'It seemed quite meaningless. He asked, "Why did they not act on the letters he sent them?"' I saw a flicker of understanding on Alauddin's face and pressed on.

'Do you know what that means?'

He did not speak for a while and looked at me as if sizing me up, assessing me with his eyes. Then he asked, 'That white man. He is dead?'

'Very much so,' I replied.

Alauddin then asked me, 'You are a holy man, are you not?'

I looked up at the sky and said neither in earnest nor in hesitation, 'I am as holy as anyone. Like everyone else, I try to seek the god in me.'

Alauddin gave a satisfied grunt and rose to his feet. I too tried to rise, but the wound on my thigh had stiffened. I fell back. Alauddin held me gently and firmly by the shoulders and helped me to my feet.

He said to me, 'Baba, I have bad news for you. My grandfather Rahat Ahmed Ali Khan is dead, as is my uncle Akbar Ahmed Ali Khan. So are Abdullah Khan. Of Iqbal, no one knows.'

My grief must have shown on my face. But I understood from Alauddin's eyes that he read it as disappointment.

'But do not worry. If Ba'azuddin's question had to be asked of anyone, it would be to my grandfather or my father. And my father lies dying in the room in the far corner of the courtyard. So you have come to the right place.'

I looked him over once more and my hand rose as if to comfort him. I checked myself and turned the gesture to one of blessing by a holy man. Alauddin bowed his head.

'You have travelled far, baba. Do rest for a while. After that, I will tell you a story which may answer some questions you have for us.' He gestured to the cot, as if bidding me to make myself comfortable there. As I sat down again, he continued to speak.

'I do not know if you have done us a service by bringing Ba'azuddin's remains here or not. There is much that I have to think about.' He smiled a sad smile and said, 'It is not so long ago that I sat playing as a child in the streets here. And then everything turned upside down. Things were barely getting back to whatever passes for benign, when the white man appeared last week and everything came crashing down again. Now my father too lies dying, and I am soon to answer for the affairs of this village. Yes, I have much to think about. We will talk soon.' He bowed and turned away. As he walked towards the door, he stopped and turned.

'But yes, the white man you killed. You performed a great deed for us. And for that, we are thankful.'

Saying this, he went away, closing the door behind him. I looked around the empty courtyard. I thought about this young man who was the nephew of my blood brother Akbar, and the weight he seemed to carry. Then, I lay down on the cot. Looking at the sky above me, I fell asleep.

[End of Part Two]

~

I finished reading the entry and closed my notebook. I sat in thought for some time.

At that moment, Jami and Nira walked back into the reading room of the library. The watchman Abdullah was still nowhere to be seen. Probably sleeping off the ill-gotten quarter of rum. At the arrival of my two lovelorn friends, I realized I had lost track of how much time had passed. It was time to head back to the hostel.

'You know, guys,' I said as I quickly packed up my stuff, 'there are some very interesting descriptions in this journal. I understand now why the fakir, this Ba'azuddin fellow, might have wanted to conceal his identity while he was at Haider Kalan.'

'Yes,' said Jami carefully, as we descended the steps and headed back to Nira's parked car. Nira was also listening to me.

'I just read two pieces in the journal. It looks like

some answers about the treasure and Haider Kalan and Ba'azuddin Bungalee would be revealed by the time I am done reading what I have.' We got into the car and Nira started the engine. Her driver seemed to have disappeared for the evening.

'The driver's duty hours were over. So I sent him away,' she explained.

I realized that it was indeed quite late. I continued, 'This could be very exciting.'

I gave a quick summary of what I had discovered so far.

'Hmm,' grunted Jami from the front passenger seat, looking straight ahead. He seemed to be thinking hard about something.

'The rest of the entries might tell us more,' I said. 'I will decipher them through the night.'

Jami nodded absent-mindedly.

As we reached the hostel, I wondered what he was in such deep thought about. I noticed Nira, too, was engrossed in her own thoughts.

When we got out of the car, Nira stepped out as well and locked the car.

Wonderful. That is why. She is shacking up here tonight.

Where the hell would I sleep, I wondered. Not that I had plans for much sleep, anyway. I wanted to finish deciphering the journal. And from the look of things, with Jami and Nira walking hand in hand up the stairs of the hostel, they did not plan to do much sleeping tonight, either.

Fine. I will go to the TV room. Good, quiet place to work. You twats romance away. I will find out more about this intriguing treasure of ours.

19

The Men of the Ninth Company

I stationed myself in the deserted TV room. I idly thought of the times when men like Ba'az would have lived, and how those times would have been so different from ours. I wondered how life on earth might be a hundred years from now. Would people look back at our accounts and have the same sense of wonder about us, as I had about men like Ba'azuddin who rode as part of the Bengal Lancers?

I opened my notebook and started from where I had left off. The next entry had been written a few days after the previous one.

Haider Kalan
14 January 1868

Part Three
The Men of the Ninth Company

I lay restless, staring at the sky, listening to the sounds of the morning. I heard a door open. It was a young woman carrying something on a plate. Perhaps a glass of water. She saw me and gave a start. She did not expect to find me here. She covered her head and face and hurried away. My eyes followed her and I saw her disappear into a room in the far corner of the courtyard.

I looked up again at the sky and continued thinking. Some sunny thoughts, some dark.

I must have dozed off. I woke to find Alauddin shaking me out of my sleep. By the look of the sky, perhaps an hour or so had passed.

Alauddin simply said, 'Come.'

He walked ahead. I hobbled behind, my stiff thigh loosening a little with the heat from the sun. Soon, I caught up with him and walked by his side. He was slender and slightly shorter than me. But the stoop I carried to make myself Lalan the fakir or pir made me equal to his height.

He stopped in front of the ruins of the mosque. The tree stood in the foreground. A light breeze made its branches creak. Alauddin began speaking.

'That man you brought to us today, Ba'azuddin – he was not of Haider Kalan. The three others you speak of – Akbar, Abdullah and Iqbal – were his friends and were from our village. The four were part of a new force that had been created by the English captain Hodson when the rising of 1857 began. No one knew what they did for him. Shady jobs, skulduggery and guile, they used to tell the others, and laugh. All that the others knew was that they had an important role to play for Hodson in the fall of Delhi.'

'The others?' I asked.

'The rest of the men of the village were soldiers as well. We have sent soldiers to fight battles for kings and emperors ever since we can remember. We also fought for the Company. Loyalty runs in our blood. We honour the code of the salt. There was never a question about the loyalty of the men of Haider Kalan. At the time when the fire of rebellion erupted in Meerut, our men were enlisted in the Third Cavalry, the same regiment that led the foray into Delhi for the rebels. But our men, of the Ninth Company, did they side with the rebellious traitors? No, they did not. They rallied, left the main column, took the road to Lucknow and reported straight to the commander there. The commander did not know what to do with them. Our men pledged loyalty, but were part of the infamous Third. The commander in Lucknow disarmed them, put them on furlough and sent them back here.

'Our fathers and uncles, they sat out of all the fighting. We heard news that Delhi had been taken. We heard of the emperor holding his durbar. We heard of the English rallying. We got news of the siege of Delhi. And then we heard of its fall. All this was from Akbar, Abdullah and Iqbal, who came and went like ghosts, running sorties for Captain Hodson. They talked of the happenings in Delhi. And they talked of happenings in Agra. One night, the three rode in and met with my grandfather right here.'

'That would be Rahat Ahmed Ali Khan, whom Ba'azuddin spoke to me of, before he died,' I interrupted. I knew all about what had happened that night, but I wanted to hear it from this young man.

Alauddin gave me an absent-minded look and nodded. He continued, 'This place would have been a grand mosque for the village. It was being built at that time. Nearly finished. Father was not around then, for that meeting. He was away for long periods, for months on end, selling our produce in the markets of Delhi. I was a boy then. Perhaps seven or eight. I had been playing a little away from the mosque that evening. I remember seeing Uncle Akbar and two others of our village – Iqbal and Abdullah – arrive on their horses. While I was leaving, I saw another rider come in and join them. Little did I know that with his arrival, he would be bringing doom to our village.'

I remembered a boy running around, playing near

the mosque the night the four of us met here. I felt a strange bitterness and regret at hearing the hatred in this young man's voice. There was very little I could do about it now. So I listened quietly.

'The next morning, the man was gone and everything went on as usual. We heard a few days later that Hodson had captured the emperor. Soon after, Hodson also captured the two sons and the grandson of the emperor and executed them in public view. We heard all this with little grief, joy or even interest. We were passive spectators in the whole affair. Rebellions would come and go. Rulers would come and go, and sooner or later, we would find new service in the side of someone who needed fighting men. The blood of the men of Haider Kalan would soak the earth of this land many more times.' Alauddin paused. His voice quivered a little. 'Little did we know how wrong we were.' He stopped, gathered himself and continued, 'It was night, at a time when the rains had gone and winter was soon to come, when the English came. There were many of them. A whole squadron of cavalry, and about a hundred foot. The foot were dressed differently from the sepoys of the Company. For one, they were all white men. And their uniforms were a different shade of red. The horsemen were our people, but a fierce-looking lot and dressed in khaki, the colour of dust.'

That would be our scouts. Hodson's scouts, I thought to myself.

'Leading the horsemen were three white officers. Two of them in red coats and one in the same khaki as the other men.'

Majors Morstan and Sholto, and my dear friend Small. What Small had said the other night seemed mostly true, I thought to myself as Alauddin continued.

'They surrounded the village and started rounding up all the men. The men were brought here, to this very spot. Some of us, who dared, stood close in the shadows, watching, curious and terrified. Before long, they picked out Akbar and Abdullah and lined them up. They kept on looking, as if for someone else. I saw Iqbal hiding in the throng of men, trying to make himself inconspicuous. The soldiers brought man after man in front of the white man in khaki and he kept making them stand aside. From afar I saw my grandfather stepping forward to talk to the officers. He seemed to be asking them what was going on. Before the two officers on horseback who were overseeing the whole affair could answer, the other officer – the one in khaki – pulled out his sidearm and shot my grandfather squarely between the eyes.' Alauddin stopped at this point and looked at me. He jabbed his finger at a point on his forehead and said through clenched teeth, 'Here.'

'Grandfather fell to the ground like a mighty tree. My grandfather, leader of our people, was the rissaldar of the Ninth Company. They rewarded his loyalty with hot lead in his head. I heard a gasp of shock from our men gathered there. Then, with a roar in unison, they fell upon their captors. With their bare hands, they clawed and bit at whoever was in front of them. I saw the surrounding foot soldiers retreat a few paces, cocking their muskets, ready to open fire. One of the commanding officers raised a hand and, controlling his rearing, bucking horse, shouted out a hoarse command. I saw the standing infantrymen hesitate. Then they reversed their muskets and charged our men, who were clawing away at our enemies. I heard the thud of musket butt over bone, a rattle of thuds, beating like marching drums, as the infantrymen went through our people. It was like a threshing scythe cutting through grass. I had heard stories of bayonet charges. This was more terrifying. In a few moments, there were a pile of writhing, broken bodies.'

Was that infantry troop the Irish guard, I wondered. I had heard of such riot charges when they took on unarmed crowds. I remember hearing news of them landing in Bombay and making their way to relieve Delhi after it had been taken again. Why were they here, I asked myself. What were they doing with Hodson's scouts?

My train of thought was interrupted by Alauddin continuing his story.

'As the groans died down, I heard a horse galloping away into the night. Nearer to the centre of the action, two of the scout cavalry lay at the bottom of the tree, dead. The white man in khaki fired into the darkness after the retreating horse. He said something to another prone man, who was clutching his bleeding side. Hearing his reply, the white man turned to the officers on horseback and said something. I heard Iqbal's name. Soon, I saw a column of maybe seven or eight horsemen take off in hot pursuit in the direction of the fleeing horseman. I think it must have been Iqbal, because we did not find his body with the rest.'

So Iqbal escaped. I knew that not even the devil could catch him if he was fleeing on a horse. I felt a ray of hope. Alauddin continued his story.

'The white officer in khaki began questioning Akbar and Abdullah. They kept shaking their heads and mumbling something in response. He kept asking them the same question. The only word I heard was "loot". He turned to the officers on horseback, who were watching intently, and talked to them. They shook their heads. That seemed to make him angry. He spat and stamped on the ground. One of the officers on the horse – the same man who had given the command for the charge – said something sharply, and the white man in khaki cringed as if he had been whipped.' At this point, Alauddin turned to me.

'The white man who was interrogating Ba'azuddin when you found him – he was asking something about loot, was he not?' he asked. I nodded. I was preoccupied, filled with revulsion, imagining what happened that night. What Alauddin said after that turned my revulsion into horror.

'They then rounded up the rest of the village, including women and children. We all watched. The officers on horseback started barking out commands to their men. A few went back there, to our houses,' said Alauddin, pointing with his head at the village behind us. 'I heard sounds of doors being broken down and houses being ransacked. The cavalrymen in khaki dismounted, and carrying picks, went into the mosque. I heard sounds of walls being taken down. The white man in khaki asked Akbar the same question, before questioning Abdullah again. They gave the same answer, weeping. I heard the name of Ba'azuddin mentioned.'

That would have been them telling Small it was only fifty mohurs, and that I had left with the money.

'The white man in khaki selected one of the men from the writhing, groaning pile of broken bodies. It was Salma's father,' said Abdullah.

'Salma?' I asked.

Abdullah did not answer. 'They put a rope around his neck and hoisted him on a horse, and then tied the rope on the branch there.' Abdullah pointed to a branch over our heads. 'The white man in khaki asked Akbar and Abdullah the same question again about the loot. They pleaded and shook their heads. The white man in khaki cropped the horse carrying Salma's father and it ran forward, causing Salma's father to dangle from the tree. His legs flailed. He spasmed and then became still. They left him hanging there. The white man in khaki asked the same question again and again, and with every answer, another man of the Ninth Company was hanged. And after that every man in the village. Some were unconscious when they were hoisted. They went quietly. The rest shouted and screamed. But hang they all did. First one by one. Then in twos, and then in threes. With every question came the same answer from Akbar and Abdullah, and with every answer came a flick of the riding crop, and the men danced at the end of the ropes.' Alauddin looked vacantly at the tree as a gust of wind rustled through the leaves. I saw ghosts in his eyes. I saw ghosts with my eyes. My heart wanted to wail and scream.

'By the time they were finishing up, the mosque had been brought down. Some of the men came from the rubble and reported to the officers on horseback. It seemed they did not find what they were looking for. The last man of the village had been strung up by then and the white man in khaki turned to the other officers. He pointed to the rest of us standing and watching, some weeping, some sobbing, some transfixed. The white man in khaki pointed to Akbar and Abdullah, and then to us, and then to us again, arguing with the officers, who looked angry and spoke some curt words, shaking their heads. I understood that the white man in khaki wanted to hang us all, children and women, but the officers did not agree.'

Thank god for small mercies, I thought, bile rising in my mouth. At least they spared the non-combatants. And left them in their misery.

'The two officers gave a command and the cavalry troop mounted. The redcoated infantrymen, too, lined up. The white man in khaki cursed, spat again, drew his sidearm, and then shot Akbar and Abdullah. The same way he had shot my grandfather. One of the officers on horseback gave a hoarse cry of anger and surprise. The white man in khaki did not reply and mounted his horse. A command rang out. The horsemen wheeled around and in a cloud of dust, at the break of dawn, the soldiers left.'

Alauddin fell silent. I did not know what to say. I thought I must say something but could not think. My mind was numb. Silence felt more appropriate.

'Come with me. You must meet the men of the Ninth Company. We buried them here,' said Alauddin and turned around. I followed him. He made a detour around the rubble of the mosque and I saw in the distance the unmistakable litter of headstones in a graveyard. Far among the headstones, I could see two forms. As we walked, I realized that the two boys who had met me at the edge of the village were standing among the stones. As we walked, Alauddin talked.

'Father was the only grown man to survive the massacre of that night. He arrived on horseback the next day in the afternoon. He had gone to Delhi. There was a matter of the sugarcane crop that needed attending to. He found us – women and children – sitting around, stunned with the happenings of the night before. He heard what had happened. He walked around among the dead. He had become ghostlike. A deep anguish hung like a cloud around him, but he did not say anything. He just shook his head and I heard him whisper to himself, "This was not to be, this was not to be."

He sent the women away to wail the song of the dead. He gathered the boys and children. While we scavenged around for picks and shovels, the skies began to fill with vultures. We fought them for the remains of the dead. We were children, digging graves through the next three days, fighting the scavengers trying to feed on the flesh of our fathers and uncles and brothers. Father worked away as if possessed, not speaking a word, only directing the burial. When we were finished and the last grave had been filled, the vultures began to leave. It was dusk that day when father told the boys of the village what he had learnt. The truth about the man Ba'azuddin.'

We were approaching the graves. I asked, 'And that was . . .?'

'Father spoke of what he had heard in the deserted bazaars of Delhi. After the emperor had been captured, he spoke of how a ransom had been brokered between

Hodson and the princes. They would give away the entire hoard they held with them, and themselves as well, in exchange for the emperor.'

A tingle went up my spine. No one was supposed to know of this. Only a handful of men. Small, Hodson, I and a few more. How could the bazaars of Delhi be talking about this? I did not say anything though and asked instead, 'The entire hoard?'

'Six chests full of gold was what father had heard. He said Ba'azuddin was part of the squad that Hodson sent to receive the gold. Matters did not go as planned. Ba'azuddin killed everyone else in his squad and disappeared with the loot. Father learnt that Hodson sent trackers and Ba'azuddin was traced to Haider Kalan, where he was said to have friends. Father said that the moment he heard of our village being named, he rode back.'

I continued to listen, my mind working hard to consider the possibilities. All this explained what Small had said. I shivered and my hands became cold.

'Father heard from me about the rider who met Akbar, Abdullah and Iqbal, and grandfather. I saw him shake in anger. He cursed Ba'azuddin. It was he who had brought ruin to our village, he said. He howled aloud, calling out Ba'azuddin by name, among all of us gathered that day. This is what he said. I remember every word of it.'

We reached the spot where the two boys were

standing over a corpse that was supposed to be mine. Except that I saw the shroud had come off.

'You will die friendless. You will die of violence. Like the men you condemned to death. Carrion will eat away your flesh. When the time of judgement comes and you rise, you will wander about blind and crippled. Till then, you will lie in an unmarked grave, unremembered by all.'

Alauddin's words rang in my ears. They had unwrapped Small. I feared my lies were about to be discovered. I was a dead man, but for nothing I had done. A chill caught me and turned me into stone. I was weaponless. My time had come. What a terrible way to go, I thought, as I waited for a blow, or a blade.

Nothing happened.

'Most of it is has come true,' Alauddin continued speaking. 'Ba'azuddin did die friendless, tortured to death by the white man you found. And fate has a way of paying one back.'

I looked at the corpse in front of me more carefully this time. It was already mutilated by the time I had brought it here, but something had picked away at the flesh since then. The eyes were gone. There were scabs of rotting flesh hanging in shreds where once there was white skin. What was in front of me looked more like a carcass from the slaughterhouses of Idgah. I heard Alauddin say, 'The vultures never left Haider Kalan. I now know why. They have been working on him since morning.'

I doubled over and emptied my stomach on a stone. Except that nothing came out. Relief washed over me, as bile trickled out of my dry throat. Relief and hunger. I could not remember when I had eaten last.

I must have passed out. When I came to, they were sprinkling water on my face. I saw that my head was cradled in Alauddin's lap and one of the boys was trying to make me drink from a small earthen pot. As the water washed down my throat, my stomach spasmed again, and I doubled over in pain.

'Baba, when did you eat last?' Alauddin asked gently. Not hearing anything from me, he helped me to my feet. I saw that the corpse was still there. A cloth covered it now.

As they draped my arms over their shoulders and helped me walk back towards the village, Alauddin said, 'Forgive me, baba. I know you are a man of peace, but I had to be sure. I had my fears that you are a soldier, perhaps working for the white men. The shoulders under your rags could have taken a musket recoil. Your arms could have wielded a sword and you could have killed people. But now I know you are not used to seeing the dead.'

I did not say anything. I just thanked my stars. I was too weak to think.

'Your horse. The one you carried Ba'azuddin on. It must have bolted when the vultures came. I have sent two herd riders after it. These two boys tell me it was a fine horse,' said Alauddin casually, as we arrived back at the house.

'It was not my horse. It was his,' I answered after a moment.

Alauddin gave a satisfied nod. 'Good. It will be mine now. Come, let us eat.'

[End of Part Three]

20

Sons and Fathers

Haider Kalan
19 January 1868

Part Four
Sons and Fathers

We sat in the courtyard of the house, eating. The sun was shining, warming the chilly air. After we came back from the graveyard, I found the cot missing from the courtyard and two mats spread out in its place. We sat down. The same woman I had seen in the morning, still heavily draped and face covered, came and laid two large brass plates in front of us. It was a simple fare. Chapattis, pickle and curd. Alauddin asked her to leave.

I ate slowly, chewing every morsel. I imagined that my stomach must have shrunk due to not eating for a day. If I ate too much food now, as my instinct was telling me, I would only throw up all of it. Then a thought crossed my mind. The simple act of eating in the house of this man Alauddin was a matter of import. The obligation of his having broken bread with me, and the duties of protection that come with it, are important. I now knew that no harm would fall on me. For the first time since I arrived here this morning, I felt safe.

As we ate, Alauddin continued the story from where he had left off.

'About a week ago, a white man came here. I recognized him. It was the same man who was dressed in khaki that night eleven years ago. He looked older and more haggard than what eleven years would do to a man. He had a missing leg. I was sure it was the same man. His face was imprinted in my eight-year-old mind. It is not something I could forget. After he arrived, he asked a few people and came here straight to visit father. What I found strange was that he sought out my father, Rafiquddin Ahmed Ali Khan, by name.'

So that is the name, I thought to myself. Strange. It sounded familiar, but I could not recall why. It rang a bell, but a very faint one. How did Small know of him if Rafiquddin was not present during the night of the hangings? And if he was Akbar's brother, why had Akbar never mentioned his name?

'I do not know what transpired between them,' Alauddin continued, 'but when he stepped out of the door an hour later, we were waiting for the white man. I had gathered everyone, old boys and young men. We, who had watched doom befall our village, had no intentions of letting that man leave alive.' Alauddin stuffed a piece of chapatti into his mouth, chewed and then swallowed it.

'It was an even match. Sticks and stones with about thirty of us and one revolver in the white man's hands. It was a standoff waiting to turn into a bloodbath on the street, when father appeared. He made us stand down.' Alauddin had some water from a brass tumbler and wiped his mouth with his sleeve.

'I have never seen my father like that. After the night of the hangings, he had turned into a shadow of his former self. But that day, he seemed pale, fragile and weak. The white man must have said something to him inside. Father seemed meek and subservient. It made my blood boil. But a father's command is a father's command. And he was the eldest man in the village. We let the white man go.'

We had finished eating. The woman appeared again and gathered the plates. Alauddin got up. I stood up as well.

'An hour after the white man left, father's heart gave way. He has been in bed since that day. He lies dying now, in the next room. He would not have lasted the evening had it not been for Salma.' He looked at the woman walking away, and then at me.

'You asked who Salma was. That is her. We got married last month. She has been keeping father alive, tending to him.'

When I had asked about Salma and he had not answered, I assumed he had not heard me. I now knew there was very little he missed. I warned myself to be more careful. I should not be lulled into a false sense of security. This was Akbar's nephew, after all – Akbar, the sharp and wily man whose wise words had saved me from a bullet in the back more than once.

'I have two things to ask of you,' Alauddin said. 'That man you brought to us, whose rotting corpse lies in the graveyard, bury him for us. No one here will touch him.'

'I will surely do so,' I said. 'What is the other thing?'

'You are a holy man, you said.'

'As holy as any of us,' I said, for the second time this morning.

'Holy enough. You were with a dying man three days ago. Comfort another now. Spend some time with father. It will give him peace as he passes.'

I nodded, thought for a moment and then said, 'That I can do. There are a few things bothering me. May I?'

'Without hesitation,' said Alauddin.

'That man you all hate and whom you refuse to bury – Ba'azuddin. Your hate may be misplaced. If he indeed was behind the disappearance of the gold, why would he want to return? And what of the letters he spoke of? If he was innocent, his innocence may lie in the letters.'

'We will come to the letters. Shall we tend to father first?' asked Alauddin.

'There is another thing bothering me,' I said with some hesitation.

'What is it?' Alauddin asked.

'See, I was in Delhi soon after it was retaken by the English. I was there when the emperor was captured . . .' I stopped, uncertain whether I should press on. But I had a burning urge to clear my name.

'I heard nothing about a ransom or an exchange, or of six chests of gold.'

Alauddin stiffened. I threw caution to the winds and continued, 'And the white man, the only man I ever killed, he was a monster. You know that. How did he know of your father by name and why did he visit him?'

There was a deathly silence. Alauddin regarded me with cold, troubled eyes. I met his gaze.

'Lalan baba, I do not know if you are holy or not. But I do know now that you are not a spy for the white men, seeking the hidden treasure. If you were, you would not be asking these questions. I do not have answers to your questions. All I know is what happened that night when everyone was murdered. And I also know that my father now lies dying, much before his time. Will you come and bless him or will you not?' Saying this, he turned and took slow, measured steps towards the far end of the courtyard.

I followed him.

~

It was a dank, musty room that we walked into. There was the familiar smell of sickness, death and disease in the air. The same smell is common to both the aftermath of a battle, as well as peaceful demise in bed. Salma was fanning the prone form that lay on the bed. There was not much else in the room, except a large wooden chest in the corner and a few utensils on a low stool near the bed, probably implements for caring. When death arrived, there would be very little to take away from here, besides the one who would be going.

When we entered, Salma covered her head again. Alauddin must have signalled to her, because Salma gathered herself and left, shutting the door gently after her.

The room plunged into even more gloom, with the one major source of light cut off. The small window at the far end of the room, above where the chest lay, cast only a pale glow of daylight. That light seemed to avoid all else and fall on the face of the man on the bed.

For some reason that I could not put a finger on, his face looked vaguely familiar. I felt I had seen him before, under different circumstances. I had never met him, but I had seen him. Alauddin knelt beside his father and shook him by the shoulders.

Rafiquddin began to wake from a restless sleep, muttering incoherently under his breath. I came closer and sat down where Alauddin knelt, my face not far from Rafiquddin's. I saw that he was not very old. Somewhere in his forties. But by the sickly pallor, it was clear he was not too far from his end. Rafiquddin's closed eyelids squinted and contorted restlessly as he mumbled something between sleep and wakefulness. Once I got used to his tone, his words became more coherent. He was speaking as if in great distress.

'The gora sahib came again . . . he knows . . . it was me! It was me! The Great Moghul – they are after the Great Moghul.'

I looked at Alauddin sharply. He was also listening intently, a disturbed look on his face. Rafiquddin kept muttering as we listened.

'Thirty pieces . . . thirty pieces! Blood money . . . I sold us all for thirty pieces.' Saying this, Rafiquddin began to weep in his semiconscious state.

Alauddin was still trying to wake up his father, but to no avail. With every shake, Rafiquddin would speak louder. 'The one-eyed man. The one-eyed man . . . the one-eyed man promised. Forgive me, Abba! Forgive me! Abba! Abba!'

Alauddin shook his father harder this time, matching the cries of the half-awake man with his own.

'Abba! Abba! Wake up!' he said. The man's eyes opened and gazed into mine. As I looked into his eyes, I began to remember where I had seen him. The man cringed in fear, retreating to the end of the bed farthest from us. He gave me a look of sheer terror and said, 'No Small sahib! No! I have not found anything! There is nothing here! No one has come!'

For a moment I feared he knew me, but then I realized he was hallucinating. 'I told the one-eyed man what I knew! I told him all I knew! Don't kill us!'

'Abba!' said Alauddin, almost shouting.

Rafiquddin's gaze turned to Alauddin and contemplated him, blinking and confused.

'The white man is dead, Abba,' said Alauddin.

Rafiquddin stared blankly at Alauddin and then broke into a grin, eyes totally vacant. 'Dead?' he asked.

'Yes, Abba,' said Alauddin. 'You can be at peace. He had caught up with the scoundrel Ba'azuddin. He too is gone. Killed.'

'Scoundrel? Ba'azuddin dead?' asked Rafiquddin blankly, raising himself on an elbow.

'Yes, Abba. Ba'azuddin. The man who betrayed us. He is dead.'

Rafiquddin broke into a cackle. Laughing, he tossed his head from side to side, shaking it as he spoke.

'Ba'azuddin dead. Small dead. Traitor dead.' His shrill laughter set me on edge. 'Now we can spend it all! Now we can spend it all!' Rafiquddin exclaimed as he pointed to the wooden chest.

'Thirty pieces! Thirty pieces. It was me! It was me! I sold us for thirty pieces!' he said in a hoarse whisper, looking at the window, his finger still pointed at the chest. He then stopped abruptly, nearly rose and grabbed Alauddin by the scruff of his neck. The exertion seemed to be too much for him and he fell back on the bed, dragging Alauddin with him.

With a whisper I could barely hear, Rafiquddin said to Alauddin, 'Forgive me, Abba. Forgive me.' A tear trickled down his cheek.

Alauddin extricated himself from his father's grasp and gently laid a hand on his forehead. 'It is I, Abba. Alauddin.'

'Yes, Abba. Alauddin will do it. He will rebuild the mosque you started. Thirty pieces . . . thirty pieces . . .' he mumbled, eyelids drooping.

Alauddin looked at me, confusion and agony writ clearly on his face. I was expected to do something. I stepped forward and laid a hand on the man's forehead. I began to mumble some incoherent words, as if in prayer. I think it was a lullaby I was repeating. It is not important, and I do not remember what it was. My mind was working on the partially coherent words Rafiquddin had spoken. Alauddin whispered into his father's ear.

'Abba, this is a great pir who has come to bless you.'

'Pir?' Rafiquddin asked weakly, eyes closed. I continued my chanting. It seemed to soothe the man and he asked in a whisper, 'Will I be forgiven?' Between my verses, I said softly, 'If god wills,' hiding some of the disgust I felt. Rafiquddin listened to my chant and after a while his eyes opened. Looking steadily at Alauddin, he commanded in a lucid voice, all signs of weakness and madness gone. 'Thirty pieces of Company gold. In my chest. Rebuild the mosque. For my father, not yours.' Alauddin nodded, uncertain. Rafiquddin closed his eyes again and lapsed into uneven breathing. Each breath was shallower than the last. I stopped my performance and looked at Alauddin. I rose and said, 'I will leave you alone with him. It will not be much longer. I will be outside.'

Saying this, I opened the door and went out into the sunlight, away from the smell of death, treachery and remorse.

~

A few minutes later, Alauddin emerged from the room. The drawn, stricken look on his face confirmed there would be two burials in Haider Kalan that day.

He walked slowly and sat down beside me, on the cot that had reappeared in the courtyard. He was silent for a while.

'It seemed that Ba'azuddin did not betray this village after all,' I said.

'It means nothing,' said Alauddin.

'It seems it was your father who . . .'

'It means nothing,' said Alauddin, his voice sharper as he glared at me. There was an unfathomable grief in his demeanour, one that comes from a world being shattered. There was also fear in his eyes.

I shrugged and said, 'What is said on the deathbed is not repeated anywhere else. Even if it is a confession. No one shall know.'

'There was no confession. I only heard father rambling in his sleep during his last moments,' said Alauddin, with an edge in his voice.

I did not say anything. I just looked away and after a while casually said, 'But now at least you have some money to rebuild your mosque.'

Alauddin did not respond for a while. Then he stood up and said, 'There is one way to know if Ba'azuddin was as innocent as you think he was. Perhaps you can shed light on this.' Saying this, he briskly walked back and disappeared into his father's room. When he returned, he was carrying a thick sheaf of papers.

'Ba'azuddin asked about the letters he sent. And why no one had acted on them. Here they are,' he said, thrusting the papers in my hands.

'A few months after the night of the hangings, these letters, addressed to my uncle, began to come in by means of a runner. The last of these came a year ago. With no one else left to take them, they came to father. You tell me that Ba'azuddin sent them. Until you came here and spoke of them, we did not know where they had come from.'

'Why not?' I asked, but I knew the answer.

'They are written in a language no one can read. Father and I took the papers all the way to the scholars of Aligarh. They told us that it was in some obscure form of Farsi. But no one could read them.'

Of course they could not read them, I thought, as I pretended to look through the pages that I had written with my own hand and sent from Calcutta. They would not understand our code.

'You seem like a learned man. Perhaps you can read the letters and tell us where the treasure is hidden,' said Alauddin, expectantly.

So he still thinks that the letters had something to do with that treasure. I looked at the letters and pretended to try to read them. I spent a few moments turning the pages over. Alauddin was looking at me with bated breath. Then I turned the pages upside down and pretended to try reading them again. I heard Alauddin exhale in disappointment. 'No. Nothing like I have encountered before. And besides, I cannot read Farsi,' I said, trying to look as stupid as I could.

Alauddin took the papers from my hands, almost snatching them.

'Then until these letters get read by someone, we know not whether Ba'azuddin was innocent,' he said.

I rose and said, 'So be it. But he still deserves a decent burial. You have your grave to dig. I will dig mine,' I said.

~

The sun was setting by the time I was done burying Small. The others had come bearing the body of Rafiquddin. They had conducted a ceremony and buried him with honour. I was left to my devices. I was asked to go to the farthest corner of the graveyard, and a little beyond, to bury Ba'azuddin whom no one cared for. The villagers would not allow him to be buried inside their graveyard. It was only because of Alauddin that they agreed, at all. The only company I had was the mangy black-and-white dog who was sitting on its haunches. After the last lot of mud had been filled back in, and I sat back to rest, the dog came and stood over the grave. He raised his head and gave out a long howl looking at the rising crescent moon of the evening. Then he raised a hind leg and watered the grave. Appropriate for that bastard Small, I thought to myself.

As night fell, I sat there thinking about the past few days, and the various pieces of the puzzle. After Small had captured me, there were two questions in my mind that had brought me back to Haider Kalan. One was the reason behind my sullied name here. I knew now what that was about. It was Rafiquddin who had informed Hodson's troops about my being in Haider Kalan. It was evident that he did not expect the retribution that was unleashed on the village. When he returned, he made up the story about me. I had a feeling that Alauddin too had realized the truth about it now.

The other question I had was a larger one and still remained unanswered.

I thought hard about where I had seen Rafiquddin before. I searched the crevasses of my mind, until I finally arrived at the answer. The one-eyed man!

Only Hodson, Small and I had known about the exchange of thirty thousand pieces of gold and the three princes. Everyone else who knew of it – the three princes themselves, their agents – were all dead. Everyone except the one-eyed man, Hodson's spymaster. It was the shadowy Rajab Ali who ran the spy ring that brought down the gates of Delhi. I remembered where I had seen Rafiquddin earlier. It was with the one-eyed beggar of Dariba, putting a scrap of paper into his bowl, while taking a coin from it. The beggar was one of the couriers who ran messages from the streets of Delhi. At that time, I did not know Rafiquddin was Akbar's brother. It is strange Akbar never mentioned him. Perhaps there had been bad blood between them in the past. I would never know.

Alert again, I thought of what to do next. It was like the old days again. My heart pounded with excitement. I would have to return to Delhi and look for the one-eyed beggar.

Would he still be alive?

There was only one way to find out.

[End of Part Four]

21

The Milky-eyed Beggar

Haider Kalan
5 February 1868

Part Five
The Milky-eyed Beggar

I watched from across the street. I had been watching him for hours now. He did nothing. Just sat like a dishevelled heap under the archway. He rattled his bowl every now and then, whenever he heard anyone approach. But besides that, he did little else. Only a soul or two had dropped a coin in his bowl during the time I had been watching him. I looked closely at those who fed his bowl, but they were ordinary passers-by. Nothing seemed to be happening here, unlike how it had been in 1857. After a while a boy working at a kebab stall a few yards away walked over to him and dropped a few chapattis in his bowl. I was suspicious, but then I saw him eat the chapattis, slowly and without hurry. And then he went back to rattling his bowl every time he heard an approaching step.

It had taken me four days of scouring the streets of Delhi and its surrounding villages to find the beggar here in Khizrabad. Delhi had transformed since I had been here last. Shahjahanabad was vastly different. I saw that entire quarters and districts had been razed to the ground. But the story of Delhi is for another day.

At dusk, he got up, picked up the stick that was leaning by him, gathered his belongings and started walking away. He tapped his stick in front of him, walking like a consummate blind man. I marvelled at his skills. If I did not know better, I would have believed he was blind.

I followed him, careful to leave a dozen or so yards between us. Soon enough, he turned into an alley. I went after him, holding my naked dagger – Small's dagger – under the heavy blanket that covered me. Unless I was mistaken, it would be in this alley that I would be ambushed. This was how they operated. But I was ready.

I turned the corner into the alley, and nothing happened. I only saw him tapping his stick on the ground ahead of me. There was no one else. Night had fallen and I hurried after him. He heard me and began to turn. It would have to be now, I thought. I closed the distance and picked up speed, running at him in a crouching stance, waiting for the attack.

What happened next threw me off. He dropped his sack and stick, fell on the ground and cringed, backing away into a closed doorway, arms raised in protection. I stood over him, uncertain, as he babbled in a whining, wheedling tone, 'I have nothing, sahib. I made nothing today.' As I stood over him in the darkness, saying nothing, he groped for his satchel and drew out a few coins, holding them up to me. In the darkness that my eyes were getting used to, I looked at his face. Two empty white eyeballs stared back at me, unseeing.

He was not pretending to be blind. He *was* blind.

Surprised, I took a step forward to make sure. He heard me tread and let out a howl, flung the coins towards me and curled up cringing. My nose caught a familiar whiff, one I had smelt many times while fighting. It was the smell a man gives out when he is in mortal fear, or mortally wounded. He had soiled himself.

Disgusted, I caught him by his shirt and lifted him. He howled again. I was surprised to feel the bird-like bones under his shirt and how light he was as I dragged him away. I was confused. But I had to take him some place I could ask him questions without being interrupted.

Soon I reached the end of the alley. It was also the edge of the hamlet. The buildings opened up to a rivulet running in the distance. The path ahead of us led to the rivulet, one of the many feeding the Yamuna. A narrow bridge, an archway of bricks wide enough for only one horse, spanned the rivulet. I dragged him along as his teeth chattered in fear. It would have to be here, I thought. As I reached the bridge, I felt him go limp. A dead weight in my hands.

~

I slapped him awake.

He moaned and raised his hands to protect his face.

'I have nothing,' he moaned feebly.

I gave him a resounding cuff behind his ears.

'You have answers to my questions, Rajab Ali sahib.'

Hearing me, he stopped cringing and cowering. He sat up slowly and leaned against the archway of the bridge where I had laid him. His blind eyes looked at me. His demeanour seemed different. With a slight trace of pride in his voice, he said, 'No one has called me that in a long time.' I waited a moment. He asked, 'Who are you and what questions do you have?'

'Who I am is not important. I want to know about Haider Kalan.'

The blind man was startled. He spoke after a moment.

'I think I know who you are. You must be the scribe. The boy.' This man was a genius!

'Not any more,' I said.

The blind man seemed lost in thought. 'We lost you at Chittagong,' he said, remembering. 'There was another one of you. They reported that he escaped. The big fellow who could not keep his hands off a woman. What was his name?'

'Iqbal,' I said.

'Yes, yes. We lost him in Lahore. But I knew he did not have it. You did, did you not?' he asked.

'What?' I replied.

He did not say anything. I shook him hard and said, getting angry, 'No more games, spymaster. I killed Small and I will kill you as well.'

The blind man asked in a hoarse whisper, 'You killed Small? When? How?'

I told him. Rajab Ali heaved a sigh.

'I will answer all the questions you have. Ask.'

I began.

'Why did the men come to Haider Kalan and kill everyone? It was me you were after. I had left the place.'

'A few nights before,' said the blind man, looking at my face with milky eyes.

He must have sensed my surprise, because he gave a hollow laugh.

'You forget, scribe. It was my business, once upon a time, to know everything.'

As I stayed silent, he spoke again. 'You think Hodson

sent a squadron of his horse, and a company of Irish foot, two ranking majors, and Small for *you*?' He spat out the words in contempt.

'How did they explain it then – the missing ransom I had with me?' I asked.

The blind man continued laughing.

'Ransom? Ransom? Fool. It was not a ransom. It was a contract. Bounty,' he said. 'It was all her doing. The she-wolf – Zeenat Mahal.'

'The empress?' I asked.

'She wanted her own son to succeed the throne. The three princes, Mirza Mughal especially, needed to be out of the way. She and I set the whole thing up. The princes thought they were ransoming the life of their father. The bitch thought she was putting her own son on the throne. There was still some illusion in the minds of women and men that the Mughal line would be reinstated in Delhi after the rebellion was quelled. It was my finest work,' he said, with a faraway look in his sightless eyes and a slight smile of pride on his lips. 'Hodson was the last piece in the plan. He was to shoot the princes on some pretext or the other after the gold had been received. The two of us were to split the loot equally. I knew Hodson needed money. I knew I could count on his need. But I was foolish. I did not estimate his greed. And his deviousness.'

I nodded. Some things were slowly falling in place.

'But I don't understand. Why Haider Kalan?' I asked.

'The two of your friends that were killed that night – what were their names?' he asked.

'Akbar and Abdullah,' I said, my jaw tightening.

'They brought a box back with them from Agra, didn't they?' he asked. 'A small carved wooden casket?'

'Yes. But it was empty,' I said, remembering that misadventure of theirs.

The blind man nodded. I thought I saw him beaming in the darkness. 'What happened to the box?' he asked.

'I took it with me when I left. It was beautiful.'

'And after that?'

'I deposited the gold in Calcutta. And then I saw the lookout for me. So I went into hiding.'

'And what did you do with the box?'

'Why?' I asked.

Then he told me what the box meant. I started laughing. I sat down and held my sides as I laughed and told spymaster Rajab Ali about what happened to the box.

'Lost? What do you mean lost?' he asked with surprise and shock in his voice.

'As good as lost,' I said.

The blind man was silent for a while.

'I told you about Hodson's greed. When I told him what I knew of the box, he wanted it as well. That is why they sent the expedition to Haider Kalan. And someone had to be held responsible for the disappearance of the gold. It was convenient to put it on you. It was all falling in place perfectly,' said the blind man.

'It did fall in place. You were blamed. We were partners and were to split the gold, but Hodson had other plans for me. I thought I was the master of cunning, but he was the lord of deceit,' the blind man said. 'When we couldn't find the box and we lost you, he moved with speed to protect his own name.'

'But why was everyone in Haider Kalan killed? Why?' I asked.

'That,' said Rajab Ali, 'that was Small's doing. Those were not the orders. The orders were only for the four of you. Small was the devil incarnate,' replied Rajab Ali.

I was completely at a loss for words.

With a vacant look on his face, and with great sadness in his voice, he spoke again. 'Hodson made sure all the loose ends were tied tightly. I ended up with my good eye, as well as bad one, skewered out. It was Small's doing, under the orders of Hodson. Small got played as well. He was framed for the disappearance of the gold. It was the Andamans for him. I found myself in the stockade of Kotla, herded among prisoners I had put there myself. I spent three years there. The Delhi I returned to had changed. There was no need for spymasters any more,' he said. 'And what use would they have for a blind man with claims of greatness?' he asked bitterly. 'I have been like this since then. Once the spymaster of Delhi, now a beggar in Khizrabad. And under this sky tonight, I will die, covered in my own shit.'

Rajab Ali sat up and then raised himself on his knees. He turned his back to me, bowed his head and said to me, 'I don't think you have any more questions. Now do me a favour, will you, scribe? Kill me.'

I looked quietly at the back of his neck. I contemplated his life, his blindness and his wretchedness. I turned and began to walk away. Behind me, I heard him first scream, then moan beseechingly and then sob two words.

'Kill me!'

~

The next morning, on the road to Haider Kalan, as I rode my donkey, I sang the only love song I had ever composed. Sung for the first time many years ago for my own true love in Udaipur, when I gifted the box to her.

A fistful of spades, that three young blades,
Gave for my many loves, numerous as the clubs.
A work of art, pieces of my heart.
For my one queen, hath she not seen,
Diamonds and rocks,
And this man as coal.
Jewel of my soul,
As nothing but a box.

What I thought then to be an empty box, a plaything for kings and emperors, was far more than that. A box that perhaps still lives a life of anonymity. As I sang, I realized how prophetic I had been when I had composed it.

22

The Treasure of Agra

Lucknow
7 May 1868

What Rajab Ali had told me a few months ago implicated the great Hodson in a deep conspiracy. This was a vile scheme in which I was but a cog. It was his plotting and scheming that had resulted in my becoming an outlaw and a fugitive. Two of my friends were dead and one was missing. Rajab Ali had said that Iqbal was last traced to Lahore. It would perhaps be wise of me to follow Iqbal's trail to find out what became of him. But before I did that, I had to visit Captain Hodson.

Numerous were his faults and flaws and he was the reason my fortune had changed. However, this was a man to whom I owed many debts. He tutored me in the ways of the sahibs, taking over from where Major Lassan had left off many years ago. This was the man who saw beyond colour of skin and trappings of race and bestowed upon me the responsibility of being his scribe. This was the officer who tuned my skills with sword, rifle and pistol, skills that saved my life more than once. This was the man who broke down the walls of Delhi with me and turned the tide of the rebellion. He died in battle the way he lived, a man of action. He died with a musket ball in his chest and blood on his lips in Lucknow. I had to take his leave before I went on my quest for Iqbal.

In the morning I went through the gates of La Martiniere in Lucknow and walked over to a secluded corner. There, on a decorated dais, was a pedestal on a grave and a slab of marble that read:

Here Lies
All That Could Die
of
WILLIAM STEPHEN RAIKES HODSON
Captain & Brevet Major
IV E.B. Fusiliers
and
Commandant of Hodson's Horse
Son of the Vcnt. George Hodson
Archdeacon of Stafford

Born
19 MARCH 1821
Fell
In the Final Assault at Lucknow
11 MARCH 1858
'a little while'
2 Corinthians 1:12

I stood at the grave and gave a salute to the man who lay beneath. I spoke to him in a low tone, one last time. 'You died well, captain sahib. And you died far from your home. Now I have to travel far and I take your leave.'

I wanted to say more, but then I thought myself a fool for wasting my time talking to a grave. In that moment of silence and dust, my thoughts went to the many layers, conspiracies and circumstances that had led me here.

~

It started with the assault on Delhi. Two days before that, the four of us trickled out with some others. We stole out from within the lines in ones and twos and went to the English entrenchment on the ridge. The captain, a brevetted major now, listened to our reports carefully. Then he read the letters from Rajab Ali which I was carrying.

'So you know the terrain around Cashmere Gate well?' he asked Akbar, Iqbal and Abdullah.

They nodded.

'This is good,' the captain said. 'Attach yourself to the sappers with the third column,' he ordered. 'Ba'az,' he said to me, 'go with them and cover them from a distance. Theirs is a task that can mean life or death for the assault that is coming.'

At dawn, our guns began their work on the walls of Delhi. After some time, in the lull between salvos, our column crept through the foxholes towards Cashmere Gate and waited. There were two fresh-faced sapper lieutenants leading us.

While one column charged at a section of wall south of the gate, the other made its way towards the Jumna Gate. Both columns were riddled with volleys from the walls and their ladders were smashed before they could find purchase. While they stormed and fell back in waves, our sappers with the third column did their work. The two lieutenants conducted the laying of gunpowder charge under the gates.

It was a terrifying time, with our column barely ten feet from the walls, death raining down all around us. Many sappers fell that afternoon, but the two lieutenants pressed on. Akbar, Iqbal and Abdullah stayed close and provided them cover, returning fire up the walls. I stayed behind and picked the men off the walls one by one, with my trusty Sharps rifle.

It was a beautiful American weapon that had come my way only a month before. Shot after shot flew with divine precision. I can say with certainty that dozens fell to my rifle that afternoon. The three sniping upwards from under their noses and I picking off the defenders from a distance gave the sappers the time they needed. I saw the first lieutenant – Home was his name, I think – run towards the charge to light the fuse. Before he could reach it, he fell. Then I saw the other lieutenant – I do not remember his name – follow suit. Both lay inches from the gunpowder charge, perhaps dead, perhaps alive. I saw the rest of the sappers cower under the hail of musketry. I heard the bugle calls from afar announcing it was time to withdraw. The other columns had been driven back and began the retreat.

Then I saw Akbar, Iqbal and Abdullah change the tide of battle that day. I saw them rally the column to return the fire up the walls. I did my part, picking off the rissaldars who waved orders from the top of the wall. The three made a glorious charge under the crossfire. It was the quick Akbar who leapt ahead and made for the fuse. The stronger brothers Abdullah and Iqbal snatched up the wounded lieutenants. I was three hundred yards away, watching them from the corner of my eye. I was more concerned about making sure no one had an aim on them from up the walls.

The gunpowder charge exploded with a huge blast and a part of the bastion wall fell with it. The gates flew open. There was smoke and dust everywhere. For a while I could see nothing. Then I heard the bugler sound the advance. From the haze of the settling dust, I saw the redcoats swarm in through the gates.

That day, 14 September 1857, the work of two brave English officers and three valiant men of Haider Kalan won back Delhi for the English. But it was how these men were treated after that changed everything for us.

~

'The two officers will be decorated well,' said Rajab Ali that day, looking at us with his one good eye. 'As for you, this is what we have.' He tossed a gold piece each at Akbar, Abdullah and Iqbal. The-one eyed man grinned as he said, 'It is just too bad. But you people do not exist, you see.'

I understood what he meant. Our troops were Hodson's left hand, doing things that could not be done by any self-respecting army consisting of officers and gentlemen. We did not exist on paper for a good reason. I saw why we would never be talked about or decorated. The others, however, did not see matters with such clarity.

After a bit of grumbling, Iqbal and Abdullah appeared reconciled to their fate. Abdullah went off to look for a skin of wine. Iqbal went off to look for a nubile young girl or boy – whatever he could find in the pillaged bazaars. Akbar, however, glowered at the ridge from our vantage atop the walls which we had captured that afternoon. He cursed the universe at large and threw his coin of gold far out into the smoking earth. 'This?' he barked. 'This is what we live for?' he asked in frustration and stalked off.

The next morning, they left for Haider Kalan. They had some well-earned furlough and decided to do their brooding among their own people.

Before they left, Akbar said to me, 'There is no honour in these men, Ba'az. They will use us as long as we serve their purpose and then cast us off.' He spat on the ground and they trotted off.

His words kept spinning in my mind while I went about my duties as a scribe to Hodson and Rajab Ali. It was by afternoon the next day, when I was sifting through some very interesting papers, that I made up my mind about what to do.

I made my arrangements. That evening, I found a fast horse and made my way to Haider Kalan. I would have to be back quickly. I was expected to be in the camp soon.

~

I reached the village in the late hours of the evening, long after the sun had set. That was the first day I rode into Haider Kalan and I knew not the lay of the land. I asked the first person I met – a strapping young lad – where the Ahmed Ali household was. When I reached there, I was told that Akbar, Abdullah and Iqbal were not there. The heavily veiled old woman I was talking to spoke in a coarse voice, 'Akbar will be in the new mosque, up to no good, with those louts he calls friends and that father of his.'

I trotted over to where she said the mosque was, wondering what sort of no-good activity they could possibly be up to. I found my answer as I approached the nearly finished mosque. While I was hitching my horse to a stump, I heard from within the hoarse laughter of men in a tone I was all too familiar with.

They was drinking. In a mosque, no less.

I was welcomed as if I was a long-lost brother, gone for years. A red-eyed Akbar introduced me to his venerable father. 'Father, this is Ba'az, a wolf of our own pack.' Abdullah poured a fiery dose of arrack into an earthen cup for me.

After some revelry and some more drinking, I told them why I was there.

'There was merit in what you said to me the other day,' I said to Akbar. 'The English will toss us aside when our use to them is over.'

'And what brings about this change of heart?' asked Akbar after a moment's pondering. 'I thought you were especially fond of them all.'

'You forget, I am scribe to both Rajab Ali and Hodson sahib,' I said. 'I can see papers that others cannot. And this is about something I have seen and read that might be of use to us.'

The others listened as I continued. 'For one, they intend to disband our unit in a few months. Our utility is over now that Delhi is back in the hands of the English.'

The old man spat on the ground at this and said to the other three, 'I told you this would happen.'

'But there is a way we can turn the tables and extract the reward they owe us, many times over. There is a treasure we can lay our hands on.'

The word 'treasure' caught their attention far more than the news of being disbanded. They all leaned forward.

'The English are low on money,' I said. 'There is a sort of quiet desperation for actual money that their plunder of Delhi cannot fulfil. Many months of back pay are due to the troops and money is also needed to buy fresh supplies and provisions for the months that lie ahead. They need to start taking back the other cities and towns that are in the hands of the rebels.'

The others nodded, as if understanding everything. I continued, 'The diwan of Agra has come to their aid, at a threat to his title, of course. I read the dispatches yesterday. There is apparently a large diamond – the size of a pigeon's egg – which he has pledged to the English, in exchange for protection.'

'Pah! That small? A pigeon's egg is not too large,' said Abdullah.

The old man responded, 'Foolish boy! You think you know diamonds?' He asked me to continue.

'A few months ago, this diamond was shipped to a far-off place in Europe to be weighed and valued. It is being brought back to Agra in a week, under heavy guard, after which it will be given over to the bankers at Marwar, in exchange for a line of credit for the English. It is at Agra that we can take it,' I said.

'How would that be possible?' asked Akbar. 'If it is under heavy guard, how will we even get to it?'

'That is where my scribing comes to aid, my friend,' I said to them. 'Tomorrow morning, the majors Sholto and Morstan reach Agra to be part of the contingent that is to receive the diamond and guard it for the next few weeks. I have taken the liberty of cancelling your furlough and putting the names of the three of you in the contingent.' I picked up my cup and watched them, smiling. 'Of course, I forgot,' I said, watching the varying shades of wonder and greed on their faces, 'I have also put you all on the sentry detail that will guard the box.'

They sat in astounded silence mixed with anticipation for a few moments. Then the old man asked, 'You will go with them too, of course?'

'I cannot,' I said, shaking my head. 'I am wanted back at the lines tomorrow.

A flicker of annoyance and suspicion crossed the old man's face. Then he turned to his sons and asked point-blank, 'You trust this boy?'

They said in unison, 'With our lives.'

I felt a strange sense of pride and elation, and writing

about it now fills my chest with a lump of lead. Two of those brothers of mine lost their lives because of me. And Iqbal – what would he say to me when he met me next, if we ever meet in this lifetime?

A few hours later, the four of us left Haider Kalan on fresh horses. I headed back to Delhi. They sped to join majors Morstan and Sholto's troop in Agra. We would meet again in two weeks was what was decided.

23

An Emperor's Ransom

Lucknow
9 May 1868

I returned to Haider Kalan three days earlier than we had planned. I was greeted by a moonless sky. I did not ride alone that night. Accompanying me were three mules laden with chests of gold, carrying what I thought was an emperor's ransom. I made my way straight to the mosque, where I saw three horses hitched outside the doorway. As I dismounted and tethered my beasts, I ran my hands over the other horses. They were covered in foam and sweat, as if they had been ridden long and hard. I tried to hear what was happening inside, but was met with silence. I cautiously stepped in to find a dimly lit interior.

Then I saw the naked blades, ready to strike. It was the three, covering the old man in a protective arc. They started when they saw that it was me. Perhaps they were expecting someone else.

The three relaxed. Akbar spoke with an edge in his voice. 'Oi! Bungalee! What brings you here early?'

I looked at the four men. Then I looked at the open, empty casket at their feet. I raised an eyebrow questioningly, looking at Akbar. He sat down and gestured me to sit. The others sat down as well, in a circle around the empty box.

Then Akbar narrated his account of their diamond heist. I write it out in his own words, trying to remember as best as I can.

~

'There was no diamond, Ba'az. For the most, it was just as you predicted. When we reached the fortress of Agra with the troops, the two majors put us all on duty to guard the armoury. On the third day, a column of heavy infantry approached the fort from the west. These men escorted a closed carriage drawn by a single horse. They were English soldiers, not like the ones in the army of the Company. For one, they spoke in a manner of English different from what we hear the sahibs speak usually. Their dress was strange. They wore a sort of cloth cut like the skirts the memsahibs wear, except that these were shorter. Their fierce whiskers and towering shoulders, however, said that they were men used to fighting. The evening they arrived, we heard of the sea voyage they had made from a town far away in Europe, famed for its diamond trade. From there, they travelled to Surat by ship. They continued the journey overland through Mewar and Jaipur. They were careful to avoid the lands held by the rebel soldiers. It was not as if they could not have put up a fight, but it seemed they were in a hurry to get to Agra.

'They put the casket in the armoury under heavy guard. What it contained was a secret, but we of course knew of the stone inside. Three white soldiers joined us to guard the gates of the armoury night and day. There were two shifts. Sometimes two of them and one of us were on duty. Sometimes it was two of us and one of them. The duty was from dawn to dusk and from dusk to dawn. Over the next few days, we made friends with the soldiers. They were not Englishmen. They came from a place called Scotland, where they distil a drink from barley, much like our arrack. These heavy-drinking men took to our arrack like fish to water. Sometimes we drank with them. We learnt about their journey. What they spoke of confirmed what we already knew.

'The munim of Agra was who they had escorted from the town of Antwerp. He was a fidgety, secretive man who rarely emerged from the cabin when at sea, or from the carriage when on the road. They did not know what he carried in the casket, but we did. The fact was that the jewel had been sent to be weighed and valued. It was to be pledged to Marwari bankers for money. We knew it was only a matter of time before it would be taken out of Agra. We had to strike quickly. We waited for a time when there would be a night watch, where there would be two of us and one of them.

'Such a time came last night. Iqbal and I were on duty. Abdullah waited at the eastern gate with fresh horses. After the second gong at night, we overpowered our Scottish friend. We broke open the door of the armoury. I stood outside while Iqbal went inside for the box. When he came out, we rushed with it to join Abdullah. It was then that temptation overcame all of us at once. We wanted to open the box and look at the legendary stone. But when we opened the box, there was nothing inside.

'We wondered what the mystery was, but there was no time for thought. The moment called for action. Iqbal wanted to put the box back where he had found it and pretend nothing had happened. But there was the matter of the third guard we had trussed up. He would identify us. We could not go back. There was only one way – forward. So we rode as hard as we could, and here we are.'

I heard Akbar out. 'This should not be,' I said after a while. 'The information was accurate.'

There was silence again.

Then I said, 'It matters little, in any case. I have news of Delhi and all is not good. After we parted last, I returned to Delhi as planned. A few days later, I rode out with the captain and a small squadron to capture the emperor. A lot has happened since. We must all disappear. Listen carefully.'

I began telling them my story of the past few days.

~

'When I returned to Delhi after meeting you here, the Red Fort had been taken over as a makeshift camp for our irregular troops. The looting, hangings and murders, that made us turn our hearts away from our oaths, continued unabated. But that was not the least of what I encountered. I returned to find a new officer attached to our company. His name was Small.'

'Small?' asked Abdullah, speaking for the first time that evening.

'Yes, Small,' I replied. 'The same man who was responsible for my flogging three years ago. The same man who testified against me in that trial. The same Small who was later tried for perjury in a military court. He was the reason for my wandering about in Delhi until I found service with you among the captain's irregulars. It is perhaps the nature of our irregulars that they take in the outlaws and the lost. I found my home there. But the unit also took in Small, as a sergeant major.'

By this time, the old man had poured fresh draught into a cup and passed it to me. I took it with a nod of thanks and continued.

'The moment I saw him, I knew there was going to be trouble. Soon enough, I sensed he was spreading poison against me. It would be whispers in the officers' mess, a slight mention here and there about cowardice and treachery, or conversation about how I had struck an officer in the past. It was all untrue and I had long been exonerated of the charges. The majors Morstan and Sholto would have laid to rest those rumours as they were a part of the court that had cleared me and discharged me honourably, unlike what they did to Small. But they were not around. They had already ridden away to join you in Agra.

'These rumours reached Captain Hodson's ears. They reached Rajab Ali as well. You know there is little that misses his ears and that one eye. It was only due to my conduct over the past year and my use as a conduit to his spymaster that Hodson gave me the benefit of doubt. "Let it pass, my young Bungalee scribe," he said one night after I had finished his letters – one to his wife, among many. "Larger things are afoot now. Tomorrow afternoon we ride to glory or death," he told me and asked me to report at noon for a sortie into enemy territory.

'The next afternoon we rode with a company of sowars to the tomb of Humayun. There, with bluff and bluster, Hodson sahib secured the custody of the

Emperor Bahadur Shah Zafar. There was promise of safe passage and conduct and long minutes of eyeballing with the captain of the bodyguard. We waited for an hour in the sun, uncertain whether we would return or be killed like dogs. But soon the emperor came out with a small retinue. The result was that we captured the emperor at the resting place of his ancestor. We headed back to the Red Fort, escorting his group. As we left rebel-controlled territory, the stragglers faded away. We came within sight of Delhi Gate. Hodson sahib turned to me and said, "By Jove, Bungalee, we did this!"

'The badshah of Hindustan was taken through Chandni Chowk and into the fort, to be handed over to General Wilson. Wilson did not seem too pleased with the capture. "I was never expecting to see any of you back," he said to Hodson. Captain sahib looked like a dog who had just been kicked by his master. Without a word, he turned around on his heels and left. I followed him. Outside, he told me curtly to summon Rajab Ali.

'That night, Rajab Ali gave me further orders. They came from Hodson himself. The rebels had arranged for a large ransom to secure the emperor and get him back with them. General Wilson had agreed, after hearing of the size of the bounty, which was six large chests of gold, to be handed over to us in exchange for the emperor. The gold was to be in denominations of double mohurs of the East India Company. There would be five thousand double mohurs in each chest for a total of thirty thousand. The plan for the exchange was laid out. Hodson would be given custody of the three princes who were still holed up in Humayun's Tomb. They would accompany him to the Lal Darwaza where the emperor would be held. The gold was to be delivered to us at the ruins of Kotla. Once the gold was secured, the emperor and the princes would be released to the rebels. Rajab Ali told me that I was to receive the gold and ride to the Lal Darwaza with the news. Then he told me who was to be with me when the gold was received and stand guard while I rode to Hodson.'

'Small?' asked Akbar.

I took the earthen cup and drank deeply. I nodded and continued.

'After everything, gora skin is more important than a black man's deeds. At least it is so for the English. Even if the white person is the devil incarnate, he is their own. The next morning, Small and I waited at the gates of Kotla. There was the discomforting silence between us of adversaries having to suffer each other. After an hour of waiting, we heard the sound of horses. Two horsemen appeared from a thicket of trees. They were accompanied by three mules, bearing two large chests each. We waited for them to reach us. The horsemen came within fifty yards, left the mules and walked back with their mounts. They went a hundred paces or so and turned around, watching us. We rode slowly towards the waiting mules. We dismounted and Small opened one chest. The sunlight reflected off the gold that lay inside. I had never seen so much of it together. Small raised a hand to the two horsemen in the distance and waved. They turned and rode away.'

I stopped and took another swig from my cup, emptying it.

'Small then told me in his vile tongue to check the other boxes. He called me a kaffir and a negro, and despite the blood that was boiling inside me, I complied. Orders are orders, after all. I was closing the lid of the last chest, when I sensed something and turned around. Small stood there, a pistol pointed straight at my heart. His expression was one of loathing and glee at the same time. He bared his teeth in a malevolent manner and fired.

'God was with me. The pistol misfired. Fear and anger came over me and I went for his throat. I bashed his head with the butt of his own pistol. He lay bleeding. There was no life left in him. I did not know what to do, so I left him there. I mounted, took his horse and the three mules and led them to the ruins of Kotla. It took me the better part of an hour to find a spot where they would remain unseen. I hid them there and then I rode as fast as I could to the Lal Darwaza to deliver the news to the captain.'

'But by the time I got there, it was all over. The bodies of the three princes were hanging at the gates of the Lal Darwaza. There was a throng around them. Of our men, there were none to be seen. I was glad I was in mufti. The agitated crowds were all men of the rebels. They spoke of how the English officer held them at bay as they waited. Then, when the crowd started getting bigger and more restless, the officer drew his revolver and shot the three princes. He had his men hang them and rode away with his hundred sowars.'

'The emperor?' asked the old man.

'Still in custody,' I said.

'So the emperor remains captured, the exchange failed and the princes are dead,' said the old man, heaving a deep sigh.

'What happened after that?' asked Akbar.

'I had no place to go. Neither forward, nor backward. Like you, when you found this box empty. I know Hodson sahib shot the princes out of desperation. But who was to believe that I was not to blame for the delay in delivering the news? And then, there was the body of Small. I have been discredited enough already. Now with his murder, I am sure to be hanged. So I did the only thing I could. I came here. I knew you would be here, sooner or later.'

There was a brooding silence. Then came the inevitable question. It was Iqbal.

'What happened to the gold?'

I began to laugh. Still laughing, I looked at all of them. 'I was wondering who would be the first to ask. I brought it with me, of course. I thought it would make a good accompaniment to what you would bring. That treasure should have gone somewhere else, but fate has its ways. Instead, we have thirty thousand gold mohurs. Double mohurs, actually. The ransom for an emperor. It is outside, on the mules.'

The old man rose quickly. The others did, too. They went out of the mosque in a rush. After a while they returned, but at a slower pace. The old man stepped forward and embraced me. Akbar looked at me and gave a short, sharp nod as a salute. Abdullah gave a low salaam. Iqbal slapped my back and kept slapping it until I complained it was hurting. All this while the old man continuously poured liquor into the earthen cups. Each time the men emptied their cups quickly. They drank in relief and fear – fear of what may befall them.

~

Akbar's father said, 'Rest for a while. Soon you must leave with the gold. There will be a price on your head. The murder of an Englishman will not go unpunished. They are sure to be looking for you and the treasure.'

'What about the three of you?' I asked. 'You are wanted men, too.'

'We will stay here. No one will think of looking for us, with you at large. Besides, all we did was steal an empty box. But you must leave and hide the gold somewhere. Return when it is safe,' said Akbar.

I hesitated. The old man said, 'Do not worry. We know you will come back. A lesser man would have kept the gold for himself rather than bring it here. Do you know what to do with it? It will be cumbersome to lead these laden mules around.'

I thought for a while and said, 'I know where to go. There is a man in Calcutta. Son of an Irish horse merchant who is like a father and friend to me. He will help me.'

'Will you be safe on the road to Calcutta?' asked Akbar. 'The fighting still rages in Lucknow and beyond.'

'I will take the long road through the mountains. No one will think of looking for me there. Besides, I still have the dispatches of Hodson. I can always say I am delivering them. There are certain advantages of being a fighting scribe, you know. My letters will take care of some dangers. My sword and rifle will take care of the rest.'

The others nodded.

Then a thought struck me and I said, 'Let us put that empty box you brought on one of the mules, shall we? I know they might not come looking for you, but if they do and find this box here, there will be no end of trouble.'

Iqbal picked up the box – an ornately carved chest with intricate silverwork on its lid. As he stepped towards the doorway, he said, 'I will load it. Before you leave, another drink for us all.'

As they all drank the last of the arrack, I began to

hum a song. A familiar piece about the path to battle and how those who ride on it never return. Akbar, Alauddin and Iqbal joined in at the second verse. We had sung this song together many times over the past few years. Once the song was finished and the drinking was done, I got up to leave.

All of us walked together to the door of the mosque. We embraced one by one and then left. I sensed the old man and his three companions watching me astride my horse and fade into the darkness, followed by the laden mules.

24

On the Trail of Iqbal

Haider Kalan
19 June 1868

While in Haider Kalan that night, I had taken the beautiful empty casket as an afterthought. It would have been a shame to just leave it around. Such a beautiful piece of work it was. And then, a year later, I gave it as a gift to the love of my life outside the temple of Udaipur where we had met. It would serve as a jewellery box for Sunanda. I promised that when we started a new life some day, I would bring her ornaments fit for a queen – my queen. None of that happened. I played my part of the mad fakir of Udaipur, and preached words of love in the temple during the day. At night, we made love under the humid night sky. One day they found out about us.

We had kept our tryst secret for long. But then, it does not bode well for a holy man, which I pretended to be, to be putting a child in a young woman. They came for me with torches and pitchforks. I ran away from Udaipur as a fugitive, unable to ever return.

So many years have passed since, and it is ironic that Sunanda perhaps still possesses the box, not knowing what it really is. The diamond, which was the size of a pigeon's egg, was not inside the box, for it had instead been sent to Antwerp to be cut up into nine pieces and polished. These nine pieces were then embedded within the lid of that box, a box which was probably carelessly lying around among her things. The diamond setter had done a brilliant job of hiding the diamonds. He had fixed them on a sliding tray of wood, which was fitted inside the lid. There was intricate silverwork on top of the lid. No one could guess what was inside.

I sometimes wonder about the child Sunanda was with when I fled Udaipur. Was it a boy or a girl? I sometimes wonder whether the seed of Bayaz-ud-din Waris Ali Khan will live on in this world after I am dead and buried.

Udaipur now bears the fruit of the many secrets that were sown during the events of the year 1857. The ransom of Bahadur Shah Zafar, which was not a ransom but a bounty that miraculously made its way into my hands. I was able to brave the snowy mountains of the

Himalayas, shake off my pursuers and give the gold to Harper for safekeeping.

Now both the box, as well as the key to the gold, are in Udaipur. I need to find Iqbal at any cost. I cannot show my face in Udaipur any more, and in my stead, it is only he who can go there. He will find the key to our treasure in the place it lies hidden. If he finds the box as well, it will be a blessing beyond compare, but I do not have high hopes of that. The gold will do for now.

Iqbal must be found.

I thought of what I could possibly do now. I could, of course, go looking for Iqbal. Rajab Ali told me of having traced him to Lahore, before losing him.

But what would happen if I am gone from here and Iqbal returns one day? My mind was filled with these thoughts as I looked at the mosque of Haider Kalan being rebuilt.

~

Haider Kalan
25 June 1868

The mosque is a far cry from how I imagined it would be. Alauddin's two elder sons have ruined whatever thought I had put into the drawings I made for them. There is a stubborn mule-headedness that simply refuses to leave them. I drafted detailed plans for what I wanted the edifice to look like. I wanted a beautiful cross-squinched dome that would rest atop octagonal beams. When I returned, I found they had applied their own wisdom. There lay a lump of a false dome on a flat slab of stone. I asked them about the drawings and they proceeded to pull them out of some dusty recess, but insisted they followed them to the letter. When I pointed out that the dome was built all wrong, they sheepishly looked at each other.

~

Haider Kalan
5 October 1868

I must leave soon, but before that I must leave a sign for Iqbal if he ever returns. A sign that only the four of us would have understood – four ghosts who served Hodson, of whom only two remain.

I sat down with Alauddin and put into motion an elaborate plan.

With him, I created a tale we could tell the villagers and everyone else around. The story would explain the events of that night in Haider Kalan. 'It will help ease the pain,' I said, to which Alauddin nodded and said, 'And it might help us find someone who can read this kind of writing in the letters that came from Ba'azuddin.'

Trying to push my luck, I hazarded, 'Of course, we need not say in the story that he betrayed the village. We do not know if there is truth in that.' Alauddin glared at me, but agreed reluctantly.

And so a story was born, that I began telling, and a story that Alauddin has learnt by heart. If Iqbal ever returns here, I am certain he will understand and know what to read. Then he will go to Udaipur and know where to look for our treasure.

Yesterday, I finished the markings on the roof of the mosque.

Something I did must have aroused Alauddin's suspicion. I do not know what. Perhaps it is the fact that I forgot to take the letters with me before pretending to copy from them on the ceiling.

I am nearing the end of the pages of this journal. It will be an extremely difficult situation if Alauddin ever discovers these journals are written in the same hand as the letters.

In a week from now, I will set off upon my hunt for Iqbal. And then perhaps to London – home to what the sahibs called their old country. That will be my new world.

I have laid out my tasks. I will first have to . . .

~

The journal entries ended here abruptly. The electricity in the TV room went out seconds after I finished this entry in the journal. Reading it through the last few hours, sitting on the hard bench, my body had stiffened. I got up and stepped out to the adjoining terrace. This was the same terrace that Jami, Nira and I were standing on yesterday, before we went to Professor Venugopal. It seemed like it was many years ago. It felt as if a large part of my world had turned upside down and inside out, as I read this last fragment of the diary.

There were two parts to the thoughts that were running through my mind. One part involved the treasure. The many treasures – the nine pieces of diamond cut from the one which was the size of a pigeon's egg. The thirty thousand pieces of gold.

The other part involved the man Bayaz-ud-din Waris Ali Khan. A man they called Ba'az. Ba'az of the Bengal Lancers, I thought to myself. I rolled the words over in my mind. They had a nice ring to them.

This will not do, I told myself. I have to think straight. So I began to collect my thoughts.

I looked at the arched bridge of Khizrabad in the waning moonlight. This was the same place where Ba'azuddin Bungalee had interrogated Rajab Ali many years ago. And here I stood today, reading the diary of the man long gone. I wondered what more must have been written in the pages that were burnt, what other stories might have been told that no one would ever be able to read again. Perhaps there were more accounts of the happenings in Delhi during the siege of 1857. Perhaps there were personal accounts of Captain Hodson. Who knows?

My eyes left the bridge and came back to the overhang of the terrace, below which I stood. The hostel had been built in steps – each floor smaller than the one below. On the first-floor terrace below, there was darkness. I could see the door of our room from where I stood. It was shut. No lights inside. No crack of light under the door.

Jami and Nira were probably asleep. Just as well. Their romance had given me a fair amount of time to read the diary in peace, without being interrupted. It would be best to summarize what I had discovered, I thought. The hunt for the treasure had now reached a critical point. I sensed we were very near our goal.

How many days had it been? I asked myself. Why, it had been barely ten days since Jami and I showed up at Haider Kalan. At that time, I was broken with grief and failure. Of having to repeat another meaningless year of studying a subject I had long lost interest in. And then, Ba'azuddin Bungalee had come into my life and breathed some purpose and excitement into it.

A great treasure lay within my grasp now. Money that would make it unnecessary to study and struggle to find a job that would pay the bills, turning my life into the same kind of life baba had led. And continue the same generation after generation. An unbroken chain of first bending over backwards to study and then spending one's life in servitude, working at a meaningless job. Whether we were talking of fifty pieces of gold or more, the treasure we would find would do so much for us. Jami would be out of his misery as much as me. Mirza and Haider Kalan would get some relief from their debt. Everyone would gain from it.

But it was not just the money. The last ten days had given meaning to my life. This Ba'azuddin Bungalee, the diaries, the treasure, was an objective to work towards. The stories of the village, truths, lies – there was so much to read and understand. So many layers, such complexity. And there was this history that had never been told before. Truths and lies mixed with what was believed to be real. I had already found the diary that was a treasure in itself. A treasure that held great import for the likes of Professor Venugopal and myself. Now, onwards. Eastward Ho, to finding treasure that would be meaningful to all.

Tomorrow I would tell Nira and Jami all that I had learned. Everything still pointed towards Udaipur. We would find a way to resume our hunt.

As I collected my thoughts about the various pieces that led to the treasure, I pondered on the gaps in the story that still remained. Perhaps Professor Venugopal would be able to help. I remembered that I had invited him to lunch as well. I wondered if he would come.

Part IV

The Great Moghul

25

Red Earth

The professor did not show up, of course.

Lunch was another satiating, deeply spiritual experience. So were the mangoes in condensed milk syrup that followed. In our food coma afterwards, Nira, Jami and I were sprawled in mashi's pleasantly cool living room.

Now would be a good time, I thought, to discuss the matter and what to do next.

I began. 'I have put together everything. The story dada-jaan told in Haider Kalan. What he told us about the fakir later. The letters we found and the diary. What I have makes sense. This is what I think happened.'

'The three – Akbar, Abdullah and Iqbal – have this friend, Bayaz-ud-din Waris Ali Khan. He is from some place in Bengal, so they, and perhaps everyone else, call him Bungalee. They also call him Ba'az.

'During the events of the rebellion of 1857, they are working for the English. Under the direct command of Captain Hodson, famous for having captured the Emperor Bahadur Shah Zafar. Hodson ran an elaborate spy network during the siege of Delhi which was instrumental in the fall of Delhi. His chief spymaster was called Rajab Ali. He was a mysterious one-eyed man, who controlled or supervised the activities of our four friends.

'Sometime soon after the fall of Delhi, our four friends get pissed off for not getting suitably rewarded, especially as compared to the goras, for their role in the fall of Delhi. Ba'az proposes that the three – Akbar, Abdullah and Iqbal – attempt to steal a diamond from Agra, where they are sent on sentry duty to protect the diamond. Ba'az hatches the plan for them. They steal the box supposed to contain the stone, but it turns out to be empty. They arrive at Haider Kalan with the empty box, on the run because they can be identified as the thieves. Ba'azuddin Bungalee joins them soon after.

'Now this fellow Ba'azuddin Bungalee has been busy. He was involved in an exchange or a ransom that was supposed to free the emperor. But the exchange went horribly wrong. The emperor's two sons and grandson were killed. Now Ba'az is on the run – with six chests of gold. Thirty thousand double mohurs. While stealing the gold, he kills an English officer – or so he thinks – and now believes he is a wanted man.

'After meeting his friends and their father, he takes off for Calcutta. Here is a piece of detail that connects to dada-jaan. The father of one of the three is the great-grandfather of dada-jaan. It is a complex lineage that I have tried to trace, but we will come to it later. Ba'azuddin Bungalee travels all the way to Calcutta. He takes a different road than usual. Through the Himalayas. Probably through Nepal and Sikkim. On the way, he eliminates one of the three who are chasing him.

'In Calcutta, he gives all the gold, barring fifty double mohurs, to an old friend named Harper, who is an agent of Lloyd's Bank. While in Calcutta, he comes to know there is a warrant against him. He hightails it all the way to Udaipur, to lie low for a while. While fleeing, he apparently kills off the rest of his pursuers and all is well. He has fifty pieces of gold and possibly a way to get to the rest of it from Lloyd's Bank. This, I am assuming, is the "key" he mentions here and there in his diary.

'While in Udaipur, he disguises himself as a fakir to escape the warrant against him. But he runs into trouble when he gets a girl pregnant. He has to leave in a hurry and ends up leaving the fifty pieces of gold and the key in Udaipur. Sometime after leaving Udaipur, he sends letters to Haider Kalan, addressed to Akbar, Abdullah and Iqbal. These are the letters dada-jaan showed us. The letters are written in a cryptic cipher which they probably used to talk to each other while doing their spying work for Hodson.

'What Ba'az does not know, however, is that a few days after he left Haider Kalan, Hodson and Rajab Ali sent a bunch of soldiers there. There is a possibility that Haider Kalan was betrayed by dada-jaan's great-grandfather – Akbar's uncle – who was also a spy for Rajab Ali. Anyway, the soldiers came to look for the diamond box that the three had stolen from Agra.'

'But you said they failed to steal the diamond. They only had an empty box,' Nira pointed out.

'I will come to that. Anyway, the soldiers torture Akbar and Abdullah, but get nothing. One of the white officers is a merciless bastard. He orders the soldiers to hang every adult male in the village. In the massacre, dada-jaan's great-great-grandfather dies, and so do all the other men in the village, but Iqbal manages to escape.'

'Iqbal escaped?' said Jami.

'Yes. At the end of that night all the adult men of the village are hanged, and the mosque is torn down before the English leave. In the meantime, the treacherous uncle, who was conveniently away all this time, returns. He is shocked by what has happened. This was supposed to have been a simple arrest of three people, but instead, the whole village lies ravaged. To save himself, he blames Ba'azuddin Bungalee for having brought ruin upon the village. Ba'azuddin, of course, knows nothing of all this.

'Eleven years later, Ba'azuddin has left Udaipur, where the key to the treasure still lies, with fifty double mohurs. Ba'az is heading back to Haider Kalan. Just before he is about to reach the village, he finds out that he would not be very welcome there and that most of his friends are dead. So he shows up in Haider Kalan as a fakir instead, carrying the body of the English officer who had ordered the bloodbath, who he says is Ba'azuddin Bungalee. He buries the officer in a grave there and sticks around to figure out why all the mayhem happened in the first place. Why Haider Kalan was targeted and why his name is sullied in the village.

'After some time he tracks down Rajab Ali in Delhi. Rajab Ali is spending his days as a miserable blind beggar, and this is where things get very interesting. Ba'azuddin finds out that the entire exchange and ransom for the emperor was apparently something else altogether. It was meant to be a bounty to kill the emperor's two sons and grandson, engineered by the empress Zeenat Mahal to put her own son on the throne. Evidently, she was under some sort of an illusion that the English would reinstate the Mughals on the throne of Delhi once the rebellion died down. She was apparently trying to manoeuvre her own child into the line of succession. Rajab Ali and Hodson played along with her delusion and agreed to the deal. In the plot, Ba'azuddin was to be eliminated as well. Hodson and Rajab Ali were to split the loot. Instead, Ba'azuddin refuses to die and disappears with the gold. Hodson sends trackers after him.'

'So why send soldiers to Haider Kalan?' asked Jami.

'Rajab Ali finds out that the three friends, Akbar, Abdullah and Iqbal, have taken the box from Agra. The three do not know that the box is not really empty, but contains the original diamond, cut into nine pieces, hidden inside.'

'Huh?'

'The original diamond they wanted to steal, something the size of a pigeon's egg, was taken to Belgium and brought back, cut into nine pieces. These nine pieces were concealed in the box. Hodson and Rajab Ali think that the box is with Akbar and his friends and therefore send troops to retrieve it from Haider Kalan. Three trackers are sent after Ba'azuddin Bungalee. But they do not find the box. Akbar and his friends refuse to squeal. The box is actually with Ba'azuddin. He takes it from Haider Kalan and carries it to Udaipur, where he leaves it with his lady-love. Anyway, the box is the reason Haider Kalan was stormed and not Ba'azuddin's gold. But the soldiers were merely to find the precious box and escort it back. The carnage was the work of an English officer who was acting pretty much on his own.'

'My head hurts,' said Jami.

'What happened to the box? And the nine pieces of diamond inside?' asked Nira. The diamonds seemed to have sparked her interest.

'Not important really,' I said. 'Not to us, or our treasure. The box is lost forever, for all practical purposes. Ba'azuddin gave the box to someone named Sunanda in Udaipur. Someone he had an affair with.

'So now Ba'azuddin has figured out why Haider Kalan was attacked. All is good, except that he cannot perhaps explain it to the people of Haider Kalan. He continues living as a fakir, a disguise he first adopted in Udaipur to avoid being recognized. Remember, he still has a warrant against him. Now, the treasure, or the key to it, is lying somewhere in Udaipur. He needs Iqbal to go get it, because he cannot go there himself. Since he was chased out of town because of his illicit romance, he cannot show his face in Udaipur.

'In the meantime, he is rebuilding the mosque in Haider Kalan with the help of dada-jaan's grandfather. On the ceiling, he leaves a message for Iqbal, in case he ever returns. Ba'azuddin Bungalee then goes off on Iqbal's trail. This is where the diary ends.'

'So where do we go from here?' asked Jami.

'Most things point towards the fifty pieces of gold still being in Udaipur,' I replied. 'It is concealed somewhere. If we are lucky, whatever we find there will also help us in finding out what happened to the rest of the gold, which he gave to the man named Harper from Lloyd's Bank.'

'So how much are we looking at now?' asked Nira. 'In terms of treasure?'

I did not understand. Nira explained, 'I mean, are we trying to find fifty mohurs, or the whole thirty thousand?'

I thought for a moment. Then I said, 'I am fairly certain – one hundred per cent – that we are going to find the fifty mohurs. We are sure to find something or the other about what happened to the rest.'

'Hmm,' said Nira. 'Fifty lakh is not so bad.'

'Fifty mohurs,' I corrected.

'Same thing,' said Nira. 'In today's market, a double mohur of the East India Company is going for about a lakh. After taxes and all.'

Smart. She had been researching things according to her priorities.

'I checked,' she explained, 'a lakh a mohur for certain and possibly more.' She seemed to be making some calculations in that head of hers.

'You are sure we will not find these diamonds you mentioned?' she asked after a few seconds.

No, Nira. Now don't be greedy, I thought. 'Most definitely not. I have no idea where to start looking for a hundred-year-old empty box in Udaipur,' I said.

'Hmm,' said Nira. 'Never mind that, then. So at a minimum, we are looking at splitting twenty-five lakh between the three of us,' she said.

How did she get to that number?

'Fifty lakh you said. After taxes,' I said.

'No. Half goes to Mirza and Haider Kalan, you

remember?' Nira corrected me. There was a tinge of regret in her voice.

I had forgotten all about that.

'Yes. Yes. After deducting the money you have spent already,' I added. If we were to be hyper-accurate about numbers, we might as well go all the way.

Nira gave a dismissive wave at that, as if it was nothing. I sometimes did not understand her brain at all.

'So what now?' asked Jami.

'Udaipur again,' I said. Seeing Nira's sharp gaze, I added with haste, 'Better prepared this time, of course.'

'What were those verses on the ceiling again? The ones you deciphered?' she asked. 'Was there mention of anything about them in the diaries?'

I shook my head. 'No, nothing. And even if it was there, it would be in some part that was burnt.' I recited the verses again.

In the red earth of Udaipur,
With the mother goddess,
By the water,
With Jagat lies the key.
Locked in the head is great treasure.

The three of us sat in silence, each lost in their own thoughts. I kept going over the verses in my mind repeatedly. I was interrupted when Jami spoke out loud.

'Where did the fakir go eventually?'

I shrugged. 'Who knows? Perhaps we will never know. Maybe he made up that story.'

I thought it would be a good idea to go see dida once before I left. 'Guys,' I said as I rose, 'I will go to dida. Even if she does not remember it later, it would mean something to her for a while.'

Jami nodded. Nira looked at him and said, 'Come. Let us go to see her as well. She will probably like seeing people, Alzheimer's or not.'

Dida was blind as a bat, I wanted to say. But Nira had a point. All of us got up.

~

Dida was sitting on her cot, fanning herself, when we entered. Hearing us come in, she squinted her cataract-ridden eyes at us and asked, 'Who?'

'Dida, it is me,' I said.

'Oh, Shumon. It is you. Who are these people with you?' she asked.

I said, 'My friends.'

With unseeing eyes, she asked me, 'You have been gone a while, Shumon. Where were you?'

Jami shook his head at Nira, asking her to remain quiet. 'We had gone to Udaipur, my friend and I. We had some work there,' I said.

'Ah, Udaipur,' said dida, 'you must drink a lot of water every morning. It is good for the constitution. Udaipur seemed so beautiful when I was a little girl.' She sought out Nira, 'Come here, Sumita. Sit by me.' Nira sat next to her. Dida held her hand. 'You do drink a lot of water, do you not?'

'Yes,' said Nira, uncertain what to do or say next. I came to her rescue. I asked, 'Have you been to Udaipur, dida?'

'What fine toys baba made for me,' said dida. 'The red clay there was perfect for making dolls. Red dolls. Sumita loved them too – those that remained.' She began to hum a song under her breath. A lullaby. She caressed Nira's hands as she sang. Finishing the refrain of her song, she said, 'This was before you met her. You must drink lots of water. It is good for her. She is with child, you see.' Nira flushed a deep maroon and gave me a piercing scowl at the same time.

Dida continued fanning herself silently. Nira rose. After a while, dida seemed to notice us, as if for the first time, and asked, 'Who?'

'Dida, it is me,' I said again.

'Who, Shumon? You have been gone a long time. You are having a lot of water, are you not? It is good for Sumita. She is with child, you see.'

'Yes,' I said. 'We will go now.' I gestured to Jami and Nira and we left the room quietly, closing the door behind us.

We went to the dining room to pick up our bags before leaving. Mashi was sitting there, a stack of papers in front of her. More exam papers that she was correcting.

Nira said, 'We must be going now, aunty.'

Mashi looked up at us and nodded. 'Right, children. Travel safe. Come again soon.'

Nira said, 'I can't imagine dida lived in Udaipur as a child. I'd have thought she is from somewhere in Bengal.'

Mashi looked at her, seemingly confused. I said, 'She mentioned it just now. After learning that I have just been there.'

There was a flicker of understanding on mashi's face. 'Oh. No, no. I mean yes. She did live in Udaipur as a little girl.'

'How is that?' I asked.

'Not this Udaipur. The other Udaipur. After fleeing Sylhet generations ago, our family settled in Tripura for a while. There is an Udaipur there. It used to be the capital of the princely state long time ago. There is a temple there, one of the Shakti Peeths. It is a major place of pilgrimage. It is called the Tripura Sundari temple, dedicated to the mother goddess.'

~

After the frantic dash from mashi's place to the hostel, I found myself in the room, surrounded by my papers, notebooks and a large atlas of India. Jami and Nira sat on the edge of the bed as I spoke.

I had to keep a calm, steady tone, or I would have been babbling mindlessly.

I pointed at a page in the Oxford India Atlas. It showed a map of India and its provinces in 1857. 'Exhibit B,' I said. 'Ba'azuddin deposited the gold at Calcutta for safekeeping sometime before 28 April 1858. That is the date on the letter he sent informing about it. The next letter is on 15 May, once he reached Udaipur after killing his remaining pursuers. He also mentions in the letter that it took two weeks. Two weeks are enough to travel by horseback from Calcutta to Tripura.' I traced my finger across the map.

'But not to Rajasthan.' I traced my finger again. 'The distance is five times and one has to travel through Kanpur, where the fighting still raged. But his bigger fear would have been being recognized on the busy highway. Remember, he still had a warrant in his name.'

Nira and Jami nodded at what I said.

'Exhibits C, D and E. The verses,' I said. 'We have "red earth". The Udaipur in Tripura is built on red clay soil. The Udaipur in Rajasthan is not. We have "mother goddess". The Udaipur in Tripura is home to the Tripura Sundari temple, which is a Shakti Peeth and has a temple dedicated to the mother goddess. In Rajasthan's Udaipur, we do not have anything as direct as that. And "by the water". The Udaipur in Rajasthan has lakes, true. But the Udaipur in Tripura has a large man-made reservoir just by the temple.' I opened a page of the *Manorama*

Yearbook where I had marked Tripura. 'So we have three hits on the verse. The best we have done so far.'

Jami nodded vigorously, looking at Nira, who nodded a little slower, brows furrowed. Then she asked, 'What about the word "Jagat"? Do we have anything about Jagat in this Udaipur?'

'No,' I said, 'not yet. But having been to Rajasthan once, I can say with certainty that the Jagat temple and the Jag Mandir there did not do us any good.'

Nira nodded, absent-mindedly, lost in thought. 'There is only one way to find out, then,' she said. 'Someone has to go to Tripura.'

'Yes.' I said. 'Whenever we can. It is not as if we can go in a hurry.'

Nira raised an eyebrow.

'The only way to get there is by air,' I said. 'Via Calcutta. It is not likely we can do that in a hurry. Tickets are booked months in advance. And besides, they would be too expensive to justify the risk.'

'How expensive and what risk?' asked Nira.

'Don't know about the expense,' I said. 'The risk is that we have not cracked what this Jagat business is. Locked up in whose head is a key. There is no mention of that in the diary I have read from cover to cover. If we go charging into Tripura, it might just end up as another wasted effort, like the last time.'

Nira nodded. 'Hmm. True. Any other way to find out then? About this Jagat thingie.'

I had no idea. I said as much.

Nira rose and said, 'I have an idea. But before that, I need to make a call.' Saying this, she left the room.

Jami and I sat looking at the pile of papers in front of me. Jami had not said much all afternoon. He had been especially quiet after our visit to dida. Finally, he asked me, 'So you guys are from Tripura, not Bengal.' It would be hard to explain to him, I thought. But I tried anyway. 'It was all the same thing once upon a time. Tripura, West Bengal, present-day Bangladesh.'

'And Sylhet? The place aunty mentioned?'

'Part of modern-day Bangladesh,' I said. 'There was an exodus long ago to Tripura, when our family moved there from Sylhet.'

'How long ago?' asked Jami.

'Ah!' I said. 'Don't know. Very long ago. Late nineteenth century or so, I guess. Or maybe just before Partition.' Frankly, I had no idea.

Nira walked back into the room. She had a triumphant air about her. 'I can get us to Tripura,' she announced. 'Can the two of you go on Friday?'

Today was Tuesday.

'Yes,' I said. 'But how did you manage that?' I was not very comfortable with how fast all this was moving. Had she gone and bought air tickets for us? That would be too much money.

'Jethu is with Indian Airlines,' she said. 'Dad's elder

brother,' she explained to Jami. 'I just spoke with him. He can get us two tickets to Agartala and back.'

I looked at her. Then I said, 'No, Nira. There is no way you are paying for this, too.'

'Who said I am paying?' asked Nira.

I continued, 'In that case, there is no way I can pay for air tickets. Not for another wild goose chase.'

'No, silly!' she said. 'These tickets are for free.'

Seeing my face, she started laughing. 'You have no idea how many free tickets a zonal director of Indian Airlines gets a month, do you? This is nothing.'

My god, I had never thought such a thing could be nothing.

'And as for the wild goose chase,' said Nira, 'I have faith in you. You have brought us so far. You will take us further.' Saying this, she pulled my cheek with one hand and ruffled my hair with the other.

The bloody indignity! Was I some kid? I must have turned red, because Jami started giggling. When Nira pressed her advantage and attacked me on the other cheek, I was caught unawares. The she planted a kiss on it.

Jami was rolling with laughter, as I felt my ears burn. Fine. Jami and I are flying to Tripura, then.

26

Johnny Walker

We settled into the aircraft. A three-hour flight to Calcutta, a brief stop and then the same aircraft would take us onwards to Agartala. We should be there by afternoon or so, we were told. As I waited for us to take off, I thought about my visit to Professor Venugopal before Jami and I embarked on what would hopefully be a step closer to our treasure.

I had deposited my treasure on the professor's desk inside the library. The journals were his to study now. I had everything copied down in my notebook, in any case.

It was a short summary of the discovery and the history that the Ba'azuddin Bungalee narrative could shed light on.

'A fellow from Greater Bengal. Soldier of fortune. Living during the times of the mutiny. Working for Hodson's spy ring. Writing in cryptic code, in English, his language and expression better than most Englishmen of his time. This is a find of a different sort altogether,' said the professor. 'I wish there was more of this diary that could have survived. Who knows what more he must have seen and written about.'

The professor had a faraway look and then was quiet for a while.

'Who knows.' he said finally. 'Who knows what lessons of history it bears. But what you did find is no less than a priceless jewel.'

'Yes,' I said, 'the role of Hodson's scouts in the siege of Delhi.'

'Fascinating . . . fascinating,' said the professor, 'and a contract it says, does it not? The murder of the three heirs of Bahadur Shah Zafar was a dastardly contract killing. No historic account captured that.'

'Yes. I too have not read about it anywhere.'

'And this diamond he mentions, and the mysterious box,' said the professor, 'it might tell us, finally, what happened to the Great Moghul.'

'You mean the Emperor Bahadur Shah Zafar?' I asked. 'I thought it was a known fact that he was captured and put on trial, and that he died in Rangoon.'

'No, no. Not him,' said the professor. 'I meant the diamond the size of a pigeon's egg. The diamond this Ba'azuddin mentions. It was probably the Great Moghul. That was the name given to the stone. It was a magnificent stone and went missing during that time. This diary lays one controversy to rest, if nothing else. The diamond was not taken by the English. It lies concealed somewhere in a box.'

The professor put the notebooks away carefully in one of his drawers and said to me, 'Once you are back, let us exchange notes on all this, shall we? I will show this to my historian colleagues as well. Then, perhaps, we can write another paper?'

I nodded. Writing papers on history seemed like a very good idea.

'That is, if you still join college next semester,' he added with a wink.

If I found the treasure that would finance my life for a few years, I would not mind sticking around in college studying history, I thought to myself. Otherwise, I would have to enlist myself as a bloody draughtsman somewhere. Eke out a living on a few hundred rupees a month.

All this conversation was from the previous evening. But now, I needed to focus on better things. The adventure ahead. Tripura. Agartala, and then on to Udaipur. What might lie ahead, I wondered.

Anyway, I had three hours or more to kill right now. I dozed off.

~

As I awoke, a voice announced that we were about to land in Agartala. I had slept through the stopover at Calcutta.

I saw that Jami was still asleep. He was drooling a bit from the corner of his mouth. I tried to shake him awake once. He smiled blissfully.

The sound of the aircraft engines increased as we began our descent. I looked out of the window and saw that we had just broken through the clouds. Agartala lay below, lush green and full of trees. I wondered what lay ahead. Would we find only fifty pieces of gold, or more? Would we find anything at all?

~

Stepping out of the small airport that served as the gateway to Tripura, I looked around. The sights and smells which greeted me appeared vaguely familiar. I had a faint memory of having been to this place many years ago. Ma and baba had brought me here when we had come to India on vacation. To meet some distant relatives. Agartala was a slushy, sleepy town back then. It was still a slushy, sleepy town. Fifteen-odd years had done nothing to the place.

Before we had left, mashi had grimaced when I mentioned going to Tripura. 'Bloody bastards of Congress – scoundrels and scum of the earth,' she remarked. 'And the communists are no better. A blight on the memory of Marx. Carry mosquito lotion, boys. That place is a swamp.'

And a swamp it was. Jami and I took an autorickshaw to the bus terminus, thinking of catching the first bus to Udaipur. We passed through what was meant to be the centre of town, the driver proudly pointing out the finest landmarks.

'And you thought Haider Kalan was a place where nothing ever happened,' I said to Jami. 'Look at this place. The capital of a state, no less.'

Jami was looking at the passing bamboo thickets, the leafy green copses in the middle of the city, the thatched hovels that were houses, the stinking open sewers flooded with garbage from the monsoon. He only said, 'There is this fable by Aesop. About a bunch of miserable rabbits wanting to kill themselves because they were so weak and pitiable. Then they chanced upon a bunch of frogs living even more pitiable lives. They found the strength to continue living, telling themselves that their fate was at least better than that of the frogs.'

'What of it?' I asked.

'I do not want to be a rabbit or a frog. I want to be the wolf and feast on them all,' Jami said.

What on earth did that mean? I shook my head. It was probably nothing. Some faff-heavy words that made him feel better.

We reached the bus terminus and took the private bus that connected Agartala to Udaipur. I had anticipated a ride of an hour or two at most, since the distance was only fifty kilometres. Five hours of pothole-ridden, broken roads later, we reached the town of Udaipur. It was a little after sunset. The noisy bus station of a sleepy town greeted us as we disembarked.

~

We went to the back of the bus, along with the other passengers, to retrieve our bag. As Jami slung the duffel bag we were sharing over his broad shoulders, I looked around the bus station. It was small, like in any small town. Two bays only. A few shops scattered across the compound. Finding a place to stay was our first task. Earlier, I was sure we would be here by late afternoon, with enough time to look around and find a place. Now, in the gathering dusk, I was not so certain. Small towns like these, I knew, in far-flung locations, usually went to sleep soon after sundown.

'Yes, sir. Hello, sir. Hotel? Hotel?' a voice enquired from behind us.

We turned around to see a small, scrawny kid. Maybe fourteen or fifteen. A loose, faded, checked shirt of an indeterminate colour, and a pair of trousers in a similar shade, hung from his lanky, bony frame, as if from a hanger. A broad, toothy smile seemed to counter the sense of sombre penury that hung over him like a cloud.

'And I thought you were thin,' said Jami to me softly. 'You can carry three of him in you.' Then he said, louder, to the boy, 'Yes. You know of any?'

Hearing Jami speak in English, the boy's eyes lit up slightly. He began to speak quickly, in broken English. 'Yes, sir. Oh, fine, sir! Very nice hotel. Five star, seven star, eleven star. Oh, man. Oh, fine hotel.'

Jami sighed and began what promised to be a long haggle. 'You have anything cheaper? Something within two hundred a night?'

'Two hundred? Very nice, very fine. Perfect hotel. Lake view.' Saying this, the boy stuck out a hand. 'You give bag, sir. I take you there. Five minutes.'

Slightly thrown off by this abrupt closure of the bargain, Jami looked at me doubtfully. I shrugged. I was tired and wanted to be done with this quickly. Jami hauled the bag off his shoulders. He looked at the size of the boy and seemed to have second thoughts about handing over the heavy bag. But the boy quickly grabbed it and heaved it on his back. He seemed to almost double up under its weight but steadied himself in time, flashing his toothy smile. 'You come now, sir. You from Delhi? Bombay? You no look like Calcutta.'

'Yes. I no look like Calcutta,' said Jami.

'Delhi,' I said.

'Oh, fine! Oh, fine, Delhi! India Gate, capital. Prime minister, Red Fort. What is your name? Kapoor? Singh?

You Punjabi? Dal makhni – shahi paneer?' the boy chattered, balancing the weight of the bag. 'My name Johnny,' he announced.

'Johnny?' I asked.

'Yes. Yes. Johnny. Like Johnny Walker,' said the boy. Then, after a pause, 'Janesh. Janesh Jamatia,' he said, extending a frail hand towards Jami and me.

I gingerly shook hands with the boy. Jami, on the other hand, gave him a vigorous handshake and said in English, 'Pleased to meet you, Johnny. My name is Jami. Your English is very good. Where did you learn it?'

The boy smiled and said, 'Thank you, sir. I watch film. And from hear.'

Jami was smiling amusedly. I felt Jami was reminded of himself. This young boy in the backwoods of the country, trying his best to learn English.

Johnny turned away and called out to us over his shoulder, 'Come, I take you to five-star hotel.'

'Sure. A five-star hotel. Here. For two hundred rupees,' I said under my breath, as we followed Johnny towards the exit of the bus stand. Suddenly a man stepped out of the shadows near the gate, a crooked half-lit cigarette between his fingers, and tapped the boy on his chest. The boy halted immediately. The man towered over the boy and began to talk rapidly in Bengali, occasionally giving him a push. The boy shrank back. Jami and I quickened our steps and reached him.

'What seems to be the problem, mister?' asked Jami,

stepping in protectively between the man and the boy. The man said something to Jami, again in Bengali, pointing at Johnny and making threatening gestures. Johnny spoke back in a whining tone, as if explaining something, pointing at the bag and then at us. To us he said, 'I tell him, brother – you my friend, no? I take you to hotel. Five-star hotel.'

The man gave a short laugh and spoke to the boy again. He sidestepped Jami and cuffed the boy under the ear with a casual, imperious whack. The boy yelped in pain and anger, nearly dropping the bag. The man began to take the bag off the boy, but before he could do so, Jami grabbed the other end of it in a vice-like grip. The man said something to Jami, his tone making it clear that he was trying to explain something patiently. He tugged at the bag, but Jami held on to it. The man then spoke out in English, 'You come with me. I take you to hotel.'

Jami did not move his hand and looked at me.

'It seems to be a turf battle,' I said. 'This fellow was telling our friend Johnny that he has no business touting hotels here.'

'He seems to be doing some touting of his own,' said Jami. 'Why is he piling on to the poor boy?'

Johnny was still nursing his bruised cheek when I turned to him and said in Bangla, 'Don't worry. We are going with you.' To the man I said, 'Mind your own affairs, mister. He is our friend.'

Both the man and the boy seemed taken aback. The boy gave a wide, beaming smile and answered, 'You are Bengali. Oh, fine!' He tugged at the handle of the bag that was still stuck between Jami and the man. The man let go. The boy victoriously slung it back on his shoulders and said to the man, 'See! I told you they are my friends. Now go mind your business.'

The man took a threatening step towards the boy. Jami, who had been following the exchange but not quite understanding the words, remained rooted between the man and Johnny, blocking the man and protecting the boy.

Cursing and muttering, the man growled, 'You will pay for this, Janesh, you bastard. The party office will have your skin for this.' He looked at me and said, 'There is a permit needed for hotel agenting here. This boy cannot take you.'

I impassively ignored him. The boy tittered and jeered and the three of us turned away, continuing on our way. The man called out from behind, 'Careful, mister. You are making a mistake. Paresh Riang cannot be cheated.'

'What was he saying?' Jami asked me. The boy, skipping ahead of us, interjected, 'No worry. He say he party. I too am party.' Then he said to me in Bangla, 'These goons don't let honest people make a living any more.'

'Party?' asked Jami as we walked.

The boy said nothing.

'Political,' I explained. 'Evidently, nothing happens in Tripura without the party getting a commission.'

'You help me, I now not take you to five-star hotel. I take you to seven-star hotel. For you, same rate,' said the boy.

Jami rolled his eyes at me behind the boy's back and said, 'Keep walking, Johnny Walker. Lead on.'

~

We turned into a dirt alley just off the larger street and stopped in front of a decrepit building. It was rundown, two storeys tall and very, very seedy-looking. A once-working backlit sign said 'Seven Star Hotel'. Below it, in slightly smaller letters was written, 'Dighi view rooms extra rate. Fully AC, hot water'.

Jami and I exchanged a glance but did not say anything. For two hundred a night, we couldn't expect anything better. I just hoped there were no bedbugs. Janesh dropped our bag on the steps outside with a thud and said, 'You wait. I go make deal.'

A while later, he emerged happy and picked up the bag again. 'You come, sir. I get best room for you.'

We walked to the reception desk, behind which stood a spectacled, bald man, scribbling away at a register. He looked up at us and turned the register around, indicating that we should sign it. I scribbled my name in the last column. I noted that against our names was written 'Delhi Party'. I raised my eyebrows a little at the room description. It said 'Honeymoon Suite'. Jami paid the man two crisp hundred-rupee notes.

Janesh led us up the stairs, taking two at a time. He stopped in front of a door and turned a key in the lock. The door creaked open and Janesh walked in, switching on a white fluorescent light in the room. The smell that greeted us as we stepped in after Janesh was one of musty dampness, mingled with the stinging synthetic odour of rose-scented room freshener. Jami turned his nose a little. It was a small room with a rickety double bed, a plastic jug on the bedside table and a solitary wooden cupboard in a corner. The bed was covered with a white bedspread that had large red roses printed on it. The same fabric had been used for the window curtains.

Janesh walked to the windows and with a flourish drew the curtains aside. 'Best room in hotel, sirs. Best view in Udaipur city – temple and dighi.'

Jami and I walked up to the window and looked out at the silhouette of the Tripura Sundari temple. In front of it was a large lake, seemingly man-made, with cemented edges. The reflection of the lights on the roof of the temple shimmered on the placid surface of the water.

Jami murmured in my ear, 'Tomorrow, we go looking. Udaipur of the red earth – check. Temple of the mother goddess – check. Water – check. Now we need to get to the bottom of this Jagat business.'

I did not say anything. I felt a sense of mild detachment. Even despair. Somehow suddenly I did not have the confidence that Jami had in this whole affair. I could not put a finger on why, but I felt a strange sense of futility. I reached into my wallet and pulled out a fifty-rupee note. I handed it to Johnny and said, 'This is for you.'

The boy looked at the note and raised his hands. He said to me in Bangla, 'From you, nothing, sir.' Pointing at Jami he said, 'This dada stopped Paresh Mastan from beating me. People do not do that.'

Jami nodded. He did not understand what had been said but could sense gratitude. Johnny gave a wide grin. He addressed Jami, 'And dada, hotel give commission. You no fear.'

He waved at us and turned to leave. 'Goodnight, sleep-tight, dream-sweet-dreams. See you. Morning tomorrow.' And he skipped down the stairs, singing at the top of his voice.

~

I lay awake. It had been about an hour since we had turned off the lights. There was total silence all around. In Delhi, and even in a place like Haider Kalan, there were sounds in the night. Traffic, and sounds of the city in Delhi. Crickets, owls and other birds of the night in Haider Kalan. Here, there was nothing.

Nothing meaning absolutely nothing. No sound whatsoever. I could even hear my heart beating, and the sound of my blood vessels pounding. I wondered how Jami was faring. I could not hear him tossing or turning. He lay absolutely still.

'Jami . . .' I whispered.

Nothing.

After a few heartbeats, I heard him ask, 'Can't sleep either?'

'No,' I whispered.

'Everything is so quiet,' he said.

'I know, man,' I said.

There was silence again for a while. Both of us lost in our thoughts.

Soon I heard Jami begin to breathe deeply, as if he was falling asleep.

Sleep continued to elude me, as I thought of Ba'azuddin Bungalee, the treasure, and what tomorrow held in store for us.

27

Jagat

A loud knocking on the door woke me up. I groggily opened my eyes. Jami was sound asleep by my side. The morning light filtered in through the drawn curtains. I got up from the smelly bed and opened the door. Janesh sprang into the room in two strides and said, 'I am ready.'

Jami was getting up, fumbling around for his slippers. Bleary-eyed, he asked, 'You are? For what?'

'I show you Udaipur. Come down.' Saying this, Janesh left as abruptly as he had arrived.

Jami and I exchanged a weary glance and proceeded to get dressed. I was hungry.

We went downstairs and stepped out of the hotel. We looked around in the alley. Janesh was nowhere to be seen.

'Now where could that joker be?' asked Jami.

'No idea. Let us walk down to the street and see. There should be something to eat somewhere around there.'

As Jami and I stepped on to the street, Janesh called out to us from a small shack that seemed to serve tea. We walked to it. It was a small, rickety stall with a few benches in front. Some early customers sat around, peering into their newspapers. A dark man with a few missing teeth sat behind the stove, heating a large aluminium kettle. When we reached, two piping hot glasses of tea were waiting for us. We sat down on a bench while Janesh hovered around, talking to the owner of the stall.

The tea was sickly sweet and tasted different. I noticed the tins of milk powder stacked behind the counter and remembered mashi saying real milk was rare in these areas.

As we sipped our tea, Janesh came with two plates of bread slices and omelettes. We mumbled our thanks and wolfed down the hot breakfast. We did this thrice.

'How is it that everyone speaks Bengali here?' Jami asked.

'Because everyone here is Bengali.'

'Have you guys been here forever?'

'I don't know. But it seems that the king of Tripura was always a Bengali.'

'What about the people who lived here before?'

'Who? Before what?'

'I don't know . . . the indigenous people. The tribals. Like there are everywhere else in the north-eastern states.'

'Pushed to the hills. Whoever remained has been assimilated into the Bengali community. I think our friend Janesh here is part tribal. His last name, Jamatia, is tribal. I think our common friend, that thug at the bus stand, is a tribal, too. But they are from different tribes,' I said.

'Hmm. Nice,' said Jami.

'What is?'

'You guys are colonists, too.' Jami smiled.

'In a roundabout way, I suppose, yes.'

'I can't imagine you guys fighting, conquering lands, though. I can't think of docile, rice-eating Bungalee babus like you going to battle, wielding swords and muskets like the British did.'

I did not say anything. We had our own share of brave warriors.

'I suppose you can conquer with word and song as well. Cultural conquest,' he said in a clipped tone, imitating what he thought passed for an English accent.

'Whatever,' I replied, getting up to pay the tea stall owner. 'They tried to take the fight out of the Bengalis after 1857.'

'Meaning?'

'In 1857, the English East India Company had three armies in India, based at their three principal trading centres,' I explained. 'The largest and most powerful of these was the Bengal Army. It was this army that had risen in rebellion against the English. All the other garrisons – Meerut, Ambala, Kanpur, Peshawar – whether or not they participated in the fighting, were part of the Bengal Army.' After a moment, I added, 'All of you – Jats, Punjabis, Sikhs – you were all our bitches.'

'What do you mean?'

'After 1857, the crackdown by the English did not merely happen in places like Haider Kalan. It was particularly brutal in Greater Bengal. Helped in part by the bureaucratic babus of Calcutta, of course. But at the end of it all, the Bengal Army was disbanded. Forever. The English Army in India was later formed into regiments made up of Sikhs, Marathas, Gurkhas, Jats. Everyone except Bengalis,' I said. I kicked the ground. 'All these jokes about Bengalis being too craven to fight battles – not much truth in them, I think. It later took a round, plump Bengali to raise another army, and take on the might of the empire.'

'Who?' asked Jami.

'Fellow named Subhas Bose. The Indian National Fuckin' Army. The Legion Freies Indien of the Wehrmacht,' I said. 'I will tell you some day about how the flag of India flew for a while over Kohima and Imphal. I will also tell you some day about how another chap from Bengal, a schoolteacher, led a ragtag army of Bengali babus and bibis and hoisted our flag over the armoury in Chittagong. But all that for later. Now let us go look for this damned treasure of yours.' I nodded to Janesh and asked him to lead. I stalked away, ears hot, probably red with indignation.

Jami followed.

~

Janesh led us down the street, towards the temple, spouting a well-rehearsed speech that described Udaipur, Tripura, the temple and the many man-made reservoirs dotting the city. Jami kept up a conversation with him. I saw him glancing at me every now and then. I was walking a little behind them, seemingly not listening and a little aloof. Blood was pounding in my head and ears. I had not felt like this in a while. I shook off the murderous thoughts in my head and tried to concentrate on the task at hand.

Soon we were near the temple. As we approached it, I was distracted by the strains of music coming from behind a derelict wall on the side of the road. A stringed instrument accompanying a high-pitched, mournful voice. There was a rickety bamboo door set in the wall. Behind the wall, an enormous banyan tree spread itself out. The song was in a language vaguely familiar to me, but strange nevertheless. I felt my heartbeat quicken.

Seeing me stop, Jami and Janesh retraced their steps.

I asked Janesh, 'What place is this?'

'This is the garden of the Mad Fakir.'

Seeing my puzzled expression, Janesh tried to explain in broken English for the benefit of his new-found hero, Jami. He tried, but faltered and switched to Bengali. 'This is Pagla Fakir's garden.'

'Who is that?' I asked.

'He is the guardian of the turtles.'

'What turtles?'

'The dighi in front of the temple – the lake. Kalyan Sagar. It has many turtles. It is a special attraction of Udaipur. They are very big. They live for many years. They are very holy. Come, we will see the temple. Then we will feed the turtles. Everyone does it.'

I felt reluctant to leave this shrine of the guardian of turtles. For some reason, I remained rooted to the spot. I asked Janesh, 'Who is singing inside?'

'Why, Pagla Fakir, of course. The present Pagla Fakir.'

'Meaning? Have there been other Pagla Fakirs?'

'There is always a Pagla Fakir in Udaipur. As long as our temple is here and there are turtles in the lake, there will be a Pagla Fakir. This one has been around for very long. He too is very old. Some say that the Pagla Fakir lives as long as the king of the turtles. Whenever the turtle king dies, Pagla Fakir disappears and then there is a new Pagla Fakir. The king is always buried near the temple. We will see it all. Come, I will show you.' The boy was getting a little impatient.

On another day, I would have scoffed at all this nonsense. But today was different. There was something in the song I had just heard that was stirring up strange, old, long-forgotten memories. Jami had been trying to follow snatches of the conversation I was having with the boy. He asked, 'What is this all about?'

I explained the story to him. The song inside had changed from the plaintive one that had made me stop. I asked Janesh, 'Can we go inside to listen?'

'Yes, of course. Many people come with offerings and listen to the songs every morning. But this is very boring. The temple is more interesting.'

I turned to Jami. 'Why don't you guys carry on? I will take a look inside.' Then I added, 'I need to clear my head a little.'

Jami gave a slight nod of understanding. 'I will watch out for clues. About our treasure. But I will need you eventually. You know the verses best.'

'I won't be long,' I said.

Jami and the boy started walking towards the temple. I went to the bamboo door, pushed it open and stepped inside.

~

In front of me stood the tree. It cast a deep shadow, blotting out the morning sun. It took a moment for my eyes to get accustomed to the change in light. I squinted to find the source of the song.

An old, withered man was singing, sitting cross-legged under the tree. Next to him, a young man in his twenties sat playing a one-stringed instrument. A few people surrounded them, some with their hands clasped in prayer. I stood for a while. Then I sat down with the others and listened.

Song followed song. I could understand some of the words, sung in a dialect of Bangla. Some of the tunes had renditions in other languages as well. I had heard them before. Songs of praise for the gods, passed down orally over generations. Some of these songs had become temple ragas and later found a place in popular music. I kept listening, a little more at peace than I was a few minutes earlier.

As the old man finished the song and started another, my ears pricked up. It was the same song that had drawn me in. A loud, high-pitched, sonorous melody. I felt I had heard it before, but just could not put a finger on where. Its memory was locked somewhere in the deep recesses of my mind. Whatever it was, it seemed to relax me, and I felt myself feeling drowsy, nearly nodding off to sleep.

The song stopped. No more songs followed. The singing was over for the morning, it seemed. The people sitting around started stirring, some of them getting up to leave. The young man who had been playing the one-stringed instrument went to them with a bowl and a bag. Some dropped a coin or two. Some handed over packets of grains that they had brought along. Offerings for the upkeep of Pagla Fakir, I reasoned. I felt about in my pockets and drew out my wallet. Without a thought, I pulled out a hundred-rupee note, folded it and put it in the bowl when it came to me. The young man's eyes widened slightly. He gave a short nod of acknowledgement and moved on.

The gathering dispersed. I walked out with everyone else into the bright light outside. I would come back later and ask about the song, I thought.

It was then that I saw Jami running down the street from the temple, waving at me. He was panting hard.

'I think I have found it. Jagat. In the red earth of Udaipur. By the water. In the lap of the mother goddess. Come with me!'

~

I walked briskly with Jami as he explained.

'Johnny boy took me to the temple. There seemed nothing important there, so we went to feed those turtles. It is a big affair here, it seems. There were throngs of people going in and out of the temple and then walking to the side of the lake, where the turtles come by. It was then that I saw these,' said Jami, pointing to the edge of the path that separated the temple from the lake.

There was a long line of graves. Too small to be

human. Some of them cemented mounds. Some more elaborate. A few had headstones. They were on a stretch where the red loamy clay stood stark in the rising morning sun.

'I asked Johnny what they were and he told me that the turtles that die are buried here. Ritually. Without fail. See what I found among the graves.'

Jami had come to a stop in front of a stone-lined platform. It looked different from the rest of the graves. The stonework was better. There was a headstone on it. On it were carved a few lines in Bangla.

Jami said, 'I asked him what it said. And guess what?'

I read aloud, 'Here lies Jagat Bahadur, Lord of the Turtles. Died – Magh, 1272.'

'For a moment, I was disappointed with the year. Then Johnny told me that the Bengali calendar dates this at about 1865,' said Jami. 'Between the time Ba'azuddin rode out that night from Haider Kalan and returned as a fakir eleven years later.'

I looked around the place and softly chanted the lines that we had memorized by now.

Rangi lal mitti Udaipur mein
Gode shakti mata ki
Jal ke kinaare
Jagat ke paas hai chaabi
Sire pe, taala bandh
Hai khazaana dhan

'Yes, it all fits,' I said excitedly, pulse racing. 'Red earth, Udaipur, right under the nose of the mother goddess, by the water. Here is Jagat and with him lies the key, locked up in the head.'

'I will bet all the treasure on earth that this grave was built by Ba'azuddin Bungalee. And built just like the one he built for himself at Haider Kalan. Whatever we are looking for lies here, inside the headstone.'

I looked around. The place was deserted. The morning service at the temple was over and the crowds had left. This was as good a time as any to step forward and look behind the headstone. I felt sure of a false panel there. Like there was in the false grave of Ba'azuddin at Haider Kalan. A thought struck me, and I asked, 'Where is your faithful sidekick?'

'Who, Johnny? I did not want him around while we looked. So I sent him off to buy some booze. This deserves a celebration, does it not?' asked Jami, nearly giggling. 'Shall we look at the grave closely?'

I thought for a second and then shook my head. 'No, not now. Let us wait till dark and come back then. I don't want to risk doing this in daylight.'

28

The Sealed Tube

It was nearly midnight. We made our way to the grave of Turtle King Jagat. I flashed the torch to make sure we were at the right place. Jami was behind me, staggering slightly. There was not a soul in sight.

'Here, hold this,' I whispered as we reached the spot behind the headstone. I handed the torch to Jami.

'Hold it still!' I whispered. I crouched on my haunches and began to feel the back of the headstone with my fingertips carefully. The light swayed unsteadily.

I had a fleeting moment of panic as the light suddenly went out and there was a rustle in the undergrowth behind me. I turned around, still crouching, to see the light make its way to a bush a few yards away, the tottering bulk of Jami behind it. The light soon settled on a spot, and I heard the unzipping of a fly, and then the unmistakable sound of a long, heartfelt piss being taken. The light eventually made its way back towards me and settled on the grave to my right, confused.

'Not there, here! Fuckin' drunkard,' I whispered.

Jami grunted and complied, shining the light at the right spot.

I examined the flat rear of the headstone. There was a healthy growth of moss and algae on it. I scraped it, trying to feel a catch or a hollow.

Soon, my fingers settled on a knot. I pulled out a coin from my pocket and scratched the knot with the coin. Some of the algae gave way, revealing a crack, just a millimetre deep, running horizontally. I scraped along the crack, removing years of accumulated moss. A rectangular etching, about the size of a flagstone, appeared. I traced the edges with my fingernails and looked for some purchase. Jami was watching intently. He was wobbling a little less now. Irritated, he said loudly, 'Let me try.'

I was about to ask him to be silent but before I could do so, Jami cradled the torch in both hands and pointed the flashlight at the spot, as if taking aim. He swung a foot back, balanced himself, and landed a resounding kick on the crack.

With a slow lurch and a crash, the flagstone fell on the ground. With a slower lurch and a louder crash, Jami too fell to the ground. The torch went out.

There was silence. I bent down lower, hoping no one had heard us. The silence lingered.

Then, I heard a rumble and heavy breathing. Jami had started snoring.

I fumbled around, groping for the torch. My fingers closed on its familiar form and I shone it where the flagstone had been. There was a small cavity, about a foot deep. The inside was dry. There was a package wrapped in oilskin inside the cavity. I picked it up. It was heavy, about two kilograms. No string around it. I rolled the oilskin open. It fell away. Inside was a foot-long metal tube. I picked it up and shone the light on the tube. It seemed to be made of brass. It had turned green with age. There was a wax seal on it. It felt heavy. I shook it. A muffled rattle inside. I shone the torch inside the cavity again to see if there was anything else. It was empty.

~

I switched off the torch and wrapped the sealed tube back in the oilskin, stuffing the whole thing inside my shirt. I felt around for the fallen flagstone and struggled to lift it with both hands. After a brief struggle, I managed to put it back in its original place.

I looked around in the darkness. Everything was quiet again, except for the steady sound of Jami snoring.

I shook him and Jami jumped out of his sleep, jabbering, looking at his surroundings confusedly.

'Come along. We are going home,' I said.

~

In the hotel, Jami lay snoring on the bed beside me. I was propped up against the pillows. I had not switched on the lights, so the room was dark as I held the tube in my hands. It had been a wild ride over the past few days, I thought to myself. And all of that had ended with the metal tube I held in my hands. I gave it a slight shake and felt something move inside. My fingers felt the red lacquer that sealed the tube. For some reason, I could not get myself to open it. It was a strange sort of feeling – anxiety and fear rolled into one. I had an idea about what I would find in there. And a fear of what I would not. And a smaller terror nested within all that anxiety and fear – about actually finding what we were looking for. What would I do then? What would come after?

I was certain that the fifty pieces of gold lay inside the tube. A part of me – the excitable twenty-something – wanted to open the tube right away. But the rational, mature part – the one that followed historical research – wanted to follow the process. A seal like that, which had remained unopened for over a hundred years, should be preserved, not broken.

Besides, I should not be the only one to witness what lay inside the tube. Jami, the drunken rascal sleeping next to me, deserved to participate in the unveiling. And Nira – she had brought us this far in our quest.

I contemplated what to do next. Sleep seemed impossible. The first thing to do in the morning would be to book the flight back to Delhi. But what would I do in the meantime? I began to whistle tunelessly under my breath. The same song I had heard in the garden of Pagla Fakir. As I whistled that lullaby, sleep overtook me.

~

The morning light was streaming in through the windows of our seedy hotel room. Jami was still sleeping. Now, however, his breathing was more gentle and regular. In an hour or so, the operator of the telephone booth would arrive and I would be able to make that call to Nira. I kept the sealed metal tube carefully in the bag. I thought it would be a good idea to take a walk by the lake.

I cursed under my breath. Once again, like many times before, I wondered why I was born in this time and place. What would I not have given to have been around during the time of Ba'az, when the way of the sword was commonplace, and I could have wielded one with skill.

Nothing to be done with pipe dreams, I thought to myself. We had our hands on a treasure, or so I thought.

Things should be better now. With the kind of money we would have, I could very well start taking up fencing classes wherever I wished. At that moment, the thought of the treasure gave rise to a nagging voice in my head. I could not put a finger on what it was, but it was a voice of doubt.

I was sorely tempted to rush back to our room and yank out the contents of the tube. But that would not be right. I quickened my steps and headed for the nearest telephone booth. It would do well to put temptation to rest. I went in and dialled Nira. It was a quick conversation.

'We found something,' I told her. 'Get us back.'

She took down the phone number of the booth I was calling from and asked me to wait there.

She called back in fifteen minutes.

'Get your asses to Agartala airport by noon. Your seats are confirmed. You should be in Delhi by sundown.'

She is a fast one, I thought. I glanced at the clock. It was a little past six. We did not have much time.

29

Fifty Pieces, More or Less

Immediately after we landed in Delhi, I made the pilgrimage to Professor Venugopal's den. There was this important detail I needed to check with him. Once that was done, I set the stage.

The drafting table in the room was converted to a spread of exhibits. My notebooks that had been filled over the past few weeks. Some books that might be needed for reference. And a red hand towel that covered the sealed brass tube.

Jami still refused to talk to me. He had stopped talking after asking me for the thirtieth time to open the tube. When I refused again, he began his cold silence. This silence had begun from Agartala airport and continued all the way to Delhi. Now, we sat at the table in our room. The two of us, for the time being. Nira was on her way. As I waited for her, I found an old, trusted friend among my things. A packet of tobacco, with things other than tobacco in it. The same packet from which I had smoked in Haider Kalan and then stumbled upon my find in the mosque. I had forgotten all about it before leaving for Agartala. Now, with a few moments to kill, and a lot of effect to build for my audience of two, I rolled one, lit it and inhaled with languid ease.

Nira arrived soon. I assumed Jami had already spoken to her about what had transpired in Udaipur. They had surely talked while I had gone to Professor Venugopal. As she sat down, I came to the point.

'This is what we found,' I said, taking out the sealed brass tube from under the red towel, 'in the grave at Udaipur. There is a reason I was hesitant about opening it so far. Mostly because of the nature of the seal, which I was uncertain about.'

I thought of expounding on the virtues of historical finds and how it was important to examine seals before they were broken. But my audience's impatient expressions told me that my academic efforts would be wasted. So instead I said, 'I showed the seal to the professor. It was just as I had thought.'

'What?' asked Nira.

'Nothing,' I said. 'It is a common, ordinary red lacquer seal. Nothing to it. It can be broken.'

I rolled the brass tube over to Nira. 'Why don't you do the honours?' I asked. 'It seems right for you to open it.' I hoped I sounded matter-of-fact.

Nira looked at the tube warily. Then she picked it up and asked, 'Why? Because I am a girl?'

'Because you are our financier,' I said. 'And I have a feeling I already know what is in there . . .'

Before I could finish, Nira gave the tube a twist and with a crack, the seal broke. She gave another twist and the tube opened – a small cylinder within another. The two parts slid apart.

A stream of coins dropped from the tube on the table. They seemed to be coming out of the tube in a never-ending stream. Discs of yellow metal, more than an inch in diameter – the size of the tube. Each one of them with the head of a balding man on one side. William IV, House of Hanover, King of the United Kingdom of Great Britain and Ireland.

'About fifty pieces of gold,' I said. 'Double mohurs of the English East India Company. The ones Ba'azuddin Bungalee retained after giving the rest to Lloyd's Bank for safe custody.'

Jami and Nira were hardly listening to me. They were both on their feet, in a daze, looking at the coins on the table and on the floor, as they rolled about before coming to a stop. Jami wore an expression that was a mix of sheer terror and delight. Nira, however, was looking at the gold around us astutely. As I sat at the table, the two of them picked up the coins. Jami's hands shaking, Nira's steadier.

The brass tube lay on the side as they stacked the coins on the table. Five neat piles. Ten coins in a pile. Each coin worth a fortune in terms of its weight in gold and much more in terms of its antique value.

Their astonishment soon began to turn into exhilaration. I had never seen Jami so happy in the time I had known him. Nira had a broad grin as she gazed at the table and then at Jami. I seemed to have been forgotten, relegated to the background, as they stood over their five neat piles of gold.

But Nira was Nira and I had confidence in her ability to get back to business. Sure enough, I saw that the calculator had begun its work in her head. Multiplications and divisions. She would be calculating the value of the gold and dividing it among us. Then, she would begin to think some more and ask the question that formed in her head.

'What happened to the rest of it? The rest of the thirty thousand pieces mentioned in the diary?' she asked.

Thirty seconds. It took her thirty seconds.

'I don't know,' I said and reached for the empty brass tube. 'I have a hunch. Let us see.'

I took the open tube and looked inside. The smell of metal wafted into my nostrils. A smell laced with many other smells. Perhaps it was my imagination, but I smelt blood, gunpowder, steel and smoke in there. I peered into the tube. I gave it a bit of a shake.

As I fiddled with the tube, I drawled in my best lecture tone, 'I imagine that Ba'azuddin made some sort of a deposit with the banker. He must have received something in return for it. Something he must have sealed in this tube along with the coins.'

I inserted a finger into the tube and felt around. My finger touched something. I pulled my finger out and along with it came a tight roll of paper.

With great care, I unrolled the piece of paper that had remained in the tube with the coins for over a hundred years. It was a thin parchment. I skimmed over its contents.

'Here is your answer,' I said, passing the parchment carefully. 'This is what happened to the rest of the gold.'

Nira and Jami eagerly looked at the parchment and read its contents.

'The man named Harper, the turbaned sahib of Calcutta, helped him deposit the gold. The representative of the Lloyd's Bank gave this to him in return for the thirty thousand pieces of gold, minus the fifty that we have here. He kept it safe for himself and his three friends, hiding it in Udaipur. This tube was something he left behind in Udaipur and could not go back to collect. But this is the treasure that he hoped Iqbal would go back and bring.'

I took the piece of paper back from them and read out aloud from it.

This agreement

Made on this date, the Twenty Sixth Day of April, the year 1858 between Neal Harper, esq. son of deceased Patrick Harper, representative of the Honourable Lloyd's & Co.

With

Ba'azuddin Waris Ali Khan, representing the interests of Dost Akbar, Iqbal Mahomet, Abdullah Khan and himself.

Depositing the sum of Twenty-Nine Thousand Nine Hundred and Fifty Double Mohurs minted by the Hon. East India Company,

Valued at a sum of

Rupees Eight Lakh Fifty Thousand Only,

Decreed to be converted into Pound Sterling of the value

One Hundred Thousand Pounds Only

To be invested by the trustees and holders of the bank, in secure recurring deposits in perpetuity till claimed by the investors.

This is to certify that the sum total of invested value may be made available to the signatory, or a bearer of this note, of which one number copy is issued to the depositors, and one number kept by the investee.

There was a smudge and a seal at the bottom of the parchment, under which there were two signatures. One had a scrawl that read Harper. The other was a beautiful, cursive hand that was all too familiar to me. Ba'azuddin Waris Ali Khan.

At the bottom was written the date 26 April 1858. 'What does this mean?' asked Jami. He seemed to have forgotten that he was not speaking to me.

'Nothing much,' I said casually, carefully handing over the paper to Nira. 'It means that the money may still lie with Lloyd's Bank somewhere in Britain, invested sometime soon after this note was written. Since then the money has been growing. It has been growing for over a hundred and thirty years now. The hundred thousand pounds would be worth at least a few million now.'

'More,' said Nira in a whisper, 'and it belongs to the bearer of this note.'

'Us,' I announced. 'All that money belongs to us. If it is still there. And if there is anyone who can pull strings in faraway London to find out what to make of this, it is you, Nira.'

Nira giggled like she was in delirium. Jami had his mouth open. 'A few million rupees!' he exclaimed. He seemed to have stopped breathing.

'Pounds!' Nira and I said together. Then we all started laughing. This had come together neatly, indeed.

'One thing we need to make sure of before we proceed,' I said after we had finished giggling like maniacs. 'We need to make sure this note is still valid.'

'I have just the person for that,' said Nira. 'Come,' she told Jami.

'We may be gone for a few hours,' she said to me. 'There is a man named Mr Raman. Our family's financial adviser. He would know how to go ahead with this document.'

'Take it all and keep it safe, guys,' I said to them, handing over the pile of coins and the piece of paper to them. 'It might not be a good idea to keep all this lying around in the hostel room.' I took a last drag of my smoke and tossed the stub inside the metal tube. As I closed the tube, the wafts of smoke began to work their magic inside my head. In a swirl, I saw Nira take great care to sweep everything into her bag. As she turned to leave with Jami, she announced, 'Tonight, we party! To celebrate our dearest wish coming true. We found our treasure!'

Dearest wish or not, one part of me wanted to warn me that this was a lot of money to just watch walking out of the door. Another part told me that these were good friends. And another part of me did not care about money any more. There was a man I needed to talk to. There were a few demons in my head that needed slaying.

30

Bungalee Partners Limited

I walked about for hours in the dark corridors of the hostel. I felt I was in a trance, going around the cobwebs and labyrinths of my miserable head. I flitted between reality and dreams, hallucinations and lucidity.

It was in one of these moments of lucidity that I found myself in the lobby, in front of the telephone.

This would be a good time to talk to baba. We had not spoken for a while now. This would be a good time to call him.

Would he be surprised? Would he be angry?

Or would he caress me on the head like he used to when I was a child?

I wanted to call him and tell him the truth that I had kept from ma and him for three long years. That I was a complete failure. That I had perhaps been wrong to study architecture, and that he was right. I should have become a computer scientist like him.

But then, baba, I would tell him, it has all turned out well. I have found a hoard of gold. There would be no need to ever worry about paying bills again. You will not have to continue doing that terrible job any more.

We can build a supercomputer, baba, I would tell him. Your great dream. Ma and you and I can sit together like old times. I will lie down, curled in your lap and hear all the stories you used to tell, like lullabies. We will get ourselves a home in the mountains, away from everyone else. And then you can make Roald Dahl come alive again. And I will become Tintin.

There was so much I would talk to him about.

Then, I remembered. I could not make a call to baba any more. There was nothing more I could say to him. I was left with the harsh words we had said to each other. I had my chance to make my peace with him, but that was lost forever now. It was lost the day he died in the hospital. It was lost long before I shoved a burning brand into where his mouth would have been.

The flames had leapt up, crackling in vehemence. The sandalwood had barely masked the smell of roasting flesh. My stomach had rumbled, and then I had thrown up.

Tears of rage and frustration welled up in me. What I would have given, I thought, to fight the enemies and shadows I could see. What I would have given to be able to wield a sword and put my demons to the ground. And here I was, instead, with my fantasy about speaking to a father who was dead and gone.

Ma then. I might as well speak to ma. Ask her how she was doing. Tell her that I was still around and that we would not have to worry about money any more.

I lifted a hand to pick up the receiver. And the phone rang, breaking the spell.

It continued to ring.

I finally picked it up and held back the emotion in my voice.

It was Nira. 'It is real. The document is legit. Valid!' she was screaming in excitement.

With dull detachment, I listened as she explained what she had just discussed with Mr Raman. He was on the job already, trying to initiate things. Depending on something called prorated rate of growth, we could be sitting on anything between a million pounds, or five times that number. I remember asking her how much exactly, but she only said that it doesn't matter, it is a lot!

So she, too, had found her threshold where, after a point, it was just a huge sum of money. My level started at a few thousand rupees. For Nira, it was a few million pounds.

'Party! Party! Party!' she shrieked at the other end of the phone. I imagined her jumping about like a little girl.

Party then. Tonight. All night. Forever.

I put the receiver back in its cradle.

I will talk to ma some other day. Now, I will walk for a few hours more. And then we will have a celebration.

~

The party, or whatever it was, was on. Two people cosying up in a corner of the terrace, and another guy – me – wallowing, deep in thought, made a party not. But Dire Straits playing their dirge out of a beaten-up tape made up for the noise we might have made.

I saw Jami and Nira full of the joy of incalculable wealth within reach. Nira's adviser, or consultant, or whoever it was that rich people used to manage their money, was sure that the document we had found was valid. I was somehow not so sure. How and why was it still valid after all these years? Why did Ba'azuddin Bungalee, or Iqbal, or both of them, not claim the money?

The barrage of questions continued unabated in my mind as I sipped on the expensive liquor provided by Nira. I was still lost in my thoughts when I realized that the two of them had walked over to me.

They needed refills and they seemed well on their way to getting more and more drunk.

'We will buy a plane!' said Jami.

'No! We will buy a bird!' said Nira, and they laughed. 'What will *you* do with the money?' Jami asked me.

I had no idea. I was trying to think of something

wise to say when a voice boomed from the bottom of the stairwell.

'Jami Ahmed Ali Khan! Tellyfoone!'

Jami gave a start. It was the hostel guard calling out his name. It seemed odd that someone had decided to call him at this time of the night.

'I will be right back, guysh!' he slurred and lurched away.

'Just a few more days now,' said Nira.

'What?' I asked.

'They will be able to tell us in a few days how soon we will be able to get the money,' she said. 'I asked them to start the paperwork today with Lloyd's Bank in London.'

She was talking about her financial adviser.

'Mr Raman was telling me that we will have to open an entity between the three of us.'

'Entity?'

'Yes. A company between the three of us,' said Nira. 'It will make things easier to manage the money among us. You know, shares and all.'

A company. Interesting. 'That sounds like a fine idea,' I said. 'What will the company do?'

'Well, nothing much except manage the money and invest it and things like that,' she said.

'What will we call it?' I asked.

Nira shrugged. 'Pick a name. You decide.'

Naming a company seemed like a fun task. I started thinking of what to call it, when Jami appeared.

'The phone call ish for you,' he said to Nira. 'Some Mr Raman. Said it ish important.' Nira put her glass down.

'How . . .?' began Jami.

'Oh, I gave him the hostel number and asked him to reach me through you,' said Nira. 'But why would he call at this time?'

She and I exchanged a look before she hurried away.

The song continued playing as Jami and I sat there guzzling our drinks. Jami mumbled to me, 'That ish our song.'

'What?'

'Me and Nira.'

'Nira and I,' I corrected.

'Yesh, you fuckin angrez!' said Jami. 'Nira and I. That ish our song,' he slurred, waving at the beat-up tape recorder that played 'New York' by Sinatra. 'We are going there, with the money you have found us. Me and Nira. Shorry! Nira and I! We are going to live there forever. Away from her shitty people and my shitty people.'

He said nothing for a while after that, as the song played on. Then, quietly, he added, 'Thank you, Bungalee babu.'

'It was not all my doing,' I said. 'The two of you had a part to play as well.'

Jami only grunted. 'We make a good team,' I said. He grunted again. We sat quietly as he listened to the song, a faraway look in his eyes.

'How does the name Bungalee Partners sound?' I asked Jami a few moments later.

'For what?' he asked.

'Nira said that we may need to form a company to manage the money,' I said. 'How does that name sound to you? Bungalee Partners?'

'Bungalee Partnersh!' said Jami, raising his glass in a toast. 'Long live Bungaleesh!' he said and downed his drink in a single gulp. 'Bashuddin forever!'

I too raised my glass in a toast. 'Ba'azuddin forever, indeed.'

We had not noticed that Nira had come back quietly while we had been talking. She stood there, saying nothing.

'Hey, Nira-bayboo. Bungalee Partnersh! A toasht!' said Jami.

Nira still said nothing. Jami kept looking at her expectantly.

Something was wrong.

There was silence, as the song too decided to finish just then.

'There is nothing,' she said after a few seconds of silence. 'Mr Raman just got off the phone with the representatives of Lloyd's Bank and called me immediately after. The document is legit, valid and everything, but it was encashed long ago.'

Jami said something incoherent that I could not quite catch. Nira continued in a shaken, broken sort of voice. 'He said that the document was made in the name of four people, represented by the signatory. It was valid if presented by any bearer, except for a small detail. If the signatory appeared at the bank, he would not need the original document,' she said. 'The bank records say that sometime between 1904 and 1905 the signatory arrived and took custody of the funds. The money is gone.'

The signatory. That was Ba'azuddin Bungalee then, who travelled to London and took charge of his money. I thought I could hear him laughing at us from somewhere in the distance.

I saw Nira break down and clutch Jami's arm as she buried her face in his shoulder.

~

Things are not so bad, I told them. We still have the fifty pieces of gold. That would be good enough for the three of us, would it not? But it did not seem to be good enough for Nira. From this moment our magnificent celebration wound down. I saw the collective spirits of Jami and Nira unravel in front of my eyes. They, in turn, rapidly depleted the spirit in the bottle in front of us.

I tried to cheer them up. Nothing worked. Nira had believed she had the treasure in her grasp, only to have everything snatched away. It was something I could not completely understand.

Soon enough, Jami and Nira mumbled their goodnights and tottered away, arm in arm.

I was left on the quiet, dark terrace, wondering where I would spend the rest of the night. Unless I was mistaken, our room was out of bounds for me for the night.

I decided to walk.

I made a complete round of the many floors of the hostel before returning to the same spot where I could see the broken arched bridge of Khizrabad. I looked up at the starlit sky, and the gloom of the horizon. I could not put a finger on some of the things I was feeling. I was a little disappointed, true. It was an immense amount of money that had slipped out of our hands. But I was not bothered. The money had never been ours to begin with. I had enjoyed solving the mystery. And whatever money was there was enough for me.

~

I paced the terrace for an hour or so. I pulled out a smoke and fumbled around in my pockets for a light.

Dearest wishes coming true. I wondered what my dearest wish was, and what would happen if it came true. Was it one thing, or was it many? A week ago, my dearest wish had been to find the treasure. Two weeks before that, it had been to make my peace with baba. Now, I did not even know what it was. Would I ever be anchored to one thing, or would I spend my life flitting about like a butterfly – from one thing to another?

I began to feel drowsy. Now would be a good time to catch some sleep. I noticed that I was whistling tunelessly under my breath and muttered some lines from a song. I froze. That song! Those words! I sat down heavily, my back against the parapet. Breathlessly, I mumbled the song. Baba's face swam before me, and so did ma's. And then dida's. The lullaby relaxed me. I began to nod off.

I woke up when it was nearing dawn. The sun was not out yet. I made my way out of the hostel gate on to the street. There was no one around yet. There was a coolness in the air. The beginnings of a slight breeze.

I needed to make it to C.R. Park. I needed to hear a song. Dida needed to be paid a visit. It was not far. Only a few kilometres. I was still young.

I started running.

31

The Great Moghul

Mashi was sitting at her table when I walked in. She was, as usual, correcting a stack of papers. She was startled seeing me so early in the morning, my face sweaty and flushed.

'Everything all right?' she asked.

'Yes,' I said quietly. 'Just thought I would come by for breakfast.' I sat down beside her on the dining table.

'Just bread and omelette today,' she said.

'Will do.'

She put aside her work and got busy. After a while, I asked, 'Mashi?'

'Yes, baba,' she said, coming back with a plate of sliced bread and omelettes.

'Tell me something about us,' I said.

'Meaning?'

'Meaning, you know, about us. You, ma. Tripura, Udaipur, your childhood . . .'

She spoke for a while after that and I listened. I had a lump in my throat when she talked of baba courting ma and whisking her away after they got married.

'He was a bit of a tiger,' said mashi, smiling. 'And he was the reason she could get away from her life and come to Calcutta and then onwards to Delhi and then to Baroda. He turned her life around – and ours.'

We sat quietly for a while, lost in our own thoughts. I went over all that she had said.

'Pity your baba told no one about his condition until it was too late,' said mashi with a deep sigh.

I gave a start and asked with a snap, 'Meaning?'

'His kidneys,' said mashi, as if explaining something I knew already. The chattering began in my head again, but I remained quiet. I had known nothing about this.

'Ma does not know about him yet,' said mashi. I realized she was talking about dida. 'She will be all broken up – if she understands anything.'

'How is she doing?' I asked, my mind elsewhere, in Sylhet.

'Same as ever. Why don't you go see her?'

I went inside. Dida was fanning herself, staring into nothingness with sightless eyes. She heard me come in and said, 'Who, Shumon?'

This time, too, everything unfolded like it had in the past. She thought I was baba. I played along. This time, however, at the end of it all, I cradled her in my arms, as if I would never leave her. I rocked her to sleep and sang her the lullaby she had sung to me when I was a child. She sang, too, her hoarse voice in tune with mine.

When I left, she was asleep, smiling peacefully in her dreams. I ran my hands over her paan box, fingers going over the wood, as I contemplated what to do next.

~

The sun was high when I got back to the hostel. I did not head back to our room immediately. I was glad that I did not run into Jami or Nira anywhere.

In my present frame of mind, I was in no mood to meet them. Or anyone else for that matter. Yet.

They might be broken and devastated about the new life they could not start any more. But there was something I could do to fix that soon, I knew I could. But for now, I preferred them being wherever they were, away from me.

~

I knocked on the door of our room. I was still whistling tunelessly under my breath.

Jami opened the door after several long minutes. Nira was up as well. They both had bleary eyes. Time to rouse these people out of their sleep. I entered the room, still whistling.

'I discovered something about myself last night,' I said, sitting down on a chair. 'Last night, a thought struck me. Early this morning, I went over to mashi and dida to check some facts about our family.'

I whistled out the first strain of the tune.

'While Bayaz-ud-din Bungalee was hiding in Udaipur, he met a girl. Her name was Sunanda. He later fled Udaipur, leaving the sealed tube with the gold in the grave. From the diary it appears that she was with child.'

I whistled out another strain of the lullaby.

'There was something about the song I heard in Udaipur the other day – in that place where the Pagla Fakir lives – that I could not identify then, but last night it came to me. I had heard that song many times. It was a lullaby that dida used to sing to me when I was a child. A lullaby set on a tune sung in Udaipur, but with words that I discovered in the diary of Bayaz-ud-din Bungalee. The poem, the first poem he says he ever composed – about spades, clubs and diamonds – for Sunanda.'

I whistled another strain of the song. Then another.

'That set me thinking about this man. Could it be that Ba'az was in hiding in Udaipur as the Pagla Fakir of his time? And had to flee when his romance with Sunanda was discovered? I asked mashi about our family. She told me of our past in Udaipur, and I began to wonder who dida could be. I started to make some calculations and realized that there is a fair possibility she could be the granddaughter of Ba'az and Sunanda's child, which means Ba'az could be my maternal great-great-grandfather.'

'What!' said Jami.

'Yes. It means that Bayaz-ud-din Waris Ali Khan, the man they called Bungalee, is an ancestor of mine,' I said.

'This is so exciting,' said Nira.

'Hey man, that means we go back so many generations, eh? Akbar was an ancestor of mine as well. This stuff is poetic,' said Jami.

'Not only poetic. There is more,' I said. 'I had to make sure. This fact ties up to other things. And has a relationship with the treasure we have been hunting. Some part of it, in any case. Listen.'

They did.

I said, 'This story goes back to Haider Kalan. Akbar, Abdullah and Iqbal returned from a failed attempt to steal the diamond called the Great Moghul. A magnificent stone the size of a pigeon's egg. Something they believed to be in a box kept under guard in Agra.

'They only found the empty box and returned with it to Haider Kalan. There, they were met by their old friend Ba'az. He had just returned from Delhi, laden with mule loads of gold.

'When Ba'az fled that night with the gold, he took the empty box with him. Later, when he came back to

Haider Kalan, his encounters with Small and Rajab Ali made him realize that the diamond had been in the box all along. Cut up into smaller pieces, concealed somewhere. But for all practical purposes, it was lost forever. This was because he had gifted the box to his sweetheart, Sunanda. As far as he knew, it was in Sunanda's possession, in faraway Udaipur.

'Well, as it turns out, it seems that the box became a family heirloom, passed on from one generation to the next.' I looked at Jami to see whether he had understood what I was saying.

No. He had not caught on. 'It is something that has been lying in plain sight all these years in front of me. You have seen it as well when we were at my mashi's place the other day,' I said to Jami.

'Huh?'

'Used as, of all things, a paan box,' I said. 'And as far as I know, the pieces of the diamond of the Great Moghul have never been found. So they must be still in there.'

Jami was sitting erect as a post, eyes agog. Nira, too, was looking at me expectantly. All signs of slumber had vanished from their faces.

'I asked mashi and brought the box with me from her place,' I said. 'Thought it correct for us to examine it together. After all, we are partners in the hunt for treasure.' Saying this, I took out the box. I whistled out the last strain and finished the song.

It was a large box. Larger than an average jewellery

box. It seemed to me that it was made of sandalwood, with intricate silverwork on it. Both wood and silver had the stains of many years of use on them. I opened the box. I had removed the paan and other paraphernalia before bringing it with me.

Nira and Jami held their breaths as I examined the box.

I turned it over. Years of oil, fluids and grime had stained the wood, making it darker. I tapped the sides. Nothing. I turned it over again and opened the lid. I felt the bottom from the inside. I rapped it with my knuckles. A dull, even solid sound. I closed the box again. I stopped. The lid. What about the lid? I opened the box again and took a closer look at the panel of the lid. Yes. It was unnaturally thick. I gave it a tap. A dull sound. I gave other parts of the box a series of taps as well. A different sound. The lid had a distinctively different ring to it.

I examined it further. There was a tiny catch at one edge on the inside of the lid. After a bit of effort and a broken fingernail, it gave way.

I looked up at my two friends. I pulled at the edge I had purchase on.

Nothing happened.

I pulled harder, clawing with all the force I could manage.

With a squeal of protest, the false compartment of the lid gave way.

Out rained stones. Some large, some small. Nine of them in all. Pieces cut out of the magnificent larger piece mined from Golconda. The stones caught the morning light coming in through the windows and formed a dazzling ocean of reds, blues, purples, greens, magentas and a few dozen other colours. I had read about diamonds catching the sunlight. What it looked like in reality was a different thing altogether.

'Bungalee Partners,' I said to them as they gaped, 'I present the Great Moghul!'

They sat there on the edge of the bed, holding on to each other. I found my pack of tobacco and gently rolled another smoke. I lit it up. I began whistling the lullaby again.

From the corner of my eye, I sensed a few shadowy forms behind me. Four of them. Akbar, Alauddin, Iqbal, Ba'az, and a fifth one, too – baba. The shadowy form of Bayaz-ud-din Bungalee stood behind me and looked on at his box and the Great Moghul. I gave him a nod and a wave, bidding him goodbye for the time being. As he faded away with the others, I continued to whistle.

Writer's Note

Some characters in this book were real persons who walked this earth like we do now. Hodson of the Horse and Rajab Ali, the one-eyed spymaster of Delhi, lived real lives. The captain-major is still buried in the compound of La Martiniere College in Lucknow, not far from where he fell during the assault of Lucknow.

Other personae in this book – Small, Sholto and Morstan – lived alternate lives in the works of Arthur Conan Doyle. Akbar, Iqbal and Abdullah are the spectres of Athos, Porthos and Aramis. Somewhere in here are also hidden Harry Flashman and the ghosts of Paddy Harper and Richard Sharpe. I figured that if I have to steal from some masters, I might as well steal from them all. Petty thefts of these sort have turned this into the grand larceny that it is. I am trying to stand upon the shoulders of many giants, and it is a terrifying and precarious perch.

The narrator of our tale, however, bears no name. Give him one if you want to. Not having one would serve equally well. Somewhere in an earlier version he had one that was thankfully lost to wordsmithery.

There are more adventures of Ba'az that will be written in the years to come. It was a wet summer afternoon in London before the Great War. I overheard a conversation that a veiled stranger was having with the young Captain Athelstan King of the Khyber Rifles. It went something like this, if memory serves me well . . .

'I have roamed the world and seen more than any man can, in many lifetimes. I have captured an emperor and had a hand in the murder of princes. I have been bought in slavery in the docks of Canton, and sold again in the jetties of Yokohama. I have walked the abandoned caravan trails of the Silk Road, and crossed it to chase a shadow of my past. I have bled in the sands of Tangiers, and the dunes of Khartoum. I have eaten dead horses and living men in the savannahs of Africa. I have been there at every turn and twist of fate of your Empire. My work has made names for men like Hodson, Churchill and Kitchener, yet no one must know mine. But if you insist, my name is Bayazuddin. Some people call me the Bungalee. Others call me Ba'az.'

I hope to tell those tales some day.

Over,
Uttiyo Bhattacharya

Acknowledgements

The making of this story has been a long expedition. On that path, many have read earlier drafts. These have been friends and lovers, family and enemies. Some strangers, too. I would like to thank them all for having been part of this journey. There are too many of you to name individually, but you know who you are.

Most of all, I would like to thank the unknown many who read this after publication, and those who would read it some day in the future. I would love to hear from you what you think of it.

Publication Credits

Writer's Unit

Pre-commissioning editor: Achala Upendran
Literary agents: Kanishka Gupta, Writer's Side Literary Agency
Screen agents: Sidharth Jain, The Story Ink

Juggernaut Books

First commissioning editor: Amish Raj Mulmi
Second commissioning editor: Sivapriya R.
Third commissioning editor: Sasha Mahuli
Line editors: Janani Ganesan, Sanjiv Sarin
Copy-editor: Cincy Jose
Proofreader: Shyama Warner
Typesetter: R. Ajith Kumar
Jacket copy: Sasha Mahuli
Cover design director: Gavin Morris
Cover photo art: Wasim Helal
Cover design: Gavin Morris
Cover model: Stock image
Marketing, sales & PR: Natasha Puri and Disha Naik

A Note on the Author

Uttiyo Bhattacharya is an architect, writer and design producer. He has worked on theatrical productions as an actor, on museum and cultural projects as design manager and on classified military installations across geographies as architect of record. *Ba'az of the Bengal Lancers* is his first novel.

The author would like to express creative dissent with the design of the cover.

AN EXTENSIVE LIBRARY

Including fresh, new, original Juggernaut books from the likes of Sunny Leone, Praveen Swami, Husain Haqqani, Umera Ahmed, Rujuta Diwekar and lots more. Plus, books from partner publishers and loads of free classics. Whichever genre you like, there's a book waiting for you.

CRUCIBLES OF SIN
HITESHA
Can a Geek ever find Love?
Finding Juliet
Toffee
Mary Shelley
Frankenstein
A FAROOQ BESHI INVESTIGATION
COLD FLAKE
PRAVEEN SWAMI
A Psychiatrist's Guide To Heartbreak
How to Heal Your Broken Heart
DR SHYAM BHAT
MOIN and THE MONSTER
BY ANUSHKA RAVISHANKAR
Mafia Queens of Mumbai
stories of women from the ganglands
S. Hussain Zaidi
with Jane Borges
Foreword by Vishal Bharadwaj
Pakistan's Queen of Romance
UMERA AHMED
Nowhere Girl
A Story of Love & Forgiveness
THE BEHEADING
This Is How He Will Bless Her
ABHEEK BARUA
THE Peshwa
The Lion and the Stallion
RAM SIVASANKARAN
THE INVISIBLE WOMAN
SAURBH KATYAL
ANGRY BIRDS FAN? READ THE BOOK!
ANGRY BIRDS TOONS
TOONS TALES
ARCHANA SABOO
ADIKOOL
in
#AfricanAdventures
i am not a bimbette
Tarana Khan
DON'T FALL IN LOVE
Vandana Shankar
KHUSHWANT SINGH
WE INDIANS

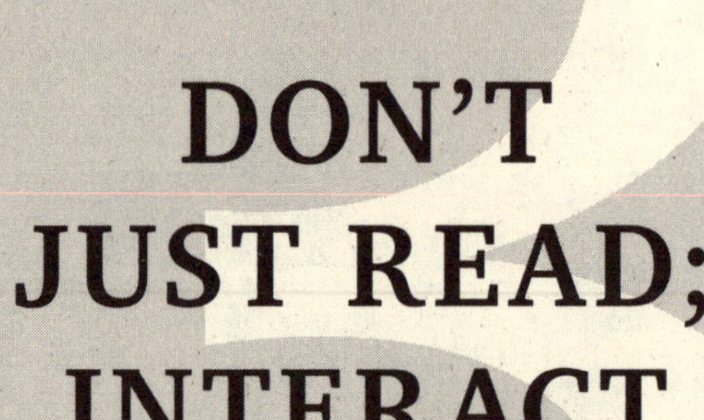

DON'T JUST READ; INTERACT

We're changing the reading experience from passive to active.

Ask authors questions

Get all your answers from the horse's mouth. Juggernaut authors actually reply to every question they can.

Rate and review

Let everyone know of your favourite reads or critique the finer points of a book – you will be heard in a community of like-minded readers.

Gift books to friends

For a book-lover, there's no nicer gift than a book personally picked. You can even do it anonymously if you like.

Enjoy new book formats

Discover serials released in parts over time, picture books including comics, and story-bundles at discounted rates. And coming soon, audiobooks.

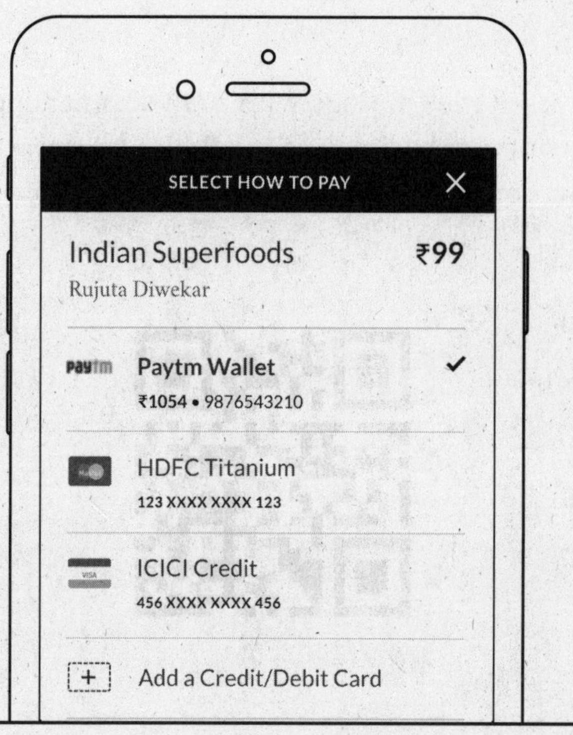

Paytm Wallet, Cards & Apple Payments

On Android, just add a Paytm Wallet once and buy any book with one tap. On iOS, pay with one tap with your iTunes-linked debit/credit card.

Click the QR Code with a QR scanner app or type the link into the Internet browser on your phone to download the app.